Fabulous!

Other Books
by Laury A. Egan

FICTION

The Outcast Oracle

Fog and Other Stories

Jenny Kidd

POETRY

Beneath the Lion's Paw

Snow, Shadows, a Stranger

The Sea & Beyond

Presence & Absence

Fabulous!
An Opera Buffa

LAURY A. EGAN

TinyFox
PRESS

Cover design and photograph by Laury A. Egan;
Execution and author photograph by Vicki DeVico
Interior design by Laury A. Egan and Jennifer Henderson

Library of Congress Catalog Card Number: 2018937849
ISBN: 978-1-946501-08-0

Tiny Fox Press and the book fox logo
are all registered trademarks of Tiny Fox Press LLC

Tiny Fox Press LLC
North Port, FL

ACKNOWLEDGMENTS

I wish to express my sincere appreciation to everyone at Tiny Fox Press for their enthusiasm, good cheer, and heroic efforts on behalf of *Fabulous!* Warmest thanks to Galen Surlak-Ramsey for his sensitive and smart editorial suggestions throughout the manuscript; to Mary Beth Surlak, for her excellent copy editing; to Jen Henderson, for her expertise with the formatting and book's production; and to Ellen Zielinski Whitfield of JKS Communications for her stellar promotional efforts.

I am also grateful to Vicki DeVico for her brilliant assistance with the cover's creation, compiling my photograph, typography, and design into digital files and withstanding my endless fussing. Additional thanks to opera singer Debra Patchell; my dear friend and poet, Karla Linn Merrifield; and to Carol Oberle and Dwight Wilson.

CHAPTER ONE

Kiri De Uwana

My psychic medium told me that it was just a matter of time. Although Madame Clara didn't elaborate on the details and said that her timelines might be a trifle off, she was absolutely positive that 2009 would be the year, confirmed by the Ouija board spirit enumerating 009. Well, that was good enough for me, Kiri De Uwana, diva divine! The bright lights were going to become downright dazzling.

My stiletto heels barely touched the sidewalk as I walked home after the session. I didn't attend to most of the whistles and catcalls from the hot men on the street, though I did flutter my pink chiffon scarf at one hunky black boy who was pile-driving to beat the band. On another day I might have invited him up for a mint julep, but today I had other things on my mind.

By the way, my name is Gilbert Eugene Rose. Although I don't advertise my place of birth, I hail from the side of Atlantic City *sans* glamour. Except for music, my childhood was a perpetual winter, one I hurried through with desperate speed. Being a gay boy and, I modestly confess, a beauty—blond hair the color of sunlight, dark blue eyes like glittering jewels, fair skin perfect as cream, and refined features (nothing too large or too small, ahem!)—I was shunned by the girls because they were jealous and taunted by the boys because I was not sufficiently rough and tumble, though a little tumble now and then held occasional appeal.

My escape happened after high school, when opera called *yoo-hoo*. I fled to the first of several music schools, leaving my mother to tend to her inebriations (my father had departed many years before). After absorbing the collective wisdom of the finest vocal, diction, and language teachers, I packed my makeup, wigs, and hats and took the bus home—my new home, New York City. That was eleven years ago. Now, at age thirty-four, I am broke, or nearly, but after emptying my purse, turning all of my pockets inside out, and searching through every hidey hole in my apartment, I have just enough cash to pay for a lesson with my voice coach, Anna Marie, who thinks I'm a soprano. Well, sort of. Anna Marie is in her eighties and didn't eat her carrots when she was young—if you get my drift. Frankly, I don't see how she can play the piano in her semi-blind condition, but she plunks away nicely with her arthritic fingers. Anyway, she knows her stuff (even if she can't tell I'm not a *female* soprano) and loves my voice and appreciates the perfume samples I liberate from Oscar's, the department store where I dress the mannequins.

So, here I am, yours truly, knocking on Anna Marie's door.

She answered after a few minutes. "Kiri, dear! How are you?" (She hasn't twigged to the fact that I'm not the famed singer, Kiri Te Kanawa, an itty-bitty misconception I see absolutely no reason to correct.)

"I'm just fabulous!" I enthused in my best breathy diva voice. "And how are you?"

Anna Marie didn't reply, having already set off, cane in hand, in the direction of her gargantuan grand piano, a black whale of a Steinway, which I swear was birthed *in situ* since I can't imagine how anyone crammed it inside her miniscule living room. Luckily for Anna Marie, the piano and its bench are easy targets for her to find. I followed her to the Steinway's curvaceous side, feeling much too big for the space—I'm six-foot-one and a weight we won't mention, though my figure is somewhere between slender and girlish. All right, a sturdy girlish.

We began warm-up scales. With the low ceiling in the living room, my voice sounded positively stentorian. Of course, I possess a very large instrument. Oh, no, how shocking! You think I meant . . . well, not that kind, but the other instrument I possess is equally impressive. Trust me.

"So, what would you like to work on today," Anna Marie asked.

"Well, I've heard some very exciting news!"

"Oh, do tell!"

"They're casting for *Così fan tutte*—"

"At the Met?" Her hands fluttered into a delighted clasp.

"Not exactly . . . but definitely, definitely uptown." No need to say how far uptown. I mean, we're not talking Albany.

"Your Fiordiligi is so fine!" Her watery blue eyes glistened with excitement. "But I'm surprised you weren't hired without an audition. I mean, you *are* Kiri Te Kanawa, after all."

Not quite, alas.

"We must practice 'Come scoglio,' then, dear, "Anna Marie said. And so we did.

—

After the session, I was flying high or as high as a girl can fly without artificial stimulation. Well, okay, Anna Marie and I did partake of an afternoon sherry served with cookie chasers that landed like rocks. I mean, we're talking seriously stale Christmas cookies that were baked before the turn of the century. And not the twentieth century, either.

As I walked to my apartment, I pictured myself on stage, singing Mozart: the warm spotlights illuminating my exquisite face; the audience hushed, thrilled to hear my sensitive, yet powerful voice; and then, after the first aria, the applause, rolling in thunderous waves toward me. And, oh, yes! The gown I'm wearing! I was considering colors, how much bosom to show, when someone called my name—my real one. It was my friend and confidant, Gal Friday, who, as her name suggests, is always available to do anything for anyone, or as I often tease, do anyone for anything. Gal is actually a real female, though bless her, she has no style at all. In fact, she's belligerently anti-fashion, always wearing black leather no matter if it's August and 96 degrees, which it was, or near zero in mid winter. And the squat heels on her engineer boots! My goodness! I wouldn't be caught dead.

"So, how's it hanging?" she asked. This passed as repartee. Well, her repartee anyway.

"Oh, Gal, I have simply marvelous news!"

She took my arm in hers, and we continued walking together, her stride slightly outdistancing mine, which was peculiar because Gal scraped five-foot-three if she was standing up straight, which was rare.

"What happened?"

"I think my great opportunity has knocked!"

"That's probably not all that's knocked." This passed for humor. Well, her humor anyway. She laughed and squeezed my hand so tightly that I feared purple bruises would erupt on my delicate white skin.

"Oh, you're such a cad," I replied, giving her solid shoulder a little punch.

Gal liked this and chuckled. "It's true. Now, what's up? Besides . . ."

I shook my head and affixed a stern look upon her. "Let's be serious, darling." I explained about the opera and the auditions.

"I don't know much about opera, but Gilbert, you're not a soprano."

"Details, details," I replied, with a fine flick of the wrist.

"But won't someone notice?" She glanced at my Adam's apple and parts south.

"Posh, tosh, girlfriend. When my golden throat opens, they won't think of anything or anyone else." I gave her a brilliant smile. "Now, how 'bout a little margarita? To celebrate?" I prayed she'd pay.

Gal clamped a meaty hand on my back. "You bet, sweetheart." She has a habit of talking like Bogart. Maybe it was because she looked like Humphrey, just a little shorter and without the five o'clock shadow.

We took off down the street, our thirst driving us like camels to the oasis.

—

The Marlene D. was our kind of place. Well, more of Gal's than mine, since it was a dyke bar, but the girls always let me in because I add class to the joint. And, heavens, it did need class. Black ceilings and black walls and black bar—*très noir*. The only bright things—other than yours truly—were a couple of disco balls spinning white dizzies around the smoky room. Gal was right at home in the color choice. In fact, she was nigh on invisible except for her face. We found two empty barstools and ordered drinks. She paid, as I hoped she would.

After licking off the salt around the glass rim, Gal asked me when the auditions were.

"Next week," I replied, "and I am so, so worried."

"About the auditions?"

"Oh, my god, no! What am I going to wear?"

"Typical girl," Gal said in her low voice. She's a baritone if I've ever heard one.

"I know. But this is serious. All my clothes are too glitzy."

"I thought the opera set liked lamé and feather boas."

"They do, but only after eight. Hmm," I said, "maybe I could go with a little color. You know, to highlight my spectacular violet eyes."

"Gil, your eyes are blue."

"Blue like sapphires, then." I thought for a minute. "Perhaps something in pink. With a few flounces and scarves."

"And long. To hide your legs."

"What's wrong with my legs?" I demanded.

Gal looked down at my shapely, firm-but-slender calves. "Knobby knees."

My mouth popped open. "I do not have knobby knees! You're just jealous."

Gal laughed and patted me on the back. "Wear a floor-length gown, and you'll be okay."

"One doesn't do gowns before sundown." I snorted, still smarting about her defamation of my knees. I buried myself in the delightful tequila concoction, then sighed a sigh that I had practiced before the mirror many, many times.

On cue, Gal asked me what was the matter.

I sighed again. "But how can I afford such a dress?"

"Broke?"

I nodded, looking at her with forlorn eyes. I'd practiced that expression almost as often.

"And what does this kind of rig cost?"

"Hundreds of dollars."

"Can you sew?" she asked.

I shook my head.

"Neither can I," she replied, without a trace of regret. "So we can chuck that solution."

I was cheered by the "we." "You mean, you'll help?"

Gal appraised me fore and aft like a racehorse she was considering at Aqueduct. "No. You're already in hock to me for big bucks."

"Oh, please, Gal! If I get the gig, I'll pay you back!"

She reached into the inside pocket of her leather jacket and removed her weenie little black book. No, not *the* black book—that one was the size of a King James Bible. After thumbing a few dog-eared pages, she squinted, tapped a thick forefinger on a notation. "You already owe me $354.69."

I gulped a large gulp of margarita. "Huh? Where did the sixty-nine cents come from?"

Gal shrugged. "Dunno."

I heaved the saddest sigh I could heave. Tears were next on the agenda. Little slow rollers that would make my eyes glisten.

"You're not going to do the bit, are you, Gil?"

"The bit?" I asked innocently. This was accompanied by a delicate sniff.

"You know. Tears and sobs and pressing your hand to your brow."

"Oh, Gal, you know me so well . . ."

She shook her head and pulled a weenie pencil from her pants to add the cost of my drink. "Okay, but this'll be the last time I spot you another dime. Business is business. Got that?"

I arranged my face into "meek" demeanor: lowering my chin and looking up at Gal kind of sideways, which was the only way I could actually look up to her. "Yes. Thank you."

—

The next morning, Gal and I stepped out together, truly the odd couple. I was wearing a demure yellow dress and pearls. From my collection, I'd chosen a nice twitchy, semi-short wig, mostly blond with a dash of darker hues. Gal wore the usual, but her hair was still wet from the shower, combed to achieve the brushed-cut look. We headed for the shops. Not *the* shops, but the ones that cater to a certain kind of woman. My kind.

I knew Luis from everywhere. Our paths crossed constantly, and his establishment, The Queen Bee, was a favorite. When he saw us approach, he opened the door and swept us inside, giving me a prim kiss on both of my cheeks. I always appreciate others taking care with my makeup and lipstick.

"Greetings!" he welcomed, kissing Gal. "What can I do for you, girls?"

Gal raised a thick eyebrow at this, always wary whenever anyone identified her sex correctly. "We're here to buy a dress."

"Ha! Ha! Ha!" Luis slapped his thin thighs and did a little hop, an old disco move that he'd incorporated into his routine. "Gal wants a dress!" Tears erupted from his brown eyes and slid down his perfectly tanned cheeks.

Gal wasn't sure whether to be insulted or amused, although she was tilting toward the former. Her mouth puckered in exasperation.

"Not for me, for chrissakes! For Gilbert."

Luis sniveled loudly and dried his tears with a dainty handkerchief he pulled from his back pocket, not that there was much room in there. "Well, that's a relief. You really scared yo' mama, honey."

"Come on, Luis," I pleaded. "I need something for an opera audition."

His eyes bugged out at the mention of the ultimate music. "A what? You got to be joshin' me, Gil."

I smiled modestly. "No, I'm not."

"Well, that's a tough nut to crack. Oops!" He giggled and put his fingers to his lips. "I shouldn't say that in front of a lady." He arched his back as if he were about to launch into calisthenics and then tapped his forehead to wake up his merchandise memory. "I have just the thing, sweetums. You've come to the right place!"

—

I tried on piles of clothes, some I would have died for, as that fashion icon Joan Rivers would declare, but, alas, they weren't what I needed. And the combo I liked best was nixed by Gal when she took a gander at the price tag.

"I don't spend that much on clothes all year," she muttered.

I bit back a pointed response regarding her wardrobe, and Luis scrunched his lips and stared at the ceiling, trying to avoid ruffling the feathers of a patron, and one who didn't wear feathers at that. I kept looking through the racks and finally selected a lime green outfit with tapered pants. We set this blandness off with a long floral scarf that I could wrap around my offending Adam's apple. I knew I could get away with this since all singers wear scarves to protect their throats. It's part of the diva-thing, tossing the end of a scarf over one's shoulder. I've practiced that, too.

Luis toted up the substantial bill and handed it to Gal, who withdrew a folded wallet that was attached by a silver chain to a belt loop. She counted out several fifty-dollar bills.

"I want a pair of front row seats to this shindig, Gilbert. And my money back with interest," she told me. "Or else."

"Oh, thank you, thank you, thank you!" I gushed.

Gal colored slightly and returned the wallet to her pocket.

After that, we went out for lunch, like all the girls who shop.

CHAPTER TWO

Guilia Hancock

I nibbled on an arugula and grilled tuna salad, and Gal set upon an earnest, four-square cheeseburger that dripped blood down her wrists. I prefer luncheons that aren't gladiator sports, but since I was once again my dear friend's guest, I could only avert my gaze and pray she staunched the red rivulets before they disappeared beneath the overhang of her leather cuff. I patted my lips gently, hoping to model the behavior to Gal, but, alas, she was beyond my primitive psychology.

As she was chomping on a crinkled French fry log, her cell phone rattled away in a deep pocket of her leather jacket.

"What's up?" she asked after flipping its thin lid. "Mmm. Mmm. Got it. Mmm. Yeah."

Well, this kind of minimalism drives me crazy. I like nothing better than eavesdropping on interesting conversations, especially ones I am not supposed to hear, so I was wearing out my pantyhose on the edge of my seat as Gal went on in this staccato vein for exactly thirty-nine seconds—timed on my lovely *faux* Cartier watch—and then she hung up.

"Friend or foe?" I asked, dithering with some fuzzy sprouts stage right in the salad bowl.

"Neither."

I shot her a quizzical glance.

"La Donna wants me."

This cryptic statement was accompanied by several vigorous swipes of the napkin and a finger snap at our waitress. Luncheon was finished, regrettably before an *après dèjeuner* drinkie.

"You know, one of these days I would absolutely love to make the acquaintance of your employer," I ventured. According to Gal, the lady I was curious to meet was reclusive because the streets harbored her enemies, of which La Donna had acquired an excessive number. Some were irate husbands of Sicilian heritage whose wives La Donna had spirited away for little afternoon trysts and quiet coercions to spill the beans on their husbands' businesses. Others were petty types who thought a quick snuff job would boost their bad-boy reputations on the street.

"Now, Gil, you know that's not going to happen."

I sighed. "Pity. And you told me she adores opera."

"I'm not mixing the two of you up. No way."

"What kind of opera does she like?" I asked.

"How the hell do I know? I don't listen to the stuff, but she's got it blaring at all hours."

"It must be a terrible strain for you, darling," I said with undisguised irony worthy of Giuseppe Verdi himself, "to hurt your ears like that."

As with most things, this flew miles over Gal's head. "Whatever. Now I got to go." She plunked down a fifty on the table.

I eyed the bill and did the arithmetic, pleased to learn that my cerebral abacus had arrived at the sum of $42.79 without the tip. I could pocket the difference if I was quick and mean, and oh, my, I am.

Gal withdrew her book and stubby pencil and wrote the cost of my lunch and clothes under the previous total. With her tongue lollygagging outside her mouth, she did the addition. When I saw the total, I almost upchucked my arugula.

She stowed her accounting supplies in various pockets and narrowed her eyes like an eagle looking upon a hapless mouse. "Remember. You don't pay, there will be consequences." Standing, Gal maintained her stern expression until finally her face relaxed into a smile. "I'll see you around."

—

After lunch, I carried my parcels to my upstairs apartment, changed into Gil, and ran over to the AIDS shelter, where I volunteer by cutting up carrots and potatoes for soups and stews. I also give benefit performances twice a year and sometimes play the piano and sing at the center. It's the least I can do, although I always feel like I haven't done enough.

When I finished, I came home, watered my plants, who were undoubtedly thinking they had been stranded in the desert, and perused purloined *Opera News* magazines, imagining myself on one of those sexy Zeffirelli sets with some nasty pasty-faced Amneris trying to steal my man. Uh-uh, girl. Not happening!

Well, the day passed until I was forced to plan the dinner menu. Was it to be pasta and pasta or rice and rice? I did have some cans of mushrooms, corn, and bamboo shoots, but that didn't tilt the decision in either direction. As I was mulling over this vexing conundrum, the phone rang.

"*Ciao!*" I said.

"Hello, I wanna speak to Miss Hancock." The voice was thick Brooklynese lubricated with a severe case of post-nasal drip.

"Miss Hancock?" I drew the name on my mental blackboard and, with an agreeable flutter of my heart, suddenly remembered the derivation of this amusing alias. "Oh, yes," I replied, assuming my *diva voce*. (For those of you unfamiliar with *diva voce*, words are enunciated with exquisite care, with round vowels, airy pitch, and the occasional rolled *r* for spice.) "This is Guilia Hancock." I'd balanced an Italian first name with an Anglo-Saxon moniker just so they'd know I was sexy but not flighty, an Italian who was, shall we say, good insurance? Maybe I should have selected "Rockefeller" so they'd think I was well endowed?

"Yeah? Well, this is Howard Lowenbaum," the man said. "From the Opera Company."

He didn't need to say which one. I knew. "Why, Mr. Lowenbaum. It's so nice of you to call." I added a *soupçon* of Louisiana breathiness to diva voice.

"We liked the sampler CD you sent us. And you had a great rep list."

"Thank you. I'm delighted to hear that." The CD was me singing—that was legit—but the repertory list was wishful. No roles I couldn't sing, mind, but other than three or four operas, I hadn't learned the other twenty-six. I mean, please, *La Finta Giardinera*? Mozart *obscura*!

"As you know, Ms. Hancock, we're casting *Così fan tutte* for a staged production. Can you come and sing 'Come scoglio' and the second act duet with Dorabella?"

"Absolutely! It would be my pleasure, Mr. Lowenbaum." Arias I had under my belt, so to speak.

He coughed loudly in the phone. "Good. You know where the theater is?"

"Yes, of course."

"Next Monday morning at eleven o'clock." He dictated his cell phone number. "Now, one other thing. We need to talk to your agent . . . a Mr. Sol Bleuchek."

Uh-oh. I'd listed an agent on my PR statement because it appeared more professional. "Ah, yes, Sol." My brain was on its toes and sprinting. "Sol is, er, traveling. That's right . . . in Russia." My knowledge of tiny Russian hamlets, ones without cellular signals, was not extensive. "In . . . er . . . Prokofievgrad." I hoped Sergei Prokofiev didn't object to having a new town named after him. "I can have Sol call you, but he's difficult to reach at the moment, as I'm sure you can appreciate. I can fax him any contracts or the like, Mr. Lowenbaum, should it be necessary."

"I need to speak with him. Protocol and all that."

"I understand. Well, I'll have him phone as soon as he's in *communicado*."

—

After I hung up, I sat down in my rocking chair and rocked. A real individual audition! Not just an anonymous casting call with dozens of other singers! I rocked some more, basking in my good fortune. It was just like Madame Clara predicted. Wait until Howard Lowenbaum heard me sing! I was so excited that I picked up the phone and did what I usually did: called my ex, William Van Allan, a dear lamb who unfortunately strayed once too often.

"William!" I said in my Gilbert voice, although *diva voce* lingered, especially the elevated pitch. "You'll never believe what happened!" I proceeded to fill him in.

He was incredulous. William tended toward negative thinking. He was the proverbial half-empty man, a gallon jug half-empty. "Gil, you can't show up in person. They'll know you're no soprano right away."

I was growing weary of my doubting William. "My dear boy," I said, with serene assurance, "I shall be absolutely convincing. Just you wait." William gave a little snort. I ignored it, pained by his lack of confidence, and continued. "I have my outfit already, courtesy of Gal, who was kind enough to support me in my moment of great need."

William snorted a second time. "You suckered her again?"

"I did no such thing!" I insisted. "You are a beast, William. A dreadful beast!"

"I know, I know. I'm sorry," he replied, inserting a thimbleful of contrition in his tone.

"Apologies accepted. Now, am I seeing you this evening at the Purple Plum?" I sing a revue on Thursday and Saturday nights.

"Sure. Douglas and I'll be there around ten o'clock."

"Douglas? Who's that?" I asked before checking my jealousy at the gate.

He laughed, savoring the knowledge that I was still interested in him. "A guy I met two weeks ago—Douglas Pierce."

"What! Two weeks ago! And you didn't tell me?" My eyebrows soared upward, probably tangling with my bangs.

"Maybe you forgot that you and I broke up," he reminded me with some satisfaction.

He had me there. I *was* trying to forget.

"Hey, and you won't believe this," William chuckled. "He's a Douglas Pierce the fourth."

"What do you mean? How could you get involved with a fourth? Does he have a personality disorder—four of him? Or is he into a *ménage à quatre*?"

"Don't be ridiculous." Quite noticeably, he didn't laugh. "You'll meet him tonight, Gil. Now, I have to run. Some of us need to work."

I hung up the phone, deflated as a three-day-old balloon, and thought of Charles Dickens. Why did it always have to be the best of times and the worst of times at the same time? It was the story of my life, minus the French Revolution. The thought of William, Sweet William, *my* William with another man made me wild. He wasn't the handsomest boy in town, but he had the most beautiful brown eyes, straight black hair cut like an English schoolboy, and shoulders wide enough to cry a river on. He was also a damned fine florist, and god knows a girl needs one of those! I was bereft, bothered, and bewildered. I rocked some more, trying to recapture my joy but found only a few wisps of it traipsing about. Saddened by my potential loss, I clutched William's 8 x 10 glossy to my breast, exhaled to calm myself, and vowed not to give up the ship.

—

On show nights, I'm careful to avoid dairy products, wheat, and chocolate. This seriously taxes my culinary ingenuity since it means cereal and candy bars are *verboten*. I opted for the aforementioned canned veggies over white rice and, though I say no to alcohol before operatic performances, I drank a half bottle of awful Portuguese rosé, a contribution from a swarthy Spaniard who spent the night ages ago. Now, tell me, is there any other kind of Spaniard except swarthy ones? They do run to my taste, however, at least on Tuesdays, which was the evening of our initial meeting, and to be honest, our only *tête-à-tête* or, shall we say, *tête-à*-something.

After imbibing this meager repast, I showered, applied base makeup—appropriate for street but not stage—warmed up my luxurious voice, and then hightailed it over to the Plum, which was slowly filling up with eager beaverettes, those poor souls pining for the briefest bat of my eyelashes or, for that matter, a quick feel, which I do not allow except on the rarest of circumstances. A girl must keep her standards, particularly Kiri De Uwana.

My repertory at the Purple Plum is a mix of Broadway and opera with a little Marlene and Noël thrown in when the mood grabs hold. Tonight, I was doing a cleverly contrived medley from *My Fair Lady*: "I've Grown Accustomed to His Face" and "On the Street Where He Lives" with a segue into *Camelot* tunes with the pronouns changed to suit the clientele. After my break, I planned to sing "Un bel dì, vedremo" and "Vissi d'arte"—fav arias of the silver-haired crowd who get teary remembering Tebaldi and Callas as Butterfly and Tosca.

As I was slipping into my red sequined gown and adjusting my *décolletage*, there was a knock at the dressing room door.

"Enter!" I sang out.

And William and Douglas did. Both appeared to be flying high on love's elixir or, failing that, on several Budweisers. Douglas was fair, flaxen-haired, and I hoped, fleeting. A mere boy. A flimsy substitute for *moi*. No comparison. Chop suey. Handsome, though. Perfect teeth.

"Greetings," I said, completing my crimson lipstick. "Kiss kiss hug hug." I did neither. Divas don't actually touch.

"Gil, this is Douglas." William's face lit up like a self-satisfied glowworm at the mention of his new *amour*.

"Nice to make your acquaintance, Douglas," I replied, studying myself intently in the mirror. There was no need to turn and acknowledge my adversary. It was beneath me.

"Well, we just came to say 'hi,'" William said. "Douglas wanted to meet you."

I just bet he did. Inside I was fuming. Outside I was cool. "I'm so glad you brought him by." I delivered this in an airy fashion, as if William had introduced me to his pet Pomeranian.

This silenced William. Douglas stared at me with large doe eyes, making me suspect he was hopelessly nearsighted and unwilling to wear glasses due to youthful vanity. My vision was 20/20. I felt smug and did a little Maggie Smith-style purse of the lips. "I hope you gentlemen have a good table? If not, I'm sure I can arrange one."

"Oh, thank you," Douglas enthused, "but William took care of it." Here, the lad glanced at his lover with admiration.

It was too, too much. "Wonderful. Now if you will excuse me, the show must go on."

The two left quietly as I heard my call announced. I did a few more scales, sang a few snatches, and made my way downstairs through the dark and dusty halls.

CHAPTER THREE

Dear William
and Little Lord Douglas

The next morning I had cash from my singer's tip box—a veritable fortune of $133.77. I called Anna Marie for a session, which we scheduled for two o'clock. Plenty of time to see her and then get to my mannequin-dressing job, a catch-as-catch-can arrangement that paid the rent with a few nickels left over.

Anna Marie was happy to see me. We worked hard on the score, although I was slightly fatigued from the outing at the Purple Plum despite the fact that I use a microphone at the club.

"Kiri, dear," Anna Marie began, "I think you have really settled into your voice." She was smiling but staring six inches to the left of where I actually was.

"Why, thank you! That's so nice of you to say." Actually, I was terrifically relieved to hear Anna Marie's opinion because—daft as she was—the lady knew her opera.

"Your voice is still a trifle dark for Fiordiligi. I don't know why exactly, but there it is." She considered this for a few minutes, gyrating on the outskirts of dementia space, and then asked if I had worked on my comportment.

Had I worked on my comportment? Indeed I had! I gave her a preview of the first act scene in which I admire my lover's portrait while singing "A guarda sorella." As I did this, I thought of William, therefore precious little acting was required, even though I was still smarting from last night's effrontery—the two of them sitting arm in arm several feet from the stage, with William cooing and billing *ad nauseum* over Douglas, who at least had the good taste to be attentive to my exceptional performance.

"Brava!" replied Anna Marie at the end of my aria. "Splendid!"

I was unsure whether she had really seen me do my rendition, but I was content with approval of any sort. "*Grazie*," I replied modestly. "So you think I'm . . . I'm ready?"

"Yes, yes," she replied, "a thousand times, yes."

With this approbation, I paid her forty dollars, pressing it into her hands. Once, I'd made the mistake of leaving the money on the piano, albeit in plain sight for those of us who can see. Unfortunately, Anna Marie can't and the next student could. He paid her with my cash, and Anna Marie accused me of not paying her. An expensive error I have never made again.

I rushed home to change out of my dress and stockings into Gilbert garb, as I thought of it. Khakis, a pink polo shirt, and sneakers. Sometimes it was difficult to make the transition, and today was no exception. While I have zero interest in making my femininity permanent, I do enjoy being a girl.

As I was wiping off my mascara, the phone rang.

"Hello," I said, trying to compromise on a voice common to Gilbert and Guilia and Kiri. The ID said "New York," which left me clueless as to who was calling and who they were calling.

"Hi, Kiri," replied a soft male voice.

"Who is this?"

"Er, we met last night at the Purple Plum. It's Douglas."

Gotcha, you little swine. "Douglas . . . hmm."

My noncommittal response threw him for a looptie-loop. "Don't you remember me?"

He sounded suitably plaintive, so I cut the boy a break. "Oh, yes. Douglas. You came with William, right?" A wicked thrust to remind him of his lover.

"Yeah." (As if he'd forgotten.) "Well, I just wanted to tell you how much I enjoyed your singing."

"Thank you."

"You were great. I mean, *really* great!" This effusion seemed to dry up Douglas' verbal well. As I was about to say goodbye after a long minute of silence, he cleared his throat and added, "I was hoping we might go for a drink tonight."

"With you and William?"

"No, not exactly."

I was not sure what he meant by "not exactly." It was either a threesome or not a threesome, therefore a twosome. "I have to go to work this evening, Douglas. A second gig."

"Oh." He deflated with disappointment. "I just thought we might get together, that's all."

"The three of us . . ."

He was quiet and then continued in a small voice. "No, the two of us."

I sighed as if put upon, which in many ways I was. How should I play this turn of events? My decision was instantaneous. "I'm free after ten o'clock, but I can't stay out late."

"Hey, really?" I could picture him grinning. "That'd be swell! Would you like to meet me somewhere?" He thought for a moment. "What about at the Rear Door?"

"Douglas, that's not quite my thing." The Rear Door attracted the S & M crowd, bikers, sailors, rough trade. I was frankly taken aback that dewy-eyed Douglas had ever flitted over its threshold.

"Oh, okay. Well, where's good for you?"

"Let me see," I considered, my tone turning into a creamy purr. "Perhaps the Flaming Flamingo? They have simply marvelous grilled capons." By this suggestion I signified place and also my intention of being properly fed.

"Sure, that'd be fine. I'll see you there."

—

Now I had a tiny conflict. Gil had to go to work; Kiri had to show up at the Flaming Flamingo without time to change since I was sure Douglas was not inviting Gilbert on a date. He was clearly star-struck with Kiri, poor boy. Cripes, I thought, this is getting out of hand. I walked to the closet and found a gray plaid overnight suitcase. Luckily, I had a traveling makeup kit and a few other items packed, to which I added a pair of white Capri pants, sling-back heels, a fuchsia knit top, a pink sweater, jewelry, wig, and a brassiere properly stuffed to a fulsome D cup. I would change at the department store and hope no one saw me.

—

I took the bus across town and the subway uptown and arrived uncomfortably hot via the store's service entrance.

"Hi, Gil," Loretta greeted me.

18

Loretta was a back-room person like I was. Not bad on the eyes, although her teeth needed capping and her hair was a grayer version of mousy. "Hi, how are you?"

"Cool." Loretta tended toward taciturn.

Since I was not cool, I walked over to one of the air-conditioning outlets. "What's on the agenda for tonight?"

Loretta consulted a list on a clipboard. "Third floor, cruise wear."

I stifled myself. I simply adore doing *cruise* wear!

—

Since we were the only store with a cruise wear collection on permanent display, I was always having to alter the male and female mannequins' bathing suits. A boy and girl need to be inserted in the beach sand next to the umbrella, according to the designer's sketch. This took me more time because I had to visit the basement for the kiddies, and then I took extra pains to pad the adult male's Speedos and tilt his body at a suggestive angle. I knew Gregory, the designer, would approve, being one of the boys himself.

As I was washing my hands after my labor of love, my cell phone rang.

"Gil, this is William."

Uh-oh. "Dear William," I said, glad for the privacy of the staff bathroom.

"How're you doing?"

"Just peachy."

He cleared his throat. "There's something I need to talk to you about."

"Oh? What?" I attempted to play the scene like Doris Day, but my feigned innocence may have been tinged with a smidgeon of guilt.

"I'll talk about it when I see you."

Something was up. "Okay."

"Are you off work in a few minutes?"

"Yes, but I have plans."

"A date?" Did he sound jealous?

"Not exactly."

My answer didn't satisfy him, which was not surprising. "Well, do you have a date or not?"

"William, I do not have a date-date."

19

"Huh?"

"Are you free tomorrow for breakfast?"

"Do you mean brunch?" William knew me well.

"Mmm. Brunch, then. Or, really, lunch," I said.

"Sure."

"Grand. At noon?" I named a favorite bistro of ours, and he agreed to time and place.

After we said our goodbyes, I hugged myself and did a little dance not unlike Luis' disco move.

—

I crashed out of the ionosphere when I remembered Douglas. Seeing him was seriously wrong because the reason I was doing it was to obtain a free dinner. For several minutes, I weighed my morality against my hunger. Then, I began to apply eyeliner. A girl has to eat, doesn't she?

Douglas was at the Flaming Flamingo's bar, twisting a pink-and-white-striped cocktail stirrer into rabbit ears. He had already shredded two damp cocktail napkins, lending support to my supposition that this was not his first Bloody Mary of the evening. And, while we're on the subject, please! A Bloody Mary after noon? My god, I stopped making that *faux pas* before my voice changed. Well, sort of changed.

When Douglas saw me, he grinned and began wiggling like a puppy. I was pleased to give him so much pleasure. Of course, I cut quite a stunning figure sashaying down the twelve stairs from the restaurant's entrance. I knew I looked good, attested to by several patrons who swirled on their stools in my direction. As I strode by, the waves of my perfume, *Passion*, that had been liberated from free counter samples, caused the gentlemen to lift their noses in appreciation.

"Good evening, Douglas," I said, offering my hand as a lady would.

He frowned, uncertain whether he was supposed to kiss my fingers or give them a little shake. He settled on the latter, confirming that he had no style, even if he was a fourth.

"I have a table reserved," he explained, standing.

"Don't forget to pay the bartender, dear," I reminded him.

As Douglas pulled out some bills from a thin wallet (I have learned that thin wallets often conceal credit cards with large credit lines), the bartender winked at me. Bart knew my dates would tip properly, and I knew he would recycle the excess into an occasional drink *pour moi*.

"Another dollar, sweetie," I whispered into Douglas' ear.

He blushed and coughed up two. We walked over to the hostess and were escorted to a curving banquette. She pulled the table forward, and I scooted along the leather bench, tapping the place beside me. "Squeeze your Weejuns in here, Dougie."

Douglas' face pinked up nicely. He was wearing a camel-colored blazer and white dress shirt open at the throat. One button undone only. Not a sport.

"Hi, my name's Francine," the waitress said, as she perused my gold necklace and the boobs underneath it. "What can I get you two to drink?"

"Hi, Francine. Nice to meet you," I replied. "Vodka martini. Up. Dry." I glanced at Douglas. "Very, very dry."

Douglas blushed again. "I'll have a rum and Coke."

Oh, dear! The only thing more *amateur* than a Bloody Mary was a rum and Coke! I stared at the ceiling to dispel my acute mortification.

After the waitress handed us menus and departed, Douglas scanned the menu. "What would you like, do you think?"

I gave him a long look. "What would I like? Oh, my, honey, you do come to the point with alacrity." I gave him a genteel but smarmy grin.

"I meant, er, to eat."

"So did I." I glanced from his face to parts below before turning to the menu and checking the right column: the prices. "How's a girl to decide," I murmured, "with so many delightful options? Oh, I don't know. The escargot sounds positively divine, and I always have a hankering for beet salad—such a lovely color!" I accompanied this with a wink. "And, let's see . . . oh, why not? The rack of lamb. Rare. Very rare." I affixed my beautiful blues on the lad and was pleased to witness how my flirtations were heating his ardor.

When Francine returned with our drinks, Douglas lifted his glass to mine and touched rims while the waitress mirrored the restaurant's namesake flamingo, alternating from one long, skinny leg to the other as she waited, exasperation creasing her vertically-challenged face.

He swallowed some of his brown, bubbly, baby drink and then ordered my selections times two. "What kind of wine should we have? I mean, if you want any wine."

"Dear boy, we must have wine." I reeled off several choices for his consideration, none of which was less than fifty dollars per bottle.

He relayed the first selection, the most expensive of the three, to Francine. It was a joy to see her smile brighten in acknowledgment of the fat bill we were accumulating and the consequent fat tip that was sure to follow. She thanked us and trundled off.

"So, what do I call you?" he asked. "Kiri or Gilbert?"

"Whatever you like," I answered smoothly.

"Kiri, then. If that's okay?"

I nodded. Such a nervous fellow. "It's very nice of you to invite me for dinner." He hadn't, but who cares about details.

"Oh, my pleasure! I guess after last night—"

"After last night?"

"Yeah. I mean, the way you were looking at me. You know, while you were singing."

I had not singled him out for flirtation. Quite the opposite. However, the footlights were rather blinding. It was possible that one of the seductive glances aimed at William had gone astray. "And how was I looking at you?" I whispered.

"You know. Kind of sexy." His cheeks colored again.

"Dare I ask, dear Douglas, about William? I wouldn't want to interfere."

He took a large swallow of rum and Coke. "We're not . . . like, an item or anything."

"I understand." And I did. Douglas cottons to me, and then William sees me again as Kiri, evoking old romantic feelings, and telephones. One thing was certain, neither was likely to tell the other that they were dating me. This looked like a lot of free dinners with Douglas, who I could no doubt stall for a week or more without any bedroom activities, and some hot sex with William, who I did not intend to stall for one second. All this and an opera audition. Wow! My ship was coming in, and it looked like the *Queen Mary*! Thank you, Madame Clara!

—

Dinner was excellent. Plenty of garlic in the escargot, plenty more on the lamb. The wine was fine, and I played poor dithering Douglas like a flapping flounder on the line. Once or twice I draped my hand on his just to feel him tense. It was so much fun, really it was!

After espresso and a slice of cherry cheesecake, I excused myself to the ladies room, leaving Douglas to manfully struggle with the bill. That's what us girls do. I prayed that he was going to do the right thing and treat me. When I returned, I was delighted and relieved to see him standing by the bar, with everything properly dispatched.

"Oh, thanks so much," I whispered. "That was absolutely lovely."

We climbed the stairs and stepped outside into the hot night, avoiding the drip from an overhead air conditioner. I leaned into him as we walked, careful not to lean too much since I was taller than he was by several inches. And, yes, regrettably, there was a bit more to me than there was to him.

"What should we do now?" he asked with hope sparkling in his eyes.

"A little stroll perhaps?"

"Oh, okay." He was disappointed that a romantic interlude was not in the offing.

It was incumbent on me, therefore, to mete out some small encouragement. I placed both hands around his upper arm. "Oh, my!" I gushed. "You must work out, don't you, Douglas?" All men fall for this line. As a result, I use it frequently. Actually, his arm felt thin and undernourished, but illusion was my stock and trade.

"No, I don't. I know I should. Maybe I'll join a gym."

"Oh, heavens, I don't think you need to."

He puffed out his chest a little. "Yeah, I think I will. I mean, I used to swim a lot when I was an undergraduate at Yale."

"At Yale! How impressive! And on the swim team?"

"No, not really. I was, well, busy with my studies."

"And they were?"

"Philosophy. I intended to go to the seminary."

Now there's one thing I am not fond of and that's religion of any sort, especially as practiced in the good old U.S.A. At the moment, Love Thy Neighbor does not seem to include me, when I am Thy Gay Neighbor.

Douglas saw my tiny frown and quickly asked where I'd gone to college.

"Oh, here and there, dear. I studied music at Mannes for a bit . . . and spent a year at Oberlin." This was true, along with stints at other music schools and workshops. Money, rather than talent, had been my collegiate adversary.

"When did you decide you wanted to sing?"

"At age four. Mother was fond of Puccini and so was I. I loved singing along with her Callas albums, but I could never decide whether I should sing with Maria or the tenor. So, so confusing. But I knew my destiny when I appeared on the stage for the very first time."

"What role did you play?" Douglas asked.

"A Sugar Plum Fairy wearing a simply divine pink tutu!"

"Er, how did that happen?"

"A fortuitous and sudden cancellation!" I smiled at him disarmingly.

—

I had negotiated the evening's end gently, but Douglas was one love bite short of smitten. Why I have this effect on the lads, I have no notion. In six years, when I'm on the far side of forty, I may not have the same magnetic allure. But then my opera career will be launched—if my ship doesn't turn out to be the *Titanic*—and Guilia Hancock's name will be on every opera devotee's lips. Or at least that's the name I think I'll be using. Who knows? Speaking of names, I had to call Howard Lowenbaum, or rather Sol what's-his-name had to call old Howie.

CHAPTER FOUR

Bruncheon with William

After a morning bath replete with bubbles and scented oils, I dressed for my luncheon date with fair William. Before leaving, I phoned Howard Lowenbaum, lowering my voice to a basso growl. At this ungodly hour of 11:15 a.m., it was not difficult.

"Mr. Lowenbaum? Hello, this is Sol Redchek."

"Oh, er . . . Mr. Redchek. I thought Miss Hancock said your last name was Bleuchek? Yeah, I got it right here in my notebook."

"That's what I said. Sol Bleuchek," I corrected.

"Huh? Oh, musta misheard you. Well, thanks for calling . . . from Russia, right?"

"Yes. It's very early . . ."

"Early?"

"I mean late." Damn, I had no idea what the hell time it was in Russia. I didn't even know where I was supposed to be in Russia. I also hoped he didn't recognize that the phone number was the same as Gilbert's, though the ID came up as "New York" and not my name.

This set Howard back a moment, but he was determined to do business. "I gotta discuss fees."

"Oh, wonderful!" At the mention of money, my voice crept up to mezzo. I lowered it like a dropped elevator. "Mmm. Yes, fees."

"We're offering $8,250 each to our four principal singers. Two weeks of rehearsal, a final dress, and four performances."

I wasn't sure if that amount was low, medium, or high. I suspected the first and knew that any agent with *cojones* would argue for more. "That's the best you can do?" I asked, pebbles rattling around in my throat.

"Well, there might be some wiggle room."

My pulse quickened. "Yes?"

"Yeah, right, but we gotta hear Miss Hancock sing first. I want to check if our offer was in the ball park before we went ahead with her audition."

"I see. Well, the fee is in the ball park." Just then a fire engine siren pierced the air.

"Hey, that's funny," Howard Lowenbaum said. "I gotta fire truck coming down my way, too. Sounds like they do in New York. Small world, huh?"

I inhaled nervously. "Small world, indeed." A coincidence since he was uptown and I was downtown.

We agreed to talk again after the audition, and I hung up feeling like I could use another bath, this time a cold shower. But William awaited, and so I donned my winged slippers and ran out the door.

—

William was late as usual, later even than me. Despite the fact that I always calculate for his tardiness, I seldom manage to best him in the game of who could arrive after the other and thus appear busier and more important. Once again, today, he won, so I cooled my jets with a glass of iced tea.

As I sipped my drink, I thought of how William and I had met at the Purple Plum—he an adoring fan, me a glamorous singer. It was a fine start all round, especially when he began sending truckloads of roses before my performances, each flower perfectly formed, its petals tucked together provocatively. And, oh, my, the boy had a nose for finding the most fragrant buds!

We dated for several ecstatic weeks, attempted to live together in his apartment for three months, and then he cheated on me with a delivery boy. When accosted, William promised fidelity everlasting. The everlasting was ten days: a customer who came in looking for gladioli out of season and found William in season. Once again, he vowed constancy—until he flung himself at the feet of his hairstylist, a slippery frippery. Can you imagine? This time, I let fly with a torrent of jealous recriminations, packed my belongings, and called a cab. Unfortunately, William watched and let me go. Ever since, I have been ruing my theatrics. William was the best beau I ever had, despite his wandering. I missed him terribly.

He was now overdue by half an hour. I was about to leave when I saw him turn the corner. Tight black jeans and knit shirt, his dark hair perfectly combed, his trim body swinging along with his loose stride. Heart be still!

"Hi, Gil. Sorry I'm late," he said, as he slipped into the chair next to me. "Clark and I had an emergency with flowers for a funeral." Clark was his shop assistant.

As excuses go, this one was on par with most of his usual ones. How could I expect him to stiff funeral arrangements for some poor dead stiff? (Sorry, I couldn't resist the pun!) "That's okay," I replied, not wishing to blow my chances.

"I see you've had a drink already."

Which indicated how long I'd been at the restaurant. "Yes, I was early."

He looked me in the eye, knowing I was dissembling, but laughed lightly. "Well, it doesn't matter. We're here now, right?"

I liked the "we're" part of the statement and felt substantially encouraged. "Right."

We discussed the attributes of the various sandwiches and waiters with equal interest and settled on corned beef. The boy we liked also fit that category, a divine redhead, but nicely lean, unlike, as it turned out, the corned beef.

After we ordered, William gave me an affectionate once-over. "Gil, it's good to see you," he said, as if we'd been parted for a year.

"It's good to see you, William," I answered. I was not going to commit to a course of conversation until I learned which way the wind was blowing.

"I bet you're wondering why I called."

"Yes, as a matter of fact."

He eased back in his chair, his big hand resting on the table. I loved his large knuckles and long fingers. They weren't graceful, but they had their own distinct beauty.

"Well, I ran into someone the other day—"

"At the shop?"

He nodded. "Yeah, a guy came in to buy some flowers for his mother."

"Dutiful son and all that?"

"Mmm. Anyway, he mentioned that he was a producer. You know me, always curious, so I asked what he produced."

I could well imagine the *double entendres* that issued forth from William's mouth. "Yes?"

"You won't believe this, but the guy—Malcolm Earl—he's got a theater near the Café Carlyle. He just enlarged the place to seat several hundred people. Anyway—"

William said "anyway" all the time. The word glued his sentences together so they flowed into one another. "Anyway what?" I asked, growing impatient.

"Anyway, he thought it would be cool to do a staged *Rigoletto*. That's his favorite opera. He's looking for a tenor to sing the Duke. I thought of you, of course."

"Of course."

"And, well, I told him your credentials—not mentioning the Kiri bit at the Purple Plum. This guy's straight, after all."

"And?"

"He wants you to give him a call to set up an audition. You can sing the role, can't you?"

Although I could compress my voice to sing countertenor or soprano, as the case might be, I was a natural tenor and, in fact, knew the music well. "Sure, but the Duke of Mantua is a real macho beast. Not exactly camp."

"Oh, I bet you could pull it off." He gave me a friendly smile, one that wasn't ratcheted up to sizzling, the level I desired.

"Darling, I can pull off anything."

He ignored my insinuation. "I think Malcolm is loaded."

"How do you know?"

"Clothes."

"Say no more," I replied.

William pulled out a card and jotted the phone number on the corner of his napkin, neatly tearing the paper with his strong fingers. "Let me know what happens."

Our sandwiches and sodas were plunked in front of us, and he tucked into the first half of his four-inch-high corned beef monster.

"Oh, you bet I will." I said, placing a dill pickle in my mouth and sliding it between my lips seductively. William, alas, didn't notice. "So what else is new?"

He finished chewing, took a swallow of his drink, and stared blissfully into space. "Ah, yes. Douglas . . ."

"He *is* very new," I replied archly.

"Gil, I think it's getting serious."

Uh-oh. "Already?" I asked, disguising my upset by crunching on a potato chip. Unfortunately, it was soggy from pickle juice and had lost its splendiferous snap.

"Mmm. He's a great guy."

"No doubt."

"I'm thinking of moving in with him."

Holy cow! "Aren't you rushing things a bit?"

William looked at me for signs of jealousy. The signs were there, green as spring grass, but thankfully William was blind with love. "No, I don't think so. When something's right, it's right. Anyway, it would save some money."

Please! "And I assume he has pots of it?"

William nodded and slurped happily on his soda. "But that's not important."

"No, of course not." I was trying to calculate my chances at wooing William back. Minus zero at this point. I would need to do some serious scheming. *Pas de problème*. Still, I was saddened and disappointed that gloating over Douglas was the real reason he'd called.

"Douglas has a nice place . . . actually pretty close to where the Earl Theater is. Lexington and 74th Street. Two huge bedrooms, a fireplace—"

"Plenty of room for your two dozen fichus plants?"

"Yeah," he replied, not catching my tone. "It isn't as posh as his parents' condo on Central Park South, but—"

"But it will do," I finished for him.

He grinned. "Beats my apartment."

I wanted to correct him: *our apartment*, for that's the way I still thought of it. I could feel the steam gathering in my ears and my eyes glazing over.

"Douglas really enjoyed your show, by the way," William went on. "He wants us to return tonight."

"How lovely it will be to see him again." I played this à la Bette Davis, with a touch of acidic sweetness, the subtlety of which sailed over William's head.

We finished our sandwiches in silence. William was thinking of Douglas, and I was thinking of William thinking of Douglas, but I was positive that William was not thinking of Gilbert. I was relieved when the bill came, ending this mental merry-go-round. We split the check since William was ultra persnickety about money, one of his wee failings compensated by his other huge attributes. I crossed my legs demurely, just thinking of those attributes.

—

Depressed about my prospects with my ex, I trudged to a bodega and then home, my blue mood bordering on indigo. There, I sat at my keyboard and did what I was supposed to do: practice, practice, practice. Both roles. It was absolute hell switching from tenor to soprano, and I don't mean just confusing. Afterward, my throat felt like it'd been bodysurfing in the Sahara. But I was a trooper and gargled, drank tea with honey, and called Malcolm Earl of the large bucks.

"Hello, Mr. Malcolm?" I began, immediately realizing my error. "Oh, sorry, Mr. Earl."

"Yes?"

"This is . . ." I wasn't Kiri or Guilia. So who was I? ". . . er, Christopher Wren."

"Like the architect?" He laughed at his joke. His voice was deep and smooth.

"Oh, that's what everyone says," I replied, floating again into dangerous vocal territory. Quickly, I regrouped into tenor. "Anyway," (to borrow from William), "I'm calling because a friend, William Van Allan, told me that you're casting for an opera."

"Who?"

There is nothing I hate more than being told to call a stranger and then be told that the person who told me to call is a stranger to the stranger. "William Van Allan. He's a florist. He said he spoke with you about me . . . about singing the Duke in *Rigoletto*."

"I thought the tenor's name was Gilbert something?"

"Oh, yes, that's my middle name. Christopher Gilbert Rose-Wren. The last is hyphenated. I usually drop 'Rose' except for accounting purposes."

I was babbling to beat the band, but I was worried that Mr. Earl might have heard my name from my cabaret show, plus I was becoming addicted to creating aliases. Hurriedly, I continued. "I know the Duke very well. Not personally, I mean . . ."

My stab at humor did not pierce his funny bone. "Thanks for contacting me, er, Mr. Wren, I mean, Mr. Rose-Wren, but I spoke with that florist over a week ago. I've already found a tenor to sing the part."

So dear William was too busy diddling dear Douglas to inform me of this opportunity when we saw each other at the Plum. As one might imagine, my competitive instincts erupted. "Excuse me for asking, but is your singer under contract?"

"Well, no, not yet—"

"Mr. Earl, you must hear me before you sign him. I'm available for an audition anytime that's convenient." I prayed it wouldn't be early tomorrow because of my late-night Kiri De Uwana gig.

He was silent for a minute then asked about my experience, which I was happy to supply in detail, embellishing here and there as everyone does, but in my case, only mentioning the opera without saying what I sang. At the end of my recounting, Mr. Earl was impressed. For god's sake, who wouldn't be? The exploits of Plácido Domingo himself paled in comparison.

"Well, okay. Why don't you come round about two o'clock on Tuesday. Madison and 75th." He gave me the street number. "Please be prepared to sing "'La donna è mobile.'"

I hung up the phone, grabbed a pillow, and waltzed happily around the room, first picturing myself begowned and smiling at the glitterati gathered to celebrate after my stunning performance in *Così*. Tall, handsome gentlemen would kiss my gloved hand and offer pink roses and share sips of bubbling champagne from my golden slippers. And, then, after *Rigoletto*? I'd be the hottest and foxiest tenor in town. The talk of New York City. Invited to the best parties and charity balls. Ladies would coo and swoon, falling into airy faints as I passed by in white tie and tails. Newspapers would run out of superlatives when reviewing my brilliant artistry.

Hmm. Well, skip me as Fred Astaire and choose Marlene Dietrich in top hat instead. Anyway, if success smiled—as surely it would—money would be bursting from my pockets. I could afford a decent apartment, fine clothes befitting both a diva and a divo, and a real piano. I'd give my mother some cash to help out, and how much fun it would be to rip the page from Gal's little book, banishing my debt forever! Maybe I'd even buy her a new pair of boots. With at least one-inch heels. As for William, he'd have to stand at the end of the line behind all my admiring beaus!

CHAPTER FIVE

Douglas, Mom, and La Donna

As I was sawing off a leg from a pre-cooked lemon herbal chicken, the phone rang. My pal Gal. She was to the point, as usual.

"Gil. Gal."

"Darling, how are you? Long time no see."

"Yeah. Hey, gotta favor to ask."

I owed everyone favors, but I was concerned about my ability to dispatch one, despite the fact that I owed Gal big time. "Sure. What can I do for you?" I asked with caution shellacked to my voice.

"Well, it's like this, see. La Donna wants to meet you."

"She does?"

"Yeah. Like soon."

"Really?"

"Yeah. I let slip I knew this opera singer, and like I told you, she's whacked about opera."

"So you said."

"But here's the catch, Gil. She's one of the girls and all, but I can't bring her to see your act. She doesn't do out very often."

"*Out?*"

"Yeah, like she doesn't like to leave her place."

"Oh, that kind of *out.* I thought you meant the other kind."

"No, she's definitely that kind of *out* all right. No doubt about it."

"And you know this from personal experience?" I asked, teasing her.

"Gil, we don't go there. Got it?"

"Oh, girlfriend, you're no fun!"

"This is serious." Gal didn't sound tickled about the whole thing. "She'll pay some big bills if you'll sing something from Handel."

"Handel?"

"Mmm. I think that's what she said."

"Dare I ask whether she wants me to sing tenor, soprano, bass, baritone, or countertenor?"

"A counter-what? Don't be smart. I don't know."

"Or perhaps a mezzo aria?" I inquired. "But, Gal, dear, I refuse castrating."

"What the hell are you babbling about? You're as crazy as she is."

From Gal's ignorance, I deduced she hadn't a clue what La Donna wanted. Of the popular Handel operas, there weren't many stellar parts for tenor. Most of the heroes were sung by women these days, in trouser roles, unless you were castrated by priests before the age of puberty. Thankfully, I hadn't been.

"I don't know," I said, realizing I needed to take into consideration some practical matters. "As delighted as I would be to meet La Donna and compare fav operas, this isn't an especially opportune time."

"Opportune time? Jesus! Are you kidding me!"

"No. I have to protect my voice right now. You know, from strain and overuse."

Gal snorted like a mad rhino. "I'll take care of your damned voice, Gil! Not only do you owe me, but no one says 'no' to La Donna. Or if they do—"

I saw her point. Both of them. "Well, I suppose I could squeeze in a little Handel. Just for you, Gal."

Gal blew a blast of air through her nose, now reminding me of a bull elephant. "I'll pick you up tomorrow at noon. And Gil, no dresses and don't be late."

I hung up the phone and frowned. If I didn't know better, Gal had just threatened me, or rather, La Donna through Gal had threatened me.

But La Donna couldn't be as bad as all that! Gal was a decent gal, and any friend of hers couldn't be that scary. Not if she was a friend of mine, too, which Gal was, wasn't she?

I shook my head at this convoluted thought, tossed my cell phone on my bed, and sighed. "Damn! Some mezzo arias to learn." I suspected these would be La Donna's preference because lesbians had a thing about watching women portraying men. Like some guys liked watching guys portraying women, an activity that benefitted me. Luckily, I had studied Handel in school, when I was considering singing countertenor, a voice type that was invading the mezzos' prized territory, much to their annoyance. But I had no Handel sheet music. I'd have to hit up my old friend Darren for that. He owned just about every score and had a great copier. And he was the only person in town who owed me a favor—I always comped him tickets at the Purple Plum.

—

Darren was delighted to bring along copies of *Ariodante* and *Guilio Cesare* to the Purple Plum in exchange for a freebie ticket. If only all my debts could be so easily satisfied! I had also promised to sing "La donna è mobile" for him as part of my second act medley, though how I was going to do this in the persona of Kiri was making my head spin. In fact, my head was spinning at heretofore unheard of revolutions per second.

I arrived at my dressing room in a tizzy, only to find some pink roses. From William? Perhaps there was hope after all. The card quickly sank that happy thought: "To Gil, with love from Douglas and William." This was not William's block lettering, however. Hmm.

I rummaged around my closet and selected a gold lamé outfit, the only clean garment available. I knew it was clean because the dry cleaner, who I hadn't paid in two months, had taken out his animosity on the round sequins, causing the dress to resemble the skin of an ailing cheetah with the lining showing through as black spots. I sighed and slipped on the gown, thinking I needed a large cash infusion ASAP, and ASAP was likely. Cheered by the prospect of new furbelows, slippers, and furs, I donned my false eyelashes and made my curtain call with a minute to spare.

Taking my place on stage, I waited patiently for the lights to come up on my face, whereupon I eyed the clientele with my special blend of calm sensuality. On my right was Darren. William and Douglas were to my left. Unfortunately, it was immediately obvious that William was paying more attention to Douglas than to me. Well, I thought, we'll see about that.

I began with my usual Broadway songs, aiming my focus on Darren, who was easy to spot with his shaved bald pate and bright white shirt. A nice, nice guy. Back in the days before William, Darren and I had once tried our darndest to be more than friends, but our chemistry sets hadn't produced chemistry.

As the first half ended, I turned full candlepower on the entwined twosome and sang Piaf's "La Vie en Rose" while holding one of the pink long-stemmed roses like a lover—a prickly one—but then again most of mine had been. Douglas, I could see, was rapt, spellbound, and nearly drooling. As much as I adore such reactions, it was a shame that his expression wasn't on my ex's face, where it would have been more welcome. So how could I achieve this transformation? If I played to Douglas, William would be miffed at me. If I played to William, I wasn't sure it would do the trick . . . well, you know what I mean. And I would lose some free yummy dinners with Douglas along the way. Still, be true to one's passion, right? I moved to the side, allowing the spot to illuminate my perfect profile. When the song ended, I looked over my shoulder at William, imbuing my glance with tragic affection, tossed the rose at him, and blew a kiss.

The applause was deafening as usual. I rushed backstage to freshen my makeup, drink some water, and quiet my beating organ. No, my heart, silly!

—

The second act curtain went up with no William in sight. Just Douglas looking like a lovesick lamb, all batting eyelashes, blushes, and squirmy-wormy posture. Other than his classic good looks and to-die-for apartment, I couldn't see why William was interested in the lad since William wasn't the type to be influenced by money—my god, he'd been seriously involved with me, which shoots that theory in the *derrière*.

Without my ex to flirt with, I gave Darren and Douglas special treatment, especially when I assayed the Duke's "La donna è mobile" aria with Bette Midler buoyancy. At the end, Darren rose to his feet and shouted *"Brava!"* and Douglas, not to be outdone, sang out *"Bravo!"* (One can always tell the opera amateurs this way.) I blew them both kisses and gave them my trademark flappy hand wave learned from the lovely damsels on QVC, my absolute fav TV show.

Backstage, I was surprised to encounter William, who was trodding the eleven boards of my dressing room like a zoo-caged orangutan. When I gave him my sweetest smile, he turned on me with very unattractive ill humor.

"How dare you do that!" he shouted.

"William, please, keep your voice down," I whispered. I doubted that he could be heard over the chorus girl number on stage, but I didn't want to risk a public airing of my love affairs.

"So you don't deny it?"

"Deny what?"

His hands clenched into fists. "You know, with Douglas."

"Douglas?"

He turned his back on me. William, too, had a theatrical bent that emerged from time to time. "Yes, Douglas. What are you trying to do?"

"Nothing, darling." I was a bit unnerved since he had yet to remark on my flirtation with him, which seemed more to the point.

"Gil," he said, facing me, "you stay away from him!"

My temper was rising. Yes, I do have one, though it rarely comes to the fore. "I am not interested in your silly young man." I was about to blurt out that Douglas was interested in me, but since I hadn't thought through the ramifications of this admission, I managed to stuff a proverbial sock in my mouth.

"He's not silly!" he huffed. "Look in the mirror. You're silly!" William flipped one of the curls on my wig and stomped out of the room.

I collapsed into my chair and fought back tears.

—

The next morning, I was so miserable that I tried to cancel my at-home visit with La Donna, but Gal wasn't answering her cell phone. Otherwise engaged, I presumed. Everyone seemed to have a partner but me. I stumped around my apartment for an hour, reading *The New York Times*, drinking coffee, and warming up my voice. Since it was Sunday, I considered calling my mother. I didn't do this regularly for the simple reason my mother was rarely regularly at home, and when she was, she was not at home, if you catch my meaning. Nevertheless, I dialed and she was there, less rather than more.

"Hi, honey," she said in her oozy-boozy smoky voice.

"Hi, Mom. How are you doing?"

She lit up and exhaled. "Hanging in there. Had a show yesterday."

My mother worked the late afternoon shift singing Broadway selections at one of the casinos. Her voice had brass or could achieve a gauzy quality, but it had been twenty-five years since she'd received top billing as a cabaret artist.

"Good. How'd it go?" I asked.

"Fine. The usual."

When she didn't elaborate, I knew she'd jump-started her morning with coffee and Irish whiskey. I could already picture her weaving about the tiny house wearing an old, see-through pink nightgown, trailing ashes on her fuzzy bedroom slippers, her dyed blond hair unraveling its beehive.

"I have a little news, Mom."

"Oh? Yeah? What's up, sweetie?"

I gave her the low-down on the opera situation, neglecting to mention that the *Così* role was for a soprano.

"That's super, Gil!" She took a hit of cigarette. "Maybe I'll come up and see you . . ."

I could tell by the way she drifted off, that by the time the end of the sentence approached, she had already thought better of the idea. My mother was like that: a split-second, short-match enthusiasm before the fire was snuffed. It made me sad to know that she couldn't muster the energy to get on a bus and hear my first staged leading role in an opera.

"I'd love that," I replied. "I'll let you know the dates."

"Great!"

We were kidding ourselves, going through the patter to support our mutual illusions. My mother still imagined herself as a sexy cabaret bombshell; I let her picture me as a sexy cabaret singer, which was true except that I wore an evening gown. My mother knew I was a gay cross-dresser, but she pretended otherwise. I guess you could say we both maintained illusions, but down deep, despite the fact that I wasn't the son she had hoped for, and she wasn't the mother of my dreams, we loved each other.

"Have you heard anything from Dad?" I asked, as I often did to change the subject.

"No. Last I heard he was in Vegas gambling away his Social Security check." She sipped some coffee.

After my parents divorced when I was in eighth grade, my father evaporated into a world that was bright shine and zero substance. He was a middling-good poker player and ran the clubs like a migrant worker chasing the crops. Other than a glam photo of him with smooth black hair, dangling cigarette, a silver suit on a slender body, and a wolfish look in his blue eyes, I hardly remembered what he looked like. All I inherited from him was his physique, his eye color, and a collection of matchbooks from various bars, casinos, and showboats.

"Has he sent you any money?" I asked, knowing he hadn't.

"Not for a long time," she confirmed, "but I don't expect it anymore now that you're grown and gone."

He hadn't contributed much to my upbringing even when I wasn't grown and gone. "That's too bad, Mom."

"So when are you coming down to see me, Gil? We could hang out at the El Paso after I do my show."

The El Paso Restaurant featured slabs of sirloin steaks, stacks of baby-back ribs, and margaritas in goblets big enough to do a backstroke in. The food was violently terrible. "Soon," I replied, lying as I always did. I hadn't seen my mother in two years. I don't think she remembered my last visit.

She excused herself, undoubtedly for a quick hit at the whiskey-filling station. When she returned, we chatted for a few minutes and agreed to talk next Sunday, which we both knew wouldn't happen.

After hanging up, I felt worse, which was true after each conversation with my mother. I breathed in the air of my apartment, relieved I was here and not home in Atlantic City, and then dressed in a blue blazer left over from some beau, khaki slacks, and a white polo shirt. Prep without pep, so to speak. At high noon, Gal Friday appeared in a big pink Caddie with tail fins NASA would envy. The car's interior was black and white, very 50s, with a flower holder bearing a red carnation. Gal, too, was sporting a red bud in her lapel. She was in an ebullient mood, all sunshine and smiles and "how are yous," probably because she loved to drive or had scored a recent success between the sheets. I explained about William, but she was determined that my rain wouldn't ruin her parade.

"Stow it, Gil, William isn't coming back. Not now. Not ever," she said in what passed for empathy.

"But Gal," I wailed, "how can I go on without him?"

"Like before. You got work to do." As if reminded about the task at hand, her happy face disappeared, or at least what I could see of it in the rearview mirror. "Remember, Gil, you gotta be polite with La Donna."

"I'm always polite," I replied, watching a cute guy go past on the sidewalk. He was wearing a tee shirt stretched tight across his chest.

"You don't get it, do you? I mean, like really polite. No screw ups or stupid comments."

I tucked in my chin. "Good as gold. That's what I'll be." I kissed my two fingers and waved them in the air.

Gal rolled her eyes. "Just don't ask her any dumb questions . . . like 'what do you do for a living.' Okay?"

I agreed, though it didn't help my jitters to contemplate the question that Gal had told me not to ask, which, of course, made me want to ask it. I fought the urge to chew on my fingernails and returned to my perusals of attractive guys until we arrived at the corner of Mott and Spring Streets, where Gal parallel parked next to two orange cones. She hopped out, moved the markers to the sidewalk, crammed the giant boat of a car in the space, and tossed the cones in the trunk, which was large enough to hold a pile of dead bodies. As I disembarked, I noted that there was a roll of plastic inside, just in case.

Shuddering at the thought of the Caddie's history, I was once again on the verge of canceling. Indeed, I even said this to Gal, who gave me a crusty look.

"Gil, pull up your bootstraps." This passed for encouragement. "Come on." She grabbed me by the arm, imprinting a sizable cleft in my bicep.

I made note of the exterior of the building lest I needed to recall it for a solo visit, though I hoped there wouldn't be any of those. Ubiquitous brownstone trimmed in black with a triangular pediment filled with gold acanthus leaves wrapping around a shell. The brass buzzers, knockers, and one wide panel were polished to a mirror shine, the latter perfect for me to check my hair before entering the hallway to the elevator, whereupon Gal punched "P" for penthouse. (I noticed she checked her hair, too, at least what there was of it.) When the elevator opened at the top, we walked to a large door, and she used a key to open it—yes, one on her silver chain. Inside, the entrance was grand, with a color scheme like the car: black-and-white checkerboard tiles on the floor, pink walls and wainscoting, and silver mirrors everywhere, presumably so no one could sneak up on La Donna. The guard sitting at a tiny desk ensured that no unwanted visitors would enter the domicile. He scrutinized me with suspicion, but Gal put up a hand.

"It's okay, Tino," she said. "She's . . . I mean, he's with me."

The guy's amber eyes stared at me suspiciously, but he nodded his bulging head. We walked twenty feet, turned to the right, and entered an enormous room filled with enough greenery to impress William. The walls were candy-striped in pink-and-white flocked paper, with gold gilt sconces and chandeliers lighting the room. A recording of *Orfeo ed Euridice* was playing, and then, somewhere behind the potted palms, I heard a rustle.

"La Donna," Gal whispered reverently. "Gil, please, watch yourself."

Since Gal rarely said *please*, I knew she was sweating bullets. We passed around a plump green sofa and came upon a petite woman sitting in a large Louis-something chair with pounds of gilt spinach carved into its ample frame.

As I gazed at her, I was astonished to see that La Donna was older than I expected, in her early fifties, with alert brown eyes and gray hair smoothly gathered in a French twist. Her black pants outfit was tailored to perfection, accentuating her modest figure, which was bedecked with gold—all good heavy stuff—necklaces, bracelets, and three rings. She was wearing little gold sandals that I would have killed for (if they were twice as big), and her second toe was encircled by an emerald ring the size of Montana. La Donna observed me with cautious interest.

"This is Gilbert Rose," Gal said.

"La Donna Giovanna Milana Gabrielli." The woman's accent was bleached of Italian or New York intonations, though her voice was slightly rough, as if she had suffered from laryngitis recently. She extended her hand to me. "It is a pleasure, Mr. Rose."

Her hand was small and cool. "Please call me Gil." I was trying to reconcile this woman's dangerous reputation with her demeanor and couldn't.

"Delighted," she replied.

"I understand you would like to hear some Handel?"

"Yes." She clicked a remote to stop the music and glided to a glossy white Yamaha.

"Oh, how nice! Do you play?" I asked.

"Sadly, not well."

I was hoping that she could accompany me since it's tricky to concentrate on singing at the same time as my fingers are at work, although certain activities I can manage with my fingers while I am singing. Details will not be supplied.

Without further adieu, I parked in front of the pristine keyboard and spread out the music for "Va tacito" and "Scherza infida" while La Donna sat on the end of a gilded loveseat. Gal stood behind her like a dark, worried angel.

"May I start?" I asked, after running through the music once on the piano.

La Donna nodded her assent, and I began the introduction.

After singing both arias twice, I nipped through another Handel song. La Donna sat gazing at the air above my head, obviously satisfied. It took the sound of Gal's creaky leather jacket to bring her back from inner space. La Donna then turned and forced her crinkly thin lips into a radiant smile, brought her small hands together in a dry clap, and stood.

"Thank you so much, Gil! What a talent you have!"

As she moved closer to me, so did Gal, who was yoked in tandem to her employer.

"You're welcome," I replied, catching a raised eyebrow from Gal and wondering what it meant.

La Donna studied me for a long, tense moment, during which I wondered if I'd truly passed her Handel test, and, secondarily, whether I really wanted to do that. I smiled pleasantly, prepared for a rejection or an acceptance.

Finally, La Donna spoke. "Will you come sing for me again?"

I glanced at Gal, who was studying her boot tops, and said, "Of course. More Handel?"

"Yes, please, but if there's something you would also like to sing, bring the music." She turned to Gal and whispered in her ear. Gal nodded, reached into her pocket for an envelope, and handed it to me. As she did so, I noticed a thin drip of perspiration sliding down Gal's forehead.

I knew that it would be impolite to open the envelope, although I was terrifically curious as to the amount inside. "Thank you . . ." I trailed off, unsure how to address my new employer.

Sensing my indecision, she told me to call her La Donna. I knew immediately we would be best pals, especially when she invited me to a charming lunch of smoked salmon, kippered herring, and a fluffy mushroom omelet.

—

Once safely ensconced in the voluptuous back seat of the Cadillac, I opened the envelope and was delighted to find six fifty-dollar bills.

"Wow!" I enthused. "Not bad pay for a Sunday." I leaned over the seat and tucked three bills in Gal's pocket. "Toward my loan."

"Thanks." Gal cranked the ignition, and the big engine came to life. "Great job."

I noticed she was staring at me via the mirror. She still looked nervous. "Okay, so why do you have your knickers in a twist?"

She sighed. "Because."

"What do you mean, girlfriend?" I was feeling sassy from my splendid singing.

"Because you're in."

This cryptic thing was wearing thin. "Okay, so I'm in. What's that mean?"

"It means she'll expect you to perform on a regular basis. Whenever she wants."

"And?"

"And if you don't . . . well, Gil, let's not go there."

I sat back and thought about this. "What could happen? I sing. She likes to hear me sing. I sing some more. She pays me a lot of money. Sounds good to me." I hesitated for a second, then added. "I mean, what's she going to do if I don't show up? Fit me for some concrete booties?" I laughed. "Gal, you've been watching too many gangster movies."

"Dense. You're really dense." Gal shook her head. "That's why I didn't want to introduce you."

"Because I'm dense? Darling, I am seriously, seriously lost."

The car stopped for a light, and Gal pivoted around to face me. "Watch the newspapers, and you won't be so lost."

This was all I could get out of Gal Friday before I was deposited at my doorstep.

—

Upstairs, I looked at my phone messages and found four from Douglas. The first was time and place, don't call me, I'll call you. Gee, I wonder why? Did he wait until William was in the shower to contact me? Coast clear? Annoyed, I listened to the other three, which sounded increasingly more intense until the last one. "Meet me for a drink at Wally's Bar at four o'clock."

It was now quarter to four, and I had to practice. Should I telephone using the number on the Caller ID? I wasn't so inclined. Let old studly Douglas stew. It's wise for a girl to play hard to get, especially when she wasn't sure she wished to be caught.

I concentrated on Fiordiligi instead of frantic Douglas.

CHAPTER SIX

Howard Lowenbaum

I woke early, aquiver with excitement. My big day! Since my last electrolysis had been painful but successful, I didn't need to do much in the way of shaving, thank goodness. I did, however, spend an exorbitant amount of time in front of the mirror preparing my face. Then, I slipped into my lime green outfit—so slimming—wrapped the floral scarf around my neck, and tucked a little green handbag that I'd borrowed from Oscar's department store under my arm.

Since I was flush with cash, I splurged and took a cab uptown. As I entered the theater, I looked around for Howard Lowenbaum, finally finding him fussing backstage in the near dark. Howard was sweating, short, and had lost his waist years ago, if he'd ever possessed one. His face looked like it had been pummeled with asteroids since his birth. What hair he possessed was coarse and black, sprouting forests in front of his ears and within them, sporadically on the broad dome of his head, and here and there on his chin where he'd missed with the razor. Around his neck dangled a pair of tortoiseshell glasses, while a second pair perched above his forehead, one pair presumably for nearsightedness and one for farsightedness. Due to the distance of both glasses from his eyes, however, the man squinted when I arrived in front of him.

"Who're you?" he asked with typical New York directness.

I regretted the heels, although they were modest, since I towered over Howie by several inches. "I'm Guilia Hancock, Mr. Lowenbaum."

"Who?" He looked me up and down. Well, mostly up.

"The soprano. For Fiordiligi's role?"

"Oh, yeah, that's right. How 'bout you come over here and sing a few."

This was not a question, so I followed him to a scratched old Steinway. Without another word, he sat on its bench, lowered his forehead glasses, and flapped a few pages until he found "Come scoglio." He played the intro without finesse but on note.

I gave it my all, trying to sound feminine, and kept my gestures simple, which was a strain. When I finished, I peeked at Howie and saw that he was flipping more pages.

"Joanne!" he yelled.

Thinking he meant me, I said, "My name is Guilia—"

"I know who you are. I want my daughter, the fuckin' mezzo."

"Excuse me?" I said, somewhat offended by his language.

"Oh, sorry," he apologized without an ounce of contrition. "Joanne?"

From the wings came an apparition in red—blood red. From her head to her nails, one end dyed and the others polished.

"What do you want?" she asked, checking me out as she did so.

"Introductions." Howard waved his hand at her.

"I'm Joanne Lowenstein-Lowenbaum. Hi."

The hyphenated last name was a doozy, and she was just short of a floozy. "Guilia Hancock. It's a pleasure—"

"Hurry up. I gotta make some phone calls." He began to play the intro to "Prendero quel brunettino," the duet for Fiordiligi and Dorabella.

"Keep your pants on, Dad," Joanne told him, as fingers to brow, eyes closed, she imagined herself in the role.

I had no idea this was going to be an amateur production, and was about to spin on my green heels, when I remembered one tiny thing. The money. My dreams of a new apartment. Of success. Of snaring dear William. I smiled sweetly at my *Così* "sister" and nodded my head at Howard to start again.

Much to my surprise, old Joanne had a perfectly glorious voice. And we sounded perfectly glorious together, a fact Howard also noticed.

"Hired," he announced in my direction as he slammed the keyboard cover shut.

—

Joanne invited me for coffee at a little Greek dive that was decorated with blue-and-white flags and faded wallpaper featuring Acropolis scenes. We parked ourselves on opposite sides of an orange leatherette booth, whereupon Joanne ordered us four doughnuts. When

45

they arrived, they oozed glutinous purple jelly. The coffee came in white mugs so thick that they only held a thimbleful of java. I carefully ate a doughnut while holding a paper napkin underneath so I wouldn't drip on my new clothes.

"So, Guilia, how'd you get started in the biz?" Joanne asked.

In the bright diner lights I was worried that she'd notice that I wasn't female. I wished we'd gone to some dark skanky bar instead. I laid down the doughnut, dabbed at my mouth with the napkin, and tightened my scarf around my throat. "School first," I replied, then explained my career in detail, omitting mention of which roles I sang, since all were tenor parts.

Joanne chimed in here and there, listing her own career highlights. We were, in fact, getting along swimmingly. Thus encouraged, I ate my second doughnut and drank more coffee, thinking that it was going to be a blast to sing with her. I liked that she smiled a lot, leaned forward earnestly in conversation, and seemed to admire yours truly in the extreme. I also liked that she wouldn't steal my spotlight on stage. She was not beautiful by any stretch, although I suspected she'd taken after her mother instead of her father, which yielded a mild improvement in the looks department. Joanne was sort of short, sort of overweight, freckled, very red-haired, enthusiastic, a wee bit tough, and tremendously hearty.

We split the bill, which I was thrilled to do without dumping a bunch of coins on the table. Feeling flush, I even left a decent tip. We left the restaurant, and, as we were standing outside, Joanne asked if I would be interested in practicing together. A splendid idea, I said.

"Where do you live?" she wanted to know.

"In the Village," I began, suddenly remembering that my apartment was swarming with telltale evidence of Gilbert's and Kiri's existences.

"Hey, that'll be fine! My place is being painted this week. Reeks to high heaven."

Uh-oh. I started to backtrack on my offer, but Joanne spied a cab, had her arm up and waving before I could say anything except "but—"

"I'll get your phone and address from Daddy," she cried, stepping into the taxi.

"Oh, god," I whispered as the cab's exhaust shrouded me in black yuck.

—

I arrived home feeling happy and worried, eager to celebrate my good fortune, but concerned when I looked around my apartment at the gay memorabilia. Then, I checked my cell phone. Two phone messages from Desperate Douglas. One—another invitation for drinks—was for ten minutes prior, at Wally's. I looked up the bar and dialed, although my internal voice was singing "Why Can't You Behave?" The bartender put me through.

"This is Kiri, Dougie dear. Just saw your message. Do you still want to get together this evening?" I asked, nauseating myself.

"Hey! That'd be decent! Can you come now?"

"In a few. I have to change. I'll be there about 5:30."

I hung up and dashed around trying to find an old frock to wear.

—

Douglas Pierce IV was decked out for the high seas in a black blazer featuring a gold crest on his handsome breast. A striped red and white shirt, white pants, and brown Docksiders completed his ensemble. Natty. And, from the glassy look in his eye, he was a bit tipsy, too.

"Kiri!" he greeted me. "I'm so glad to see you!"

I gave him a chaste kiss on his smooth cheek. "Nice to see you."

He insisted I join him for a vodka martini, probably his new choice of drink in imitation of my more sophisticated alcoholic preferences. I hesitated, both for his sake and mine, fearing what troublesome behaviors would be fueled by more liquor. Old Dougie was already soaring on the fumes of previous cocktails, unless it was my presence causing him to seem all atwitter.

"Sure, I'd love one," I replied, smiling shyly at the bartender, who was hiding a smirk under his moustache.

No big tip for him, I thought, crossing my long, long legs in Douglas' direction.

"So how did the audition go?"

I was surprised he'd remembered. "Wonderful!" I exclaimed. "I got the part!"

"Wow! That's super!"

I smiled at his enthusiasm. "Yeah, it is. Rehearsals begin on September 3, then four performances." I gave him the dates. "It's a ton of singing." Which was true, especially considering my tenor audition and whatever demands La Donna intended to make on my Handelian talents.

"Too bad I'll be on vacation then," he said.

On vacation with William, I wondered, as our martinis landed as swiftly as supersonic jets? My anxiety made me thirsty, which was a dangerous thing with these little babies. I moved the bowl of peanuts closer to hand, hoping to deaden the effects of vodka. Douglas dove into some pretzels as we chit-chatted for a few minutes.

"You know, I've been thinking," he said, playing with a toothpick thrust through a jumbo green olive.

Alarm bells went off. "What have you been thinking?" I asked in my soft diva voice.

"I've been thinking maybe we should . . . well . . ."

The boy needed help, but I wasn't Florence Nightingale, at least not since sixth grade. Loved that snazzy navy cape and white headscarf. "Yes?" I stifled a grin.

"I guess what I'm saying is . . . I'd like to go to your place."

Oh, dear. What to do now? Thinking-cap time. "I would like nothing better, honey," I replied, waiting for inspiration, "but . . . my apartment is being painted at the moment. We could always go to yours . . ." I drifted off suggestively. He wouldn't agree to this because William was installed there.

"I see." He gave me a smile that intimated how much he'd like to kiss me. "We could arrange that but not tonight, Kiri. Very soon." He pressed his knee against my thigh, edging my dress higher. "Are you sure I can't tag along home with you? Just for an hour or so?"

For a quickie before he met Willie? I knew the florist shop closed at eight o'clock. "It's just chaos in there," I said. "Paint cans and tarps and all my furniture covered."

"I bet we could uncover one piece of furniture," he whispered in my ear.

"You will just have to be patient with me, Douglas. I'm very cautious about such things."

"That's what I like about you," he said with ill-disguised guile.

His lips brushed my neck, sending chills down my leg. Luckily, the bartender came to the rescue and asked if we wanted another round.

"No, thank you," I replied, straightening on my bar stool. "Now, dear, I really must toddle off. It's been a long day."

—

A long day, indeed! My god! After scrounging in the nether regions—oh, there you go again—I meant in the refrigerator!—I found an edible tomato, bid fond farewell to some Bibb lettuce that looked limper than I felt, and ate the rest of the hacked-up chicken with a chaser of mocha-mint, chocolate-chip, fudge-swirl ice cream. A night of mindless television was all I desired. But oh, no, no peace for me. The downstairs buzzer bleated. A voice came through the intercom.

"Lemme in, Gil."

I did and then opened my apartment door a minute later. Gal strode in like a gunslinger at the O.K. Corral, all crackling leather and heavy boots. Perhaps I should buy her some spurs for Christmas or would that be too kinky?

"Need a drink," she said. "Anything."

My liquor store was not in the best shape nor was my wine cellar stocked. I was also out of mint julep fixings, leaving only some crème de menthe and a pint of Scotch. I offered both.

"The green stuff."

This astonished me, but then again Gal did have sweet teeth the size of a lion's incisors. I found two wine glasses and poured a tot for her and a tot of Scotch for me. (Green was dandy for dresses but not drinks, except for the occasional julep.)

"How'd the thing go?" she asked, slugging down the liqueur and holding her glass out for a refill.

"Great!" I told her about the afternoon audition, including about Joanne Lowenstein-Lowenbaum. "Ever heard of her?"

Gal considered this for a minute. "Nope. Gay or straight?"

"I'm sure she's straight."

"Do you want me to scope her out?"

I was wondering why I bought such lousy Scotch, but then I remembered I hadn't. It was from cheap William. "Oh, not necessary," I replied, concerned to keep Gal and Joanne far, far apart. The less the Opera Company knew about my playmates the better.

"Still, I could make some inquiries."

"Really, Gal. Not needed."

She swallowed the rest of the emerald sugar. "Okay, then, I got business to discuss."

"La Donna business?"

"Yeah. That kind." She looked distinctly unhappy, frowning wrinkles as she stared down at my moth-eaten fake Oriental rug. "We need you for a little soirée tomorrow night. You, me, and several dozen others."

"La Donna's girls?" I guessed.

"Yeah," Gal replied. "Give me some more of that soda pop."

I filled her glass. "But Gal, I need to rest my voice."

"Not tomorrow, you don't. Say, you got anything to eat?"

I handed her a bag of bendable potato chips.

"And I also have an important audition at two o'clock," I added, remembering Malcolm Earl.

"Plenty of time. I'll take you wherever you want, Gil, so long as I deliver you at seven sharp." A tiny smile crept around her mouth. "So are you femme or butch for tomorrow's gig?"

I frowned, almost too tired to recall. "Tenor. I'll be dressed in . . . oh, something nice." I went to my closet and pawed through the dresses sheathed in plastic and pulled out the blue sports jacket.

"Do you have a tie?"

I looked at her helplessly, thinking she was more likely to own one than I was, and finally located a loud floral tie from a drawer. "A present from my mother."

"Okay, I'll take care of the tie, Gil. Got shoes and pants?"

I shrugged and finished my Scotch. "What should I sing?"

"Hell if I know. But it better be good."

CHAPTER SEVEN

Malcolm Earl

True to her word, Gal cruised by in the pink Cadillac at 1:15. She double-parked, ignoring the horns blaring behind her. As if she had all the time in the world, she got out and opened the back door for me. Feeling like gentry, I stepped in. A red silk tie lay on the back seat.

"It'll match your eyes." Gal chuckled.

"Thanks," I replied, flipping up the collar of my shirt and looping the tie around my neck.

Gal gunned the behemoth uptown to the address I'd been given, deposited me at the door, and promised to return when I called.

"Break a leg, Gil," she said as she drove off in a puff of exhaust.

"Hi-ho, Silver," I muttered.

After ringing the bell, I gave my name and waited until I was buzzed into the side door. At the end of the hallway, I found a sign that said: "The Earl Theater Company." Before I could knock, the door opened upon a gray-haired, debonair man housed in an expensive gray suit embellished with a black and gold tie. I felt instantly shabby, with not a sequin or feather to bolster my morale.

"Christopher Rose-Wren?" he asked.

"Yes. Mr. Earl?" The man nodded. "Thank you for taking the time to hear me." I kept my voice lower than usual, in baritone range as a precaution against sudden elevations due to excitement. I also kept my shoulders squared and board-stiff and quelled my usual hip action.

"Well, ordinarily I wouldn't have done so, but there was something about you that I liked. You sound like a real go-getter. That's the kind of guy I want in my company. Not like that pansy Patagonian tenor I almost hired." Malcolm Earl slapped me on the back hard, almost dislodging my tooth fillings. "Let me show you the place." He opened one of two swinging doors and proceeded into a large dark area. Seconds later, he flipped switches and the place lit up. Several hundred burgundy velvet seats, in three sections, curved around a stage hidden behind a red curtain. Crystal chandeliers hung from the ceiling.

"They rise just like at the Met, except they're smaller," he explained, pointing upward. "Austrian crystal."

Everything was new and very expensive. I complimented him on the design of his theater. As we approached the orchestra pit, I could tell the acoustics were first rate and said so.

"Yeah, I spent a lot to achieve that," he replied.

"It's a real accomplishment."

"Thanks, Mr. Rose-Wren."

"Call me Christopher."

Mr. Earl patted my back again. "Now, the assistant conductor is here. Are you ready?"

I was. I moved to the piano and gave it my best, singing the bejesus out of the music. Malcolm Earl thought so, too, and offered the part to me. I started to gush with happiness, sounding like a spinto soprano on speed, and stopped. Mr. Earl smiled at my enthusiasm and explained that six rehearsals were scheduled, including the final dress, and three performances. Anxiously, I asked the dates and was relieved to learn that they alternated with my *Così fan tutte* nights. What a lucky duck!

"Do you have an agent?" Malcolm Earl asked, as we sat down in the first row.

I took a chance. "No, not at the moment."

He tucked in his chin. "Well, I must say, that's a surprise. Especially with all your experience."

I wasn't sure whether he thought being agent-less was an agreeable or disagreeable state. "I had one," I began, "but I had to let him go."

"Skimming?"

I nodded.

He laid a hand on my arm. "Sorry to hear that, but you won't need an agent. Mark my words, Christopher, you'll go places with me."

A figure of speech or was he planning a touring company? I didn't ask.

"Yes, sir," he continued, "this is only the beginning. My little pocket theater. Eventually, I want to build an eight-hundred-seat hall to compete with the Met. Here on the East Side." He looked me over carefully. "You're a handsome fellow. Great voice, tall. The ladies will go for you. I'll make you a box office star."

With all the money he'd spent on the theater, I wondered what he would spend on handsome old me. As if he read my mind, Malcolm Earl laughed.

"I bet you want to know what you'll be paid, right?"

I nodded.

"How about $9,500 for the whole thing? Does that sound okay?"

I gulped. Between the two operas, I would make almost as much as I had all of last year; throw in the loot from singing Handel, and I would be sitting in the lap of luxury. Maybe even in William's lap. I kept my voice level. "That's fine."

"Great." He gave me his hand. "Deal. Come tomorrow at one o'clock for costume and wig fitting. You can meet the rest of the cast. Bring your head shots, too."

I floated out of the theater. Visions danced merrily in my head. Of singing Don José, Rodolfo, Hoffmann, Roméo, and maybe even Werther, though Werther was a bit of a soggy, weepy lad. And then I remembered that I didn't have any PR photos of Christopher Gilbert Rose-Wren or, for that matter, of Gilbert Eugene Rose, only portraits taken during my college years. What I possessed were Kiri De Uwana glam shots.

I called Gal and waited by the theater entrance. A few minutes later, the pink Cadillac came barreling down the street. Maybe Gal could help.

"How'd it go?" she asked.

I was once again seated in back, although why I couldn't sit in the front with her was beyond me. "Very well. I have another job, but I don't know how I'm going to manage both."

"You'll manage."

"I suppose." I sighed. "Two problems. I don't have a Social Security number in the name of Christopher Rose-Wren."

"Who the hell is that?"

"Me."

"No sweat, Gil. Use your real number and put down G. E. Rose."

"Okay, I guess," I said. "And I need a head shot right away. Any ideas?"

Gal negotiated two pedestrians with inches to spare. "Hmm. Yeah. Can do. Hold on."

Before I could slap my hand on the padded armrest, the big car swerved lanes and shot through a crosstown street. We zigged and zagged until she stopped short in the Bowery at a derelict brownstone decorated with three winos on its crumbling steps.

"Here?" I asked.

"Yep. This is the place. Now let me park this monster, and we'll go see Jean-Paul."

"Jean-Paul?"

She nodded. "He owes us."

I knew better than to ask who *us* was. "I can pay. I mean, I don't want to owe anyone for this." Especially not La Donna. Being in her little black book of debts held zero appeal.

Gal turned and gave me a sour look. "That's not the way it works. Enough said."

A stab of anxiety jolted through me. Things were getting way too chummy with mummy for my comfort level. "But, Gal, really—"

Before I could utter another syllable, Gal held up her hand to silence me, whipped into a miniscule parking space, pulled out her cell phone, and fast-dialed a number. "Jean-Paul. Gal."

I opened the door for some fresh air, since the interior of the Caddie suddenly seemed stuffy. In unison, the winos rolled red eyes my way.

"Hey, buddy," one said, "got a buck?"

I mused whether it was better to chip into their liquor ante or try to pass through them with a starchy look. As I wondered this, Gal got out of the car and took me by the arm, leading me like a stray sheep through the thicket of winos. She buzzed Jean-Paul, and we were inside without paying off the boys on the steps.

Four flights of filthy stairs later, a metal door opened, and a skeletal-looking guy with a torn black turtleneck answered, a cigarette glued to his gray lips. Without a word, he led us down a chipped gold-and-black linoleum hall—or at least gold might have been the color once. At the end, we entered a large room stuffed with cameras on tripods, banks of lights and soft boxes, batteries, and dozens of black wires snaking around the floor.

Jean-Paul reluctantly withdrew the cigarette, letting the ash fall on the floor. "Here," he said, pointing to a powder room. Inside were three-quarter-high mirrors, a makeup counter replete with cosmetics, a blow dryer, combs drowning in a blue solution, and a roll of paper towels. The sink was crying rusty tears, and from the stain below the faucet, it appeared that the weeping had been a long-term jag. I sat down on the tiny stool and tried to decide how to do my face as a tenor. Less is more, I thought, applying some liquid cover to my skin, which was thankfully clear and unblemished.

As I prepared for my portrait, my case of anxiety about the whole deal with La Donna grew, although my reaction seemed unrealistic considering how nice she'd been, how small she was, and how much she liked me. Even so, Big Ben bells were donging warnings in my head as I walked into the studio. Jean-Paul guided me to the center of the room, to a bench that was only eighteen inches high, thus necessitating a substantial amount of bending and folding of my long legs. Jean-Paul circled around like a black turkey buzzard, all angles and sharp edges, his hands creating a little square through which he squinted with an analytic, bloodshot eye that made me wonder if he'd been indulging with the boys on the stoop. Finally, he retreated to the wall and threw on the lights, blinding me momentarily. He waited for my blinking fit to end, grabbed a camera, and began clicking away, occasionally moving lights or my head, as whim dictated. Without asking, Jean-Paul pulled off my tie, ruffled my hair, and flipped up my collar for that rugged, windblown look. He snapped some more frames, and we were done.

"Give me five," Jean-Paul said.

I did, though for a moment I thought he meant five bucks.

Jean-Paul lit another cigarette and disappeared into a room behind the studio.

Gal was leaning against the wall, arms crossed. "He's good."

"He is?"

"Yeah."

A few minutes later, Jean-Paul waved us into his side room and showed us the photos on a computer screen, which was the first time I'd ever dealt with digital images. "You pick," he told me.

We scanned through them once, then again, tossing out the blurry ones or ones where the lighting made me look like a Met Life blimp. Of the ten left, I chose two poses and asked if he could convert them to black-and-white photographs as well as print them in color.

Jean-Paul nodded. "Ready tomorrow morning."

"I'll pick them up for you, Gil," Gal offered.

"Could I have forty of each?" I asked, thinking that photos of me as a tenor might eventually be more useful than my "soprano" portraits.

"Yeah. No problem." He eyed Gal for confirmation. She nodded. The deal was struck.

—

Gal was taciturn on the ride home and said little. She promised an evening E.T.A. of 6:45 and told me that formal wear was rented for me at the tuxedo shop two blocks from my apartment. All I had to do was fetch my outfit.

As much as I like dressing up, my tastes run to bright hues and shimmery things, not monkey suits. In fact, other than a high school prom to which I'd been dragged by a desperate cousin, I had never donned a cummerbund. Well, maybe once in fun. Hmm. Maybe twice.

The store was dingy, dusty, and dated. After providing the owner with my name, he scrutinized my body, taking visual measurements, disappeared for a few minutes, and returned with a shawl-collared white dinner jacket, a white wingtip shirt, and black satin self-tie bowtie, pants with satin stripes, and a cummerbund. Eyeing my brown shoes, the man shook his head and proffered a pair of black patent leather dress slippers. Now, we were getting somewhere! He asked if I knew how to knot the tie, and I, not wanting to admit the truth, said I did. Oh, my god, who'd have thought it would be so *très difficile*!

I carried the ensemble to my apartment and laid everything on my bed, wondering how in the world I'd gotten myself into this mess. Of course, I had to try the fancy wingtip shirt on immediately and the satin tie. Alas, the page of instructions accompanying the bowtie were fine for knotting it on my bedpost but not backwards on me. I was growing red in the face after my ninth try when the doorbell rang. Cripes! Not somebody else! I instantly thought it was Douglas and crept to the windowsill to peek over the edge. No one there. Whew. But then: *knock knock knock*. Tentative knocks, not quite like Douglas would knock.

With the tie dangling around my neck, I opened the door to encounter Joanne Lowenstein-Lowenbaum, who was grinning away like she'd won the New York Lottery.

"Hi," I said, wishing once again that my landlord would install a security peephole and that the other tenants would stop allowing strangers into the building.

"Oh, excuse me," she began, squinting at me not unlike her father had done. "You're not Guilia."

Oh, my god! She was right! I wasn't Guilia. I'm Gilbert or Christopher or some guy or other. "Er, no . . . ah . . . ah . . . she's not here at the moment." I opened the door a little wider.

"You must be her twin brother!" Joanne exclaimed, pushing the door forward.

"Her twin brother? Um, yes. Yes! Of course I'm her twin brother."

"Pleased to meet you." She told me her name. "I'm singing with Guilia in *Così*. At the Opera Company."

"Ah, well, nice to meet you." I looked around the room wildly and saw the front page of the newspaper featuring a photo of last night's winning run scored by a Yankee. My name is . . . Derek . . ."

"Hancock?" she supplied the rest.

"Yes, Derek Hancock." I gave her my most infectious grin and then added lamely, "Guilia and I have the same parents."

Relieved at this consolidation of my identity, I offered her a chair. Joanne sat down, her eyes circling around the room at my poster collection, a few of them featuring yours truly in drag. I had to make a quickie executive decision: either my sister was a woman pretending to be a drag queen—this might cast doubt on her sexual authenticity—or else I was the drag queen, now partly got up like a straight male guy about to go to a formal dinner party. I opted for the latter and explained this in overwrought detail to Joanne, who took it in stride.

"So you're what? Straight or gay?" she asked, with typical New Yorker forthrightness.

"The Million Dollar Question," I replied, with a touch of sadness.

"You're not sure?"

I shook my head. "Mostly straight, but I do enjoy dressing up from time to time." I almost added "as does my sister," but I nipped that blurt in the bud.

"That must be so confusing for you," she empathized.

"Yes, it is." I stifled a theatrical sigh.

"Will Guilia be coming home soon?" As she said this, she eyed the double bed, the only bed in the apartment.

"Er, no, I don't think so. Was she expecting you?" I didn't remember Joanne and I setting a time to practice today.

"Sort of," Joanne replied. "We're supposed to work on the score together."

"I see. Guilia did mention something about that. She's so excited about doing the role and your duets and all." I was starting to sound gushy. I lowered my chin to deepen my tone.

"She's got a rare voice," Joanne said.

"Why, thank you, that's so nice to hear. I'll tell Guilia."

"Do you sing, too?"

"Yes. Opera, cabaret, Broadway. A little of everything."

"What operas?"

"Well, Joanne, I'll let you in on a little secret. I'm going to do the Duke in *Rigoletto* at the Earl Theater Company."

"Hey, that's great!" she enthused, patting my arm. "When?"

"At the same time you and Guilia are singing *Così*." In my enthusiasm, I told her the dates.

"What an amazing coincidence! Guilia and I can run over and see you on our nights off!"

This brought me down to *terra firma*. "Wonderful." Since I didn't manage much exuberance, Joanne examined my face with more scrutiny than it could bear.

"Well, I guess I better go," she said after the silence became too long. "I didn't mean to hold you up, Derek. May I leave Guilia a note?"

I nodded, calculating how I was going to be in the same place, as two different sexes, and two different people if Joanne came to *Rigoletto*.

Joanne ripped out a leaf from a notebook and wrote her telephone number and name in a large, floppy handwriting. Big lower loops, I noticed; money or sex or both.

—

I was in such a sweat after Joanne left that I showered again. Hoping to eat a *boffo* meal at La Donna's, I had a light repast of an apple, a few Wheat Thins, and two glasses of water. Then, I dressed—all except for the tie, which I left undone around my neck. After combing my hair, I heard a *toot toot* and knew it was Gal.

She was slickered up good, sporting a shirt like mine, a tied tie, and the whole nine yards of formal wear, with a lovely aubergine waistcoat that I coveted. Gal wouldn't trade her vest for my cummerbund, but she did fix my bowtie, straightened my collar, tucked a red carnation boutonnière in my lapel, smacked me on the rear, and told me to board the boat.

On the way to La Donna's, Gal offered some information on Joanne Lowenstein-Lowenbaum. "Gil," she said, "watch out."

"Huh?"

"She's trouble or rather her father is."

"Howie? Come on! Don't be ridiculous."

"He's playing footsies with the Russkies."

"What?"

"Yeah. The Brooklyn boys."

"Nah, you've got it all wrong."

"Suit yourself, Gil. I'm just telling you to watch your behind."

"I'd rather watch someone else's . . . preferably someone tall, dark, and handsome."

Gal exhaled and shook her head in disbelief. "I got to watch over you like a damned mother hen, don't I?"

I smiled sweetly. "And you do it so well, darling."

CHAPTER EIGHT

The Soirée

The limos lined Mott and Spring Streets, disgorging gorgeous ladies left and right. No men, I noticed, except me, although there
were some dykes decked out like Gal, one even wearing lavender
spats, tails, and a matching hat. Hadn't I seen that outfit at Ascot
Day in *My Fair Lady*?

Gal abandoned me on the sidewalk so she could park the car
at whatever marina would accommodate its bulk. I didn't know
whether to wait or follow the other guests but decided I might be
in the "hired help" category and should enter with Gal. She arrived
a few minutes later and up we went.

Bulging Head Tino was dressed for the occasion, nearly busting
the seams of a white dinner jacket. He greeted me with a professional once over. Gal put a hand on my shoulder and told me to go
in since she had to welcome the guests.

"But what am I supposed to do?" I whispered.

"Sing, for chrissakes." She rolled her eyes at the rococo ceiling.

With the music scores under my arm, I straightened to my full
height and sallied forth down the hall. In the Potted Palm Room, as
I thought of it, everyone had cocktails in hand and were gathered
in little knots. Our hostess was not in sight so I sidled up to the
bar and asked for champagne. One couldn't go wrong with bubbly,
could one? I was on my third glass, accompanied by some pleasant
pâté and a rotund shrimp, when Gal grabbed me.

"What the hell do you think you're doing?" she demanded.

"Enjoying myself," I grinned, hoping no shrimp bits were mar-
ring the effect.

"You're not supposed to be drinking, Gil! Damn, you're dumb!
Get over to the piano. La Donna hired a pianist for you and
everything."

I didn't like being scolded and thrust out my lower lip in a show of stubbornness. "Artists should be treated with courtesy and respect."

"Can it, Gil." Either Gal's collar was too tight, or she was angry because her face was turning an uncomely shade of pink. She jerked her thumb and her head toward the piano.

Not to be rushed, I swallowed the last of my champagne and strolled over to the white Yamaha, only to find a woman in black tails sitting on the bench. She was tall, slender, and stunning, much like myself. We looked great together, a fact both of us appreciated, for she—her name was Raffaella—was undoubtedly as aware of her beauty as I was of mine. In fact, I wondered whether we'd been chosen because of this, as well as for our immense talent.

When I began singing "Va tacito," La Donna slipped through a thicket of potted palms like a sly jaguar, her eyes gleaming. Tonight, she was garbed in a form-fitting, tangerine gown that extended past floor length and trailed around a terracotta urn filled with some kind of sprouting greenery that may or may not have been a lotus plant. Only my ex, William, could tell. Thinking of him saddened me. As Raffaella and I marched into more Handel, I envisioned William standing across the crowded room, hearing me laugh and wanting to make me his own. Alas, it was not to be, at least not this evening.

While the alcohol had roughed up my voice ever so slightly, no one seemed to notice. La Donna clapped with real enthusiasm, as did everyone else. Sometime after midnight, saturated with stuffed mushrooms and champagne and five-hundred smackeroos the richer, Gal dropped me off at my street and left. I climbed upstairs, growing sadder with every step. Drunker, too, as my depression seemed to intensify my intoxication. After fumbling with the keys, I opened the door, took off my jacket and tie, and collapsed on the bed, feeling like my hangover had started already. All I wanted was to be with William. I'd trade the money, the singing, everything for him. Then, I recalled Madame Clara intoning, "It's just a matter of time." Did she mean he would come round, and all would be sublime once again? But, in truth, I was growing tired of his betrayals and rejections, his wandering eye and straying heart. Maybe Madame Clara was predicting that a new guy was about to appear, one who would make me forget William.

—

In the morning, or the last dregs of it, I felt ill. I felt sicker when I checked my phone messages. Howie for Sol. Since I'd called Howard Lowenbaum (as Sol) using my cell phone, he must have recorded the number and assumed it was my agent's and, hopefully, forgotten it was mine. Howard wanted to be called back to discuss perks and where to send my retainer fee. How was I going to get the check without a real agent?

I sat on a kitchen chair and held my aching head. Sol needed to make a quick return from Dr. Zhivago-land. Hmm. I had an idea, but it was probably going to cost me.

"Gal. Gil."

—

Before my *Rigoletto* costume-fitting, I arranged to see Howard Lowenbaum so he could meet Sol. Gal arrived looking haggard after a late night, but she was resplendent in a man's double-breasted gabardine suit. Her hair was slicked back smooth as a duck's behind, although her head was hidden under a fedora that made her look like the kind of guy Elliot Ness would nab. A cigar case resided in her breast pocket.

"You look perfect!" I exclaimed, as I lugged my suitcase containing a cosmetic bag, mirror, jacket, shirt, red tie, and trousers into the car along with the rented formal wear.

"So do you," Gal replied in a wry voice. "Like that skirt and blouse combo. And the pearls, Gil. Really 60s."

"Thanks." I wasn't sure if she was putting me on or giving me an honest compliment. I didn't ask since Gal had already shoved the Caddie in gear. After dropping off the tux at the rental store, she turned uptown and we rocketed to the Opera Company.

The interior theater lights were off except for a few spots on stage—lucky for me with my hangover, lucky for Gal for obvious reasons. To add to her agent disguise, she had donned a pair of dark sunglasses. I left her in the rear of the theater where it was darkest and found Howard taking a nap in one of the four orchestra boxes that flanked the stage.

"Hi, Mr. Lowenbaum," I said.

"Who're you?" No glasses were on his nose; pairs were on his head and around his neck.

I remembered this bit from before. "Guilia Hancock. Your Fiordiligi?"

"Oh, yeah. You was gonna bring your agent. Where is he?"

"Sol is back there," I pointed. "Unfortunately, he's got an eye infection. One of those Russian bugs or something. Can't handle being in the light."

"Oh. Yeah. Right. He was over there in Russkie Land. Musta just got back, huh?"

"Last night, as a matter of fact."

Howie grunted. "Okay, so let's go meet this guy."

I did the introductions without a hitch. We chatted about the state of opera in Russia, a topic that was thin ice for Gal, but with my help, we skated along fine. Then, Howie grabbed her arm and pulled her aside, telling me to take a hike.

"We gotta talk some business here," he explained. "Man to man."

This worried me, but I knew better than to interfere. I removed myself to a seat ten rows away and turned and watched. One piece of business was an instant success. Gal offered Howie a cigar, which I suspected was a real Cuban. All smiles, they lit up and soon were puffing away, a gray cloud of smoke enveloping their two heads like wreaths around a volcano. There was gruff, manly laughter—from which of them I had no idea—then some chuckles, backslaps, nods, and more backslaps. They were getting on like bosom buddies. Good old Gal!

When they finished, Howard Lowenbaum came down to where I was sitting. "Hey, great guy you got there, Guilia. Drives a hard bargain. I like that. Yeah, I like that." He nodded in agreement with himself. "Now, I gotta split. My daughter's meetin' me for lunch. You wanna join us?"

"Er, thanks, Mr. Howen . . . Lowenbaum. Sol needs to get to the eye doctor, and I promised to take him. He can't see a thing in the daylight."

"Okay, hon. Rain check. See you next week for the first run-through, okay?"

"Absolutely. Bye."

I patted his hand like a true lady and zipped up to Gal. "We have to get out of here *pronto*, girlfriend, because the mezzo is on her way."

"The mezzo?"

"Yeah, come on, Gal." I grabbed her arm, and we high-tailed it to the theater entrance as a cab pulled up with Joanne Lowenstein-Lowenbaum.

"Uh-oh! Here she comes." I looked around the foyer and spied the coat closet. I hauled Gal in there just as the front door opened.

We waited for a few minutes until the coast was clear and then ran out to the Caddie. I dove into the back seat, stripped off my skirt and blouse, opened my suitcase, and began wiping the makeup and lipstick from my face, while Gal nosed the Caddie into the traffic.

"Gil! What was that all about?"

"There wasn't time to talk to her. I have to go to the costume-fitting and . . . oh, no!"

"What?"

"Wigs. They're going to fit me for a wig!"

"What's wrong with that?"

"I'm already wearing one!" I wailed as I ripped it off my head.

—

Gal had to circle the block a few times before I was finished transforming Lois Lane into Clark Kent. I was beginning to feel like a comic book character, changing with every frame.

"So what happened with Howard?" I asked.

"Told him you won't need a dresser and will do your own makeup. Said you were a real shrinking violet."

"God, I didn't even think of that! Thank you, thank you!"

"And I sweetened the pot by six-hundred dollars. You also get to wear your own wigs."

I couldn't believe none of this had occurred to me. "Thank you, thank you!"

"And here is the costume rental company they've hired. It's a couple blocks from your place."

My hands flew to my cheeks. "Oh, my god! I hadn't thought of that, either! As soon as they see me and take my measurements . . ."

"You'll figure out something," Gal said, swerving around a van. "Also, they gave you six comp seats per performance."

"I don't know that many people who would come."

Gal parked the car and looked at me. "You got a lot of friends."

"I guess."

"And even though La Donna don't go out much, my bet is she'll come to opening night."

"Really?" I was pleased to hear this because it meant she loved my singing.

"Yeah. Really." Gal frowned. Finally, she gave me a grim smile. "Which means I got to be there, too, and you know how I feel about opera."

"Sorry," I replied in a meek voice.

"You better be," she muttered. "I also arranged for the check to be sent to my place unless Howard hands it to you in person. Figured that'd be the easiest."

"But it'll be in your name . . . the agency's name."

"Nope. Took care of that. Told Howard to make it out to G. Eugene Rose, my assistant who handles finances."

"He bought that?"

Gal nodded and chuckled. "Cuban cigars are very persuasive."

"How will I ever repay you, Gal?"

"For starters, I get an agent's fee. Fifteen percent of your take."

"Okay," I said sadly.

"And that cut don't count against what you owe me. That's for paying the compounded interest on your I.O.U., carting you all over the place, and general aggravation. You keep giving me cash until we're square on the original bill or else we got a problem. Understand?"

"Yeah." I dipped my head. While her terms were fair, I was dismayed to see my cherished money winging away before I even clutched it in my hands.

"Good. And, Gil, here are the head shots, the tickets, and the card of the costume company." She handed me everything.

I tucked the card and tickets in my pocket, grabbed the large envelope, and opened it. The portraits made me look like a million bucks, which was what I hoped to make soon.

"You're the best!" I leaned over and gave Gal a kiss on the cheek, then stepped out of the car by the theater entrance, and told her I'd get home on my own. With my overnight suitcase in hand, I disappeared into Malcolm Earl's amazing new hall.

The soprano playing Gilda was a willowy Swede named Oletha Svenson. Big blue eyes, plaited blond hair, pale skin. The baritone, in the role of her father, Rigoletto, was built like a short-legged plow horse with a stringy mane of gray hair that would require no wig. Chester Boone, no relation to the frontiersman, he informed us, though no one asked. Malcolm Earl made the introductions. His accountant sat at a separate table, so when I filled in my forms, the guy didn't know about my fake hyphenated last name and wrote the starter check to G. E. Rose and then handed me my comp tickets for the performances. I was going to like this gig a lot.

After we were fitted for our wigs (I had to stifle myself not to advise the wigmaker) and our measurements taken for our costumes, we were shown to the piano and given a once-through. Oletha had a fine voice, much to my surprise, though she couldn't act her way out of a box. Since Gilda is supposed to be the girl in a gilded cage, I guess that's okay. Chester was solid, or perhaps I should say stolid, but had a mature sound that fit the role. I was in excellent fettle and dashed through my arias with a devil-may-care regality appropriate for the Duke, who is either a roguish seducer or a rapist, depending on one's perspective.

At the end of the rehearsal, Liberio Lazarre, a skinny Portuguese guy who was playing the assassin, Sparafucile, waved a newspaper article at Chester Boone.

"Did you know Ben Silverman is in the hospital?"

Chester read the clipping. "My god! Somebody pierced his eardrum with a screwdriver. That's terrible!"

"What's going on?" Malcolm Earl asked.

Chester showed him the paragraph and turned to me. "Silverman was scheduled to sing Don Alfonso in that new production of *Così fan tutte*."

"Sounds like a mob hit or something," Liberio offered. "It says a policeman found him unconscious Monday night with some Handel sheet music in his pocket. That's strange. Ben wasn't a Handel singer."

Oh, my god! Was that what Gal meant by *check the newspaper*? I collapsed into an aisle seat.

"Christopher . . . are you all right?" Oletha asked, but her voice didn't register, in part because I'd forgotten I was Christopher. Instead, I was Gil with a screwdriver through my ear.

—

After I left the Earl Theater, I hardly recall taking a bus to the department store. Loretta was there and remarked that I looked as if I'd seen a ghost. I had. My own. How was I going to extricate myself from La Donna's treacly tentacles? At least I didn't have another singing engagement with her, although that could change in a flash. I wondered what Ben Silverman had done to displease the tiny mobsterette. Obviously something outlandishly disrespectful. I wouldn't do that, I reasoned. No, of course not.

Feeling a trifle better, I returned my borrowed green purse to Handbags and took the elevator to the fourth floor in order to set up a men's sporting goods display replete with big-chested male mannequins. Usually, I loved to run my hand over these bulky boys, but the thrill was gone tonight. All I wanted to do was go home and find William in my bed. Was that so much to ask after the day I'd had?

—

The next morning, melancholy surrounded me like an English fog. I knew I should call Joanne Lowenstein-Lowenbaum to practice, but I could scarcely move from the bed even though there was laundry to do, dusting, and general housecleaning. Yicky things like that. But then a better idea occurred to me. First, I would go to the costume store—not as Guilia, the soprano, but as her twin brother, Derek, who was helping his sister because she was caring for a sick relative. After that, I'd cruise by to see Luis. Money was burning a hole to China in my pocket, and I needed a new dress for my Guilia role, plus my Fiordiligi costumes might need some alterations, even if theatrical outfits were rigged with Velcro, snaps, hooks, and other mechanisms to let out or let in, shorten or lengthen clothes.

These plans got me up. The phone message from Douglas, which I hadn't noticed last night, got me down. He was inviting himself to my place for cocktails and a late afternoon liaison before, presumably, he met William for a late dinner. Luckily, Douglas didn't know my address, unless he had wormed it out of William or had stolen William's little black book, which was actually red—yes, I'd peeked in it a few times. Fortunately, since I wasn't an official resident anywhere, Dougie couldn't use the internet to find me in the halls of cyberspace.

CHAPTER NINE

Costumes, Dresses,
and a New Beau

The costume shop was a short hop from my apartment. An ancient seamstress greeted me at the door. She was bent in half and sporting a wrist pincushion that looked like a porcupine had nested there. I explained that my twin sister had been cast as Fiordiligi in Howard Lowenbaum's *Così* production.

"So what are you doing here?" she asked in a voice that might be described as querulous.

"Unfortunately, my mother is very ill, and my sister is unable to pick up her costumes. But I have her measurements. She's a 38 chest, 32 waist, and 34 hip—I think."

"Hold your shirt on." The woman beckoned me into the bowels of the store, where racks of clothes and boxes of shoes crowded the narrow aisles. She headed for a table in the rear, sat on a rickety stool, and grabbed a pad of paper and a pencil. "Now, gimme those again?"

I did. "I'm not sure about the hip measurement."

"Don't matter. Adjustable," the woman muttered. "How tall?"

"Very."

This raised the brow of the elderly lady. "Like you?"

"Rather like me, yes. She's my twin," I repeated inanely.

"Don't matter. Adjustable."

"Shoe size?"

"Eleven and a half, I think."

"Not adjustable. Gotta look." She glanced at my feet, which made me wonder if she was on to my deception, shook her head, raised herself from her stool, muttered something incomprehensible, and tromped off, returning with a box containing ivory satin pumps with a gold, rectangular buckle. "Only got tens. But here's what they look like. Your sister'll have to buy her own."

I was relieved that I wouldn't have to try the shoes on and thus expose my male feet to her gimlet eyes, though my feet are very dainty, if I do say so myself.

"Thank you. I'm sure I'll—er—my sister will find a pair to match."

"Close enough is good enough." The woman tossed the shoes in the box and headed off. Upon her return, she carried two outfits: an ensemble composed of a pale blue under-blouse with a high crinolined neck and a full-length navy gown for act one, and a similarly designed ivory blouse and a gold brocade gown for act two. She demonstrated how the dresses could be altered, placed them in plastic sheathing, and took down Guilia's name, address, and phone number. I left, doubling the dresses over my arm.

—

At my apartment, I tried on the costumes and was pleased that they were easy to adjust. I then hurried to Luis' store. He greeted me with double kisses and a huge smile. He knew I was flush, otherwise I'd never show up on his doorstep.

"How's life, girlfriend?" he asked.

"Just fine. Just dandy."

"And you need some dandy new threads to wear for a dandy new beau? Uh-huh!" He poked me in the ribs.

"No new beaus that I want."

"New gig?"

I explained about the two operas and the arrangement with La Donna. At the mention of her name, he whistled long and low.

"Not good, Gil. Not good at all."

"What do you mean?"

"She's one heavy hitter for a boa-wearing featherweight like you. I'd watch my tushy."

"Oh, come on, Luis."

He placed his hands on his hips and clucked. "You need to mind your mama. Ever heard of Leonora Parking? The lot over on 34th?"

"No. What about it?"

"Named for one of the lady's lovers."

"So?"

Luis shook his head. "Well, honey, guess who's lying in state under the cement."

69

"Oh."

I thought about the Silverman story in the paper. I'd convinced myself that Ben had developed a sudden passion for Handel and then tried something stupid like shaking down La Donna, something I would never, ever do.

"Well, I won't be gracing her bed anytime soon," I said with a lightness I didn't feel.

"True, dearest boy, but La Donna's rep is, shall we say, reptilian? Like as in the alligator variety?" Luis sighed and then moved from the murderous to the mercantile. "But enough about her. You're here for a new frock, right?"

"Yes. And shoes."

"Okay! So, what can I get you? Or what can I get you for? A dime, a dollar, a C note?"

I laughed in spite of my anxiety. "I need seriously stylish, Luis. To go with pearls."

"Suit or dress?"

"Maybe a nice suit . . . with a high collar."

"Have one in ecru that is very Brooke Astor," Luis said, grinning.

"Just the thing . . . and maybe a dress, too. Let's take a selection into the dressing room."

"I wouldn't mind being taken to the dressing room with the selection." He winked.

"Oh, you cad!" I was feeling friskier at the thought of new clothes.

—

I purchased the ecru jacket and skirt ensemble with matching two-inch heels—I would have to stand quite a bit during rehearsals and needed comfortable shoes. There was also a dress that was a deeper blue than the deep blue sea, an absolute must, and a scarf with red and gold griffins prancing through a thicket of fleur-de-lis. And, with great good luck, Luis found some ivory pumps in my size, with a lower heel than I would have liked, but since I was taller than Gareth, they would do. After rummaging around in some boxes, he shrieked with glee and produced a pair of oval gold buckles. As the seamstress had said, "close enough." He inserted them on the shoes.

These expenditures took a big chomp out of my net worth, but what's a girl to do? Laden down with my packages, I stopped at the grocery store for a newspaper, sandwich, and some boneless breast of chicken for dinner. As I approached my apartment, I applied the brakes *pronto*. Joanne Lowenstein-Lowenbaum was doing push-ups on my buzzer. Before I could vamoose, she spied me.

"Oh, Derek! Hellooo!" Her voice rang out over the quiet street and set several dogs off. What was there about mezzo-sopranos that the four-legged set loved to imitate?

I was stuck. I plastered a happy smile on my face and went to greet her.

—

What could I do but invite Joanne upstairs? I was going to have to work closely with her (as Guilia) and couldn't afford to be rude (as Derek).

"Would you like water? An iced tea?" I asked, hanging my plastic-sheathed suit and dress on the back of the bathroom door.

"That would be very nice, thanks." Joanne checked out my new blue duds. "Great color!"

"Oh, yes, isn't it? It'll go so well with my . . . Guilia's eyes."

Joanne looked my way. "You *do* have beautiful blue eyes, too, Derek."

"So does Guilia," I added.

Joanne gave me an odd look, one I would have given me had I been in her shoes. Speaking of which, they were gorgeous: Bruno Magli white slingbacks with a black patent leather heel and "vamp" hardware, as the ads described the brass and black decorative rectangle. I had drooled over these only two weeks ago, thinking they were so, so stylish and yet sensible at $303.99.

I poured tea and handed her a glass, explaining how I'd picked up my sister's clothes for her, all the while wondering which of the two of us Joanne really wanted to see. I was growing suspicious that the object of her interest wasn't my sister, although once again Joanne was packing the *Così* score to give that impression. We sat at my kitchen card table.

"I was hoping to catch Guilia," Joanne began. "Because of the house painting, I moved out of my place and then realized I'd given her my apartment phone number rather than my cell."

Lame, lame, lame excuse, I thought. In fact, crippled. "Guilia is visiting her cousin, er, my cousin. Fred. He's in . . . the hospital."

"That's too bad. What's wrong with him?"

"He's laid up."

"With what?"

"Oh, with . . . cancer." I said this with a small measure of relief.

"Sorry to hear that. Will he be okay?"

"Sure. I mean, after treatment. Would you like some more tea?"

"No, thanks." My breezy attitude about my sick cousin raised a tiny frown on her forehead. She sipped her drink.

"Hey, Derek, I just had an idea. You've got a keyboard, and I need to practice a little. I haven't been able to sing in my place because of the paint fumes."

"They can be terrible," I sympathized.

"Could you sing Guilia's role . . . I mean, so I can work on the duets?"

"The duets? I would absolutely love to help you out, Joanne, but I have to save my voice for tonight."

"Tonight?"

Damn! "Well, yes. I—"

Joanne saw my photo on the Purple Plum poster, which thankfully listed Kiri De Uwana's name and not mine. The dates for the summer were on the bottom.

"Are you doing that?" she asked, pointing to the announcement.

"Yeah, sort of."

"I've never been to a show at a gay club." Joanne gave me a suggestive smile.

I could see where this was headed and was terror-struck. "I wouldn't advise going to this one. It's too raunchy. Not what I do, but the other entertainers. They exceed the level of propriety. Frequently."

Unfortunately, this had an unintended effect. "I think that sounds like fun," she enthused, her eyes sparkling with mischief. She stood up to read the time and address on the handbill.

It was tricky enough if Joanne heard me singing the Duke's tenor role, which would sound significantly different than my counter-tenor-ish impersonation of a soprano and was also rakishly masculine. However I didn't want her to see me in a dress, singing as Kiri. That was too close to Guilia. I sent my brain scrambling for a solution, and it retrieved an answer, albeit not a very brilliant one.

"I would love for you to come tonight, Joanne, but the show is sold out."

"Sold out?"

"Mmm. A bus tour of gay lads from . . . Tuscaloosa. One is the nephew of another soloist."

"Are you sure?" she asked suspiciously.

"I am. In fact, I tried to get two tickets for friends and was sadly unsuccessful."

"Gay friends?"

"No, just friends."

Joanne moved a few inches closer to me. "That's good to hear, Derek, that you have some straight people in your life. You do, right?"

"Absolutely! Lots of them. So does Guilia."

"I thought Guilia was straight?"

"Oh, yes, she is, but she has many, many straight friends." I was getting in deeper by the minute. I had to get old Joanne to leave before I was in real trouble. "I'm so sorry, Joanne, but I have to rush off. I have to meet someone. Do you want to give me your cell phone number? I'll have Guilia get in touch when she returns." I gave her paper and pen and watched as she wrote.

"Maybe I could come for the Saturday performance?" she suggested.

"I may not be on the schedule this weekend. Management switcheroos." I bolted upright and nearly sprinted for the door.

"It must be a difficult business."

"Very." I stopped myself before I raised hand to brow.

"Well, okay. Tell Guilia I stopped by."

"I will."

After shutting the door, I sighed with relief. No mention of Ben Silverman, though there was no reason Joanne would tell a stranger about the attack. Now, if I only could deter Douglas, I'd have a pleasant afternoon until my revue at the Purple Plum.

—

I worked on Fiordiligi and ignored three phone calls from Douglas, each of which grew more desperate as the hours passed. After I finished my chicken and was dressing for the evening, the phone rang again. Despite my better judgment, I picked up. Douglas sounded teary.

"Oh, thank god!" he said.

"What's the matter?"

"It's William!"

My heart pole-vaulted into my throat. "Is he okay?"

Douglas' voice sounded choked. "Yes, but he left."

"Left?"

"Yes. He left. What am I going to do?"

What thrilling news, I thought! Now maybe I stood a chance with my ex. "What happened?"

"He caught me calling you and accused me of cheating on him."

Not good. Bad for Douglas, badder for me. "I hope you told him we weren't involved."

Douglas was silent for way too long. My chickie din-din did a tippy-toe flip in my stomach. Finally, he told me what I really, really didn't want to hear.

"Kiri, I'm sorry, but I couldn't lie to him! I said we weren't lovers—"

"Saints be praised!"

"But I did say we were seeing each other . . . that ever since that night at the Purple Plum I could think of no one else."

"But you let him move in with you!" I protested.

"Only halfway."

I wanted to throttle the lad. "Douglas, we're not seeing each other. Not really. We had dinner and drinks. No sex. No commitments."

"I know," he said sadly, "but I thought maybe tonight . . ."

How was I going to repair the damage between William and myself now that he thought I had stolen Douglas away and was a house-and-heartbreaker? "No, not tonight, Douglas. You need to do some serious thinking."

"I just want to be with you," he pleaded.

"I have to go. I'll talk to you later."

"Later when? After the show?"

"No. Not then." I didn't know how to get rid of him without being cruel. "It's just bad timing at the moment. My cousin Fred is in the hospital with cancer. I'm too upset right now."

"He is? I'm sorry."

"Thanks. Now—"

"I'll call you tomorrow?" he asked hopefully.

Thick as a brick, the boy was. "Okay," I agreed.

"Oh, thank you, Kiri!"

I hung up and had to re-apply the Luscious Coral lipstick I'd chewed off.

—

Friday was my free day except for mannequin-dressing duty at Oscar's. I decided to skip out to Washington Square Park and dangle my legs in the fountain. Maybe read a few pages of a mystery novel I'd started at least nine times over the last month. Not that the book was poorly written, but my own life was so challenging that I was unable to add one more straw to the camel's back of my overtaxed mind.

The day was hot and steamy, a sexy sort of late morning. By the way, I went as Gilbert since I desperately needed to rest my feet from wearing high heels. At the park, there were the usual assortment of druggies, kiddies, folkies, and oldies plus a few fab abs and gabby girls with babies. Espying a hot blond guy wearing a blue-and-white-striped, boat-necked shirt and denim cut-offs rolled high on his long legs, I headed for him. As I dipped my toes in the tepid water, he turned my way.

"Hi," he said.

"Hi," I replied.

We were silent, trying not to look at each other.

"My name's Hank," he said, flashing his ivories at me.

"Gil." I simply adore the name Hank—so manly, friendly, and hunky. "Water's pretty warm." Minimal dialogue is usually best, allowing time for perusal and estimating.

"Yeah." He was of the same school of playwriting.

We sat by the fountain, watching it splash. Finally, Hank interrupted the comradely quiet.

"Beautiful day."

"Yes. Too nice to stay inside." Well, okay, pretty trite, but this guy was attractive, and my brain was short-circuiting slightly. He was about forty, in shape without being outlandishly fit. (I will lift the occasional weight and do a set of reps now and then, but Kiri has to maintain a feminine figure.)

More silence and splashing of feet.

"So, do you live around here?" he asked.

"I do. A few blocks away." Was Hank soliciting a quickie? It had been a long time since I'd contemplated such a thing. Weeks.

Instead of following up with an invitation, however, he asked me what I did for a living.

I liked that he was in no rush to hit the sheets. "I'm an opera singer. And I also do a cabaret show at the Purple Plum on Thursday and Saturday nights." A little advertising never hurts.

"Really?" He turned toward me and smiled. "I love opera. What do you sing?"

I explained about my two roles, causing him to hoot with laughter when I admitted to singing soprano.

"I'll have to catch that," Hank said, wiping his eyes. "And no one has figured out that you're not a woman?"

I shook my head. "Nope. Not so far." Since he was such a good listener, I provided some of my other musical accomplishments.

"Wow. I really would love to hear you sing."

"Maybe Saturday?" I asked, hope knitting a cozy little nest in my stomach.

He thought about this for a few minutes. "I think I could make that. Yeah."

"What about you? I mean, what do you do?"

"Absent-minded psychology professor. N.Y.U."

This was getting better and better. "Off for the summer?"

He nodded. "I run workshops, though, and I'm writing a book on men."

I grinned. "Men?"

"Yeah. I'm doing research."

"Right now?" I couldn't resist flirting.

Hank threw back his head and laughed. "Yes!"

I laughed with him. And as I did, all thoughts about William vanished.

CHAPTER TEN

Hank Braylock

Hank Braylock invited me to lunch. Wow, did we have a marvelous time! He was funny, smart, and modest—just like me, except for the modesty. (I admit to a wee failing in this department.) As we delayed parting, sipping cappuccinos and then draining our water glasses dry, I knew this was a man I could count on, not another footsie-straying, fooling-around William. In fact, as I gazed upon this green-eyed professor with the dimpled square chin and slow smile, I hit the delete button on my ex. I was so in thrall with handsome Hank that I even picked up the tab.

As we strolled away from the restaurant, I asked where he lived, hoping that maybe his place was closer than mine.

"I have a condo on Bleecker Street."

"I live on Jones Street," I said, "but I haven't seen you in the neighborhood before."

"Well, that's because I recently moved in."

"Oh?"

"Yeah. I'll tell you about it when I have more time."

A crescendo silent scream starting in B flat filled my head. I wanted to stop him in his tracks and find out what was too time-consuming to tell me. Was he living with someone? Instead, I measured my stride and asked where he grew up, an inconsequential question meant to disguise my panic.

"Lambertville, New Jersey," he told me. "Went to Princeton undergraduate, N.Y.U. for my master's and doctoral degrees. I haven't moved far from home."

I was impressed with his education and said so. Then, wondering if his dark secret had to do with his family, I asked after them.

His green eyes clouded. "I only have a younger brother. Both my parents are dead."

"I'm sorry to hear that." I was now curious about his brother and asked about him.

His voice turned soft. "Kenny . . . I'll tell you about him soon."

I wasn't advancing my knowledge much, but something was definitely wrong with Kenny. Better dealing with a brother problem than a lover problem, though the possibility of a lover hadn't been discounted.

Hank put a hand on my arm. "Hey, Gil, I hate to go, but I have an appointment in a few minutes. Maybe I'll see you tomorrow night?"

"Oh, yeah, sure. By the way, I hope you're not turned off by drag?"

"No, not at all. But when it comes to relationships, I prefer a guy in my bed and not a woman." He gave me that warm, easy smile.

I liked that we were talking about guys in bed together. "I do, too," I agreed, wondering if I should ask for his phone number since he hadn't asked for mine. Perhaps it would be too pushy.

"See you, Gil. And thanks for lunch. I had a great time." He squeezed my shoulder, like he was consoling me.

Despite his comment that he'd enjoyed himself, I went home and fretted, positive Hank wouldn't show up at the Purple Plum, sure that he had a partner, and sure that I would never see him again.

Churning with anxiety, I took myself off to work at the department store.

—

Saturday passed slow as cold molasses. I vacillated between hope and pessimism, usually landing on the latter. The only bright spot was a call from Gal. She had my retainer fee from Howard Lowenbaum and said she would drop it by at three o'clock. When she arrived, I told her about Hank.

"Hmm," she finally said.

Gal could be so exasperating. "Is that all you have to say?"

"Yeah, until I see this guy."

"Well, come tonight."

"Can't."

"La Donna?"

Gal nodded. "And she wants you to sing after your show."

The bright spot went out. "No! Please! This might be my big chance with Hank!"

She shrugged. "Sorry. I'd say bring him along, but it's not a good idea."

"She doesn't have the right to order me around like this!" I protested.

"Did you read the newspaper like I told you?"

I sat down. "Ben Silverman?"

Gal didn't confirm or deny or explain. "Here's your check from Lowenbaum. I'll pick you up at 10:30 sharp." She gave me a meaningful look and left.

Stunned, I sat down on the edge of my bed and worried away the rest of the afternoon.

—

When I walked into my dressing room at the Purple Plum, I hoped for a sign. A spray of flowers, a box of Godivas, a romantic card. *Nada*. Not even from Douglas. Crestfallen, I wondered if I could go on. The zip had been zapped from me. I felt lower than a snake's hips. Pro that I am, however, I slapped on the powder and wig and waited for my call.

I arrived on stage and immediately noticed Douglas, grinning madly. I gave him one of my QVC waves and searched for Hank's blond head. Unfortunately, the back of the room was dark until after the bows, and he wasn't in the first few rows.

I sang a Broadway mix and ended with an especially haunting rendition of "My Man," aiming my eyes toward the rear of the crowd in case Hank was there. At the break, the lights came up, but I couldn't see him. I escaped to my dressing room and refused to invite Douglas in when he knocked.

The second half was opera as usual. After the performance, everyone wildly applauded and then charged the bar like a herd of thirsty buffaloes. From backstage, I didn't have a good view of the crowd and decided Hank would come to my dressing room if he was at the club. I hurried down the cramped hall and into my room, changed into Gil's clothes, and looked at my watch. Oh, god! I was twenty minutes late for La Donna! But what about Hank? Maybe he met someone and was finishing a beer, about to tap on my door? I pictured his gorgeous face . . . he'd give me a sexy smile and maybe a sultry kiss.

I grabbed my bag and the Handel sheet music, and was about to go look for him, when the knock came.

"Hank!" I cried, throwing open the door.

There stood Gal, scowling, arms crossed. "You're late!"

"But . . . but . . ."

"It'll be your butt and mine if you don't get your ass into the car." She clutched my collar and dragged me toward the club's rear exit.

"Oh, Gal! Please! Let me see if Hank is inside!"

She poked her tongue in her cheek, contemplating my request for all of one second, and then shoved me out the door and toward the street, where the pink Cadillac was moored. After another shove, I got in the back seat, and Gal throttled up and off we went. I felt as rotten as a three-month old Halloween pumpkin.

After a few minutes of silence, Gal asked, "How'd it go tonight?"

"Don't want to talk about it." I refused to glance at the rearview mirror in case she was watching me.

—

When we arrived at La Donna's, Gal escorted me into a room with lavender upholstered furniture, which was coordinated with the pink and violet wallpaper. The Yamaha had been wheeled in, unless it was a clone of the one in the salon. I sat down on the bench and ran through some arias. A few minutes later, La Donna silently appeared. We said our *good evenings* and then she requested more Handel.

After I finished several arias, she clapped politely. I turned to her, wondering if I was now dismissed.

"Gil," she began, "I really appreciate that you came and sang for me. Gal—"

Gal immediately stepped around her employer's chair and handed me an envelope.

"Thanks," I said, beginning to rise from the piano bench.

La Donna smiled. "Sit, Gil."

I did. I was already overheated from singing, but now I was becoming overheated from the hot glare emanating from La Donna's eyes. Her friendliness had flown.

"I want to tell you two things," she said in a low voice.

"Oh?"

"First. You were half an hour late."

"I'm sorry . . . my performance ran—"

"I don't care," she cut in, rising from her chair. "Don't do it again."

I squirmed on the piano bench. A drip of perspiration sashayed down my temple and died a slow, ticklish death under my shirt collar. "I won't."

"And the second thing. About Howard Lowenbaum. I understand he's hired you for an opera."

"Yes," I replied tentatively.

"Well, I wouldn't do it if I were you."

"What?"

"He's trouble."

I waited for her to elaborate, but she didn't. "What kind of trouble?" I bit back asking about Ben Silverman.

La Donna raised her hand to stop the discussion and looked away. Gal cleared her throat and jerked her head, indicating it was time to leave.

—

Gal refused to speak until we were outside, perhaps because La Donna had bugs hidden everywhere. As soon as my loafers hit the sidewalk, I peppered her with questions.

"Gil, I can't tell you any more." She rubbed her neck. "Sorry."

I was incensed. "I don't get it. That opera role is a big break for me. Is La Donna jealous? Is that the problem?"

Gal pulled out the car keys and studied them like uncommunicative tea leaves.

"Come on, Gal . . . what's up?" I pleaded.

"Just do as she says."

"Why? I mean, how did she even hear that I was singing for him?"

"She hears everything."

"You mean you told her."

"I didn't know she had a problem with Howard Lowenbaum."

"Well, she seems to have a problem! And you said she might come to opening night. What happened between coming to my performance and not allowing me to perform?"

Gal shrugged. "That was before."

"Before what? Are they rivals or something? All of a sudden?"

"We don't talk about business."

"Who is *we*—you and me? Gal, I'm your friend!"

She gave me a brooding Bogart look. "Got no idea why La Donna wants you to quit. Just don't do the opera."

"This is complete nonsense!" I shouted. "I'll walk home!" I slapped two fifties in her hand as additional payment on my debt and headed for my apartment. Gal didn't follow me.

—

In the morning, I did an online search for both Howard Lowenbaum and La Donna Giovanna Milana Gabrielli. He was listed as an impresario, with an import-export business in Brooklyn and stores in Manhattan. No combination of La Donna's names produced a hit. She didn't exist in cyberspace. I also checked N.Y.U.'s psych department and found Henry Braylock, assistant professor. His bio dovetailed with what he'd told me, so he'd been truthful, and at the bottom was an office e-mail address. I wrote this down but didn't send him a note.

With nothing to do except practice, which I didn't do because my voice was tired, I decided to walk along Bleecker Street, humming "On the Street Where You Live" and hoping for an accidental meeting with Hank. I even stopped for coffee at an outdoor café, in case he might stroll by. No luck. I paid the bill and went to Washington Square Park. Unsuccessful there, too, I deposited my check at an ATM and withdrew some cash, then returned home, read the Sunday paper, and stared at the phone that wasn't ringing.

—

Dateless on Labor Day. I slept late, studied the *Così* score, and when Douglas called in the early afternoon, upset that William was rejecting him and hoping that I'd invite him over, I didn't. Even when he offered to take me out for sushi, I said no, nicely and firmly. By nine, I was on the border of crazy. Okay, crazier. I fired up the old computer and sat at my desk, composing an e-mail that was calm, cool, and collected:

Dear Hank,

I don't know if you'll get this, but I wanted to say hi. The show went well on Saturday—I was hoping to see you. Sorry if I missed you. Any chance we could meet for coffee or a drink?

Gilbert

I read this over six times to measure the pathetic factor and finally sent it, adding my cell phone number. Since I was used to being the chasee in relationships rather than the chaser, this felt strange and uncomfortable. I prayed it wouldn't sound desperate.

I kept the computer on until a few minutes before midnight, but Hank didn't reply. My night was mostly sleepless, worrying about Hank, Howard, and Herself and Herself's intentions.

CHAPTER ELEVEN

First Rehearsal

I wore my elegant ecru suit to the first rehearsal of *Così*. With double-stranded pearls, modest makeup, a leopard-print scarf, and low heels, I looked quietly assured. As I entered the theater, for the hundredth time since our visit last night, I considered La Donna's warning about singing in Howard's production, and, as I had done each time, I dismissed her attitude as competitive possessiveness. Obviously, she wanted me and my talents all for herself, but my destiny lay before me, starry and grand, and a bit of jealousy wouldn't waylay my breathtaking ascent. I wasn't some rough-and-tumble gunrunner for the mob, was I? And, besides, La Donna liked me, so long as I was prompt and polite and sang Handel with fire and flare.

Howard Lowenbaum, his glasses missing entirely, greeted me with enthusiasm.

"Hey, thanks for coming, Fiona."

"Mr. Lowenbaum, I'm Guilia Hancock."

"Who?"

"Your Fiordiligi," I said in a loud voice, as if blindness equated with deafness.

"Oh, yeah. Right." He patted me on the back. "C'mon down and powwow with the rest of the singers."

Not everyone in the cast had met, so we all introduced ourselves quickly. Fiona O'Sullivan, a coloratura soprano from County Cork, our Despina, pumped my hand like she was milking an unproductive cow. She was tall and reedy and blushy, grinned a lot, and seemed pleasant. My initial love interest in the opera, Guglielmo, was played by a bear-like Russian bass, Ivan-something unpronounceable ending in *sky*. He, too, mangled my fingers with enthusiasm. His English was passable; his body odor was not. I backed up a few paces, wondering how we were going to sing duets, and ran into the tenor who was singing Ferrando. This guy was wearing elevator shoes and still came up to my chin. I could have picked him up and chucked him across the orchestra pit without any trouble.

"My name ith Gareth Kerr," he said, "and I am *tho* glad to thing with you!"

His lisp had my tongue in knots. "Nice to sing with you, too, Gareth," I replied, thinking that the last thing I needed to mess up my soprano impersonation was a gay guy, and if this wasn't a gay guy, I'd chug-a-lug antifreeze from an Ugg boot.

When the replacement for Don Alfonso stepped forward, Howard explained that Ben Silverman had been attacked and was currently in the hospital, his singing career most likely ended. No reason for the assault was offered, though Fiona asked. Our new Don was Nate Lowenstein. A relative of Joanne's mother, I deduced. He was average weight and height, but his protruding eyes bounced around like they were on pogo sticks. Nate was older, probably in his late 50s, as befitted the role, and stuck to Howard tighter than a tick.

The conductor was also in evidence: a scrabbling little mouse of a man who was half-hidden by the Steinway. Despite the summer heat, he wore a threadbare tweed suit, tweed tie, and a little Irish tweed cap pulled down over wisps of curly gray hair. Heavy black glasses pressed down on his tiny nose, which pressed down on an oddly lush handlebar moustache, which drooped over his mouth. Maestro Cavendish MacDougal. I shook his hand and nodded deferentially.

Except for the Russian, I was taller than everyone, a fact that caused me some concern since I was supposed to be a girl. I was also a tad worried about this collection of misfits. Well, at least Joanne Lowenstein-Lowenbaum had a worthy voice. And speaking of her, where was she? I asked her father.

"Oh, Joanne is getting doughnuts."

Joanne, the Doughnut Queen.

"Okay, I'd like to hear you all," squeaked Maestro MacDougal. "Please gather around the piano."

We did and the results were mixed. Gareth lost his lisp when singing in Italian, leading me to assume that the lisp was an affectation rather than a real impediment—I've encountered this before in gay men who don't want to be identified as homosexual and opt for "straight" speech in certain situations and then revert to lisping to emphasize their gay identity. Gareth, however, seemed to be quite cozy with his sexuality in public and was also onto me, having scanned me with his gaydar and determined I was a club member, a fact he signaled with mischievous glances. As a singer, Gareth was on pitch but woefully underpowered. When the two lads switch lovers later in the opera and he becomes my *innamorato*, we would be physically and vocally ill-matched.

Ten minutes into our workout, there was a commotion and in came Joanne, bearing a huge white box of doughnuts. She flew down the aisle with her wings of red hair and duster-style Indian gauze dress flying, plopped the goodies on a table, and trilled, "Good morning!"

Her star-quality thus established, she opened the box. Everyone dove in like ravenous bluefish, much to the irritation of the conductor, whose authority she had successfully usurped, causing our maestro to harrumph and sniff in mild protest.

—

After two hours of doughnuts and singing, Howard Lowenbaum ended the rehearsal. He appeared pleased with what we'd accomplished, but the real boss was his daughter, who was less than happy. As I was gathering my things, she pulled me aside and clucked her tongue in exasperation. "I can't believe that idiot conductor hired some of these people."

"I thought your father selected the cast."

"Just me and you and MacDougal. Oh, and now Nate Lowenstein—he's my mother's cousin."

"Well, Fiona is passable and Ivan isn't too bad."

Joanne made a face. "No, he isn't, but oh my god does he smell!" She giggled and laid a hand on my arm. "And that Gareth guy! He's too much."

"You mean he'th a louthy thinger?"

Joanne doubled over with laughter. I laughed, too, but in a more ladylike fashion. I have, after all, an image to maintain.

"You're a scream!" she whispered.

"I am!" I agreed. "So how did this project get started?"

"Because of me. I couldn't find an agent so my father said he'd take care of things."

This brought me back to La Donna's warning that Howard Lowenbaum was trouble. Did this also apply to his daughter?

Joanne looked around, as if someone might be listening. "Would you do me a favor?"

One of those pesky favor-things again. "What?"

"I hate to ask, but I think your twin brother is really gorgeous. I mean, handsome. Anyhow . . . is he gay or what?"

I knew where this garden path was leading. "Derek? Oh, I'm not really sure." Hedge, hedge.

"But how can that be? Has he dated women?"

I nodded. "Sure, lots."

"And men?"

"One or two, once or twice."

"And he really doesn't know?"

I shrugged.

"Well, could you ask him if we could go out? I even told my father about Derek, and he wants to meet him. Said to bring him to dinner one night—with you, of course."

"Oh, I'm not sure that's a good idea," I replied. "Derek, is, er, the nervous type. He doesn't like to meet fathers of any kind."

Joanne stared at me for a minute, parsing what kinds of fathers there were, and then relaxed her furrowed brow. "Okay. Cool. But a date would be okay, wouldn't it?"

"You'll have to talk to Derek yourself, Joanne."

"He's just so good-looking! I mean, you're pretty and all, but he's amazing."

I was becoming jealous of myself. "He's not that good-looking."

She pushed at my shoulder. "Yes, he is! Hey, I have an idea. Why don't I give you a ride home, and we can surprise him?"

"He isn't there. He's at . . . the hospital, which is why I didn't call you to practice."

"With your cousin?"

"Yeah, with my cousin Frank—"

"I thought his name is Fred?"

"Mmm. Frederick Franklin . . ." I had to escape by using my exemplary wits. "Besides, I have a gynecological appointment this afternoon."

Her voice became more hushed. "Anything serious, Guilia?"

"Just one of those little girl things," I confided. "Nothing to worry about."

"That's good," she said and then began to tell me about an enormous fibroid tumor she'd had, which in the telling seemed to enlarge to the size of a watermelon. Now, I have always been a mite squeamish and cannot handle this sort of thing at all. Joanne didn't notice, however, and kept piling on the gory details. Finally, just short of a swoon, I begged off, saying I had to go home and shower before seeing the doctor. Actually, I did need a shower to revive myself.

"Oh, okay," she replied. "I guess I'll call your brother later. Could you give me his number?"

Reluctantly, I did, praying she wouldn't realize Derek's and Guilia's numbers were the same. I watched as she entered the number in her phone list under "D," hopefully on auto-dial, which would mean she might not compare the two.

"Good," I said. "I'll see you on Thursday for the next rehearsal."

I ran out of the theater and greeted the polluted New York air as if it were pure oxygen.

—

After grabbing a hot dog from a street vendor, I rushed home to check my e-mail messages and was disappointed to find only a few from other entertainers who were sending around mass notices of their performances. We all did this, all the time.

I contemplated a promenade down Bleecker Street. Instead, I made an appointment with Anna Marie for three o'clock, which was pushing my voice big time, but I was worried about how the Duke of Mantua was surviving the soprano onslaught. When I arrived, I noticed that Anna Marie's blouse was inside out, with the neck tag flapping like a dog's tongue.

"*Ciao*, Kiri, dear. What shall we work on today?"

How could I explain that I wanted to sing the Duke? I had been pondering this on the way over. "Well, Anna Marie, I have a strange request." I paused, thinking furiously. "I have this crazy fancy dress party to go to, you see—a charity event—and I've been asked to perform."

"How much fun! I haven't been to a fancy dress party since the war."

"Mmm. Yes. Anyhow, I know this is ridiculous, but I'm supposed to sing two of the Duke's tenor arias from *Rigoletto*."

Anna Marie giggled. "But that *is* silly!"

"I know, but there it is. Can you help?" I was taking a risk by singing in my true tenor voice, but I needed what guidance she could give me.

"Of course I can, Kiri."

And so we started in. At first, I tried to sing tenor like a soprano, but this soon got my vocal chords in a twist, not to mention the effect on my head. Slowly, I let my true sound come forth, much to Anna Marie's amazement.

"My, my," she exclaimed. "You are so good! I can't get over it!"

After she improved my *legato* in two phrases and corrected rough spots in my Italian, I thanked her and opened the bottle of cream sherry I'd brought. I poured us two glasses and toasted to the Duke. She clicked rims and began to reminisce about great *Rigolettos* she'd seen at Paris Opera, Covent Garden, and the Met. Then, Anna Marie said she wished she could come hear me sing Fiordiligi, but that she didn't get out much because walking was difficult. I told her I understood completely and kept refilling her drink, hoping she would become sufficiently inebriated so that all memory of my tenor voice would evaporate. Unfortunately, the old gal could put it away, and it was I who nearly lost his—excuse me—her memory.

After four large tots, Anna Marie said she was sleepy. I helped her locate her bedroom and then let myself out, finding the stairs down more difficult to negotiate than the stairs up.

As I approached my abode on Jones Street, the sun broiled the top of my head, well, the wig on the top of my head, and my vision danced in the summery late afternoon light. A kind of mawkish sentimentality swilled around with the sherry, producing an amber kind of melancholy that seemed to rise and fall as I stepped in and out of the shadows. My state of ill-being was enhanced when I started across the street and saw Bulging Head Tino waiting in an alley two doors down from mine.

CHAPTER TWELVE

Sticky Wickets

I spotted Tino the second he spotted me. His eyes narrowed as his dinosaur brain slowly sent electrical impulses throughout the vast domain of his skull. I retreated immediately, but he ran across the street with surprising speed for such a humongous brute.

"Hold it," he commanded.

I considered raising my hands in surrender but thought it might look a tad too campy. I stopped.

"Who . . . who are you?" I let my voice quiver.

Tino tilted his enormous noggin. "You kinda look like that Gilbert guy I'm supposta find."

"Who? Oh, my brother? Is he in trouble again?" I was about to tsk-tsk, but Tino wasn't the type one would tsk-tsk to.

He took my arm and squeezed it like his hand was a monkey wrench. "I ain't got time to yak with you, lady. Where's Gilbert?"

"I have absolutely no idea whatsoever."

"Yeah? Well, how come you was crossing the street to go to his place, huh?"

"Why was I crossing the street to go to his place?"

"Yeah. That's what I said."

"I was crossing the street to go to his place . . . to get my umbrella."

Tino craned his head on his massive body and stared up at the blue, blue sky. "I don't think so. It ain't gonna rain all week."

"Oh, I know. You're so right," I told him, "but this is a *sun* umbrella. It wouldn't do for me to get a sunburn on my fair, fair skin." I sugared up my speech, adding a dollop of drawl.

"A sun umbrella?" he asked, looking suspicious. "I ain't seen many of them around."

"And I bet you haven't seen too many ladies with such pale, pale skin around town, either," I whispered, as I watched a pink flush creep up the tree trunk of his neck. I had the boy on the run.

"No, ma'am, I guess I haven't." He scrutinized me carefully, still unsure.

"Should I give Gilbert a message or something?"

Tino grunted.

"What was that?"

"Nah, no message." With this, he turned, and as he did so, I saw his jacket flip up to reveal a blackjack tucked in his belt.

Uh-oh. La Donna really, really wasn't happy with me singing for Howard Lowenbaum. Had the assault on Ben Silverman been payback to Howard rather than to Ben? And was I next?

—

I was shaking like an aspen leaf by the time I triple-locked my apartment door. My life was out of control. I had Joanne Lowenstein-Lowenbaum amorously stalking Derek; Douglas pining after Kiri; La Donna sending goons after Gilbert; Gareth, the tenor, who could expose Guilia; and all I wanted was to crawl into Hank Braylock's arms. I sank face first into my bed pillows.

Two hours later, I woke and looked at my Kiri watch. Oh, my god! I had to be at the department store! I replaced her watch with my knock-off Rolex, raced into the bathroom, flinging clothes left and right, scrubbing my face until it was crimson, and brushing my matted hair. At a full run, I took the stairs and popped out the door into the thick chest of Bulging Head Tino.

He stared at me in shock. I backed up like a Ferrari and stripped gears down the sidewalk. Tino took a second to consult his feet before following suit. As I raced around the corner, I could hear the heavy thuds of his high-top sneakers pounding pavement. Desperately searching for an escape route, I saw an uptown bus about to depart. I ran and squeezed through its doors.

By the time I arrived at Oscar's, I was drenched with perspiration. Loretta banned me to the children's department—my least favorite place. My assignment was to put together a stupid seesaw with two insipid tykes glued to it, one up and one down. As I figured out how to attach the mannequins and make them look realistic, I wondered why La Donna was so upset. It couldn't be because the opera would take so much of my free time since she wasn't nettled about *Rigoletto*, which I assumed she also knew about. So why was there bad blood between her and Howard? Whatever it was, I was sure she wasn't going to confide in me and neither would Gal, whose sympathy seemed to be in short supply. My most pressing issue, however, was how to come and go safely from my apartment with Tino staking out my door.

After weighting the boy mannequin down and wiring the girl in the up position, I thought of a solution to the Tino problem. I would do what I do best. I finished the *tableau* and scampered to the men's department where I absconded with a summer straw hat, a big red-and-white-checked sports shirt, a mannequin's gray wig and matching chin beard, and a cane. In the shipping department, I grabbed some bubble-wrap and tape and headed for the bathroom.

It was late when I cautiously approached my street, but Tino was there all the same. I added a little sailor's roll to my gait—Popeye meets Amish farmer—and crossed over to the door to my apartment, which was also the entrance for nine other units. Tino couldn't have memorized all of the tenants yet, I hoped. He let me go past with only a quick squint.

—

Despite the prediction for no rain, it was drizzling the next morning, with a swirling breeze that refreshed the air. I peeked through the Venetian blinds and didn't see old Tino. Maybe he didn't like to get wet. I decided I better go buy a set of extra-large clothes and a better wig for my comings and goings. A new pair of pants and a shirt for Gil might also be a good idea, so that Gil didn't look so shabby. For my later return, I packed last night's costume and padding in my overnight bag.

By the time I finished shopping, the rain had stopped. I decided to call Gal Friday to see if she would speak to me. No answer. This could mean something or nothing. I assumed it meant something and a not-good something at that. Cautiously, I returned to my apartment disguised as the overweight sixty-year old. Tino was across the street, drooling and sweating, but he didn't pay me any attention.

I'd left my cell phone at home and now saw I two messages. One from Douglas and one from Joanne. I called Mr. Yale first and made it short and sweet.

"Oh, Douglas," I said. "I am so, so sorry not to see you the other night, but I was upset about my cousin."

"What happened?"

I might need old Frederick Franklin as an excuse so I couldn't kill him off. "I simply can't go into details. Reliving it is too painful." Kiri's diva voice.

"Sorry to hear that."

I could tell my act wasn't completely convincing. "My cousin took a turn for the worse."

"Sorry to hear that," he repeated.

No Academy Awards were going to be given for this starring role. "Thank you." When in doubt, keep it simple.

"So who was that guy that came to your dressing room?" he asked.

"What do you mean?"

"Blond hair. Tall. About forty."

"Who?" Hank? Heart be still.

"I didn't get his name. I told him you weren't answering your door."

I wanted to scream at Douglas. I mean a real throat-tearing, blood-curdling diva scream. "It must have been a fan," I replied through clenched teeth.

"That's what I figured." He was silent for a minute. "Hey, you know William and I kind of patched it up."

"Really?" Just peachy. He ruins my big chance and then goes off with my ex.

"Yeah. He's moved back in . . . well, this time with his things. I wanted to let you know so in case we come to the Purple Plum some night you won't flirt with me or anything."

Who, pray tell, was flirting with whom? "I wouldn't think of it, Douglas. Do not, please, give me another thought."

"Oh, Kiri, I don't want to hurt you," he began. "I know you and I had a little thing started—"

"It was a *very* little thing," I retorted in a bitchy tone. "I hope you and William will be very happy together." I disconnected.

The nerve of that wimpy weasel! I was so incensed that I marched around my apartment yelling at Douglas—and William, too. They deserved each other. Good riddance! I opened a bottle of water and drank it, hoping to cool myself down. Then, the phone rang. Joanne, the second sticky wicket in town beside Douglas.

"Hello, this is Derek." I figured it was safer to let Joanne know which twin I was in case she had noticed we shared the same phone number. It didn't hurt to remind myself, either.

"Hi. This is Joanne. How're you doing?"

We chatted for a bit before she popped the dinner question.

"Er, I'm not free until maybe one night next week, Joanne," I said. "I have rehearsals and a second job, which I do at night. I'm sorry."

Joanne, however, was more powerful than a locomotive, able to leap all of Manhattan in a single bound. "What about tonight? We could go to Bernadin for an early dinner."

Oh, that's hitting a guy in the slats. I'd been to Le Bernadin once and had fallen madly in love, but the restaurant was seriously out of my price range. "Joanne, that would be great, but I hate to admit that I can't afford a place like that."

"That's okay, Derek. Dinner's on me. I'll meet you there at six." She did a fast, fleet-footed exit before I could refuse.

Damn! I sighed in frustration. Out of the Douglas campfire into the Joanne towering inferno. I stomped around the apartment some more, but it didn't help. Then, I remembered that I hadn't checked my e-mail. I flipped on the computer. There, at the bottom, was a reply from Henry Braylock. I clicked on the message.

Dear Gil,

Sorry not to get back to you sooner, but I had to deal with some family issues. I did see your revue on Saturday night and was very impressed. You have a fantastic voice—especially in the operatic selections. I came to your dressing room after the first half, but I was told that you weren't seeing anyone.

I would enjoy having a drink with you, or maybe we could have an early dinner tomorrow night before your show?

Best, Hank

He had appended his phone, cell, and office numbers plus his home e-mail address. The fact that he gave me all four made me ecstatic. He was definitely interested!

I accepted via e-mail for dinner at six o'clock and told him to pick the place and let me know. Just in case, I wrote my phone number again. I was flying so high that I almost forgot Joanne.

When I finally climbed off Cloud Nine, I donned my blue sports jacket, pale blue shirt, and red tie. Good god! I looked like a Republican! This thought gave me the willies and so, too, did the view out my window. The rain had stopped, and Tino was posted two doors down on the opposite side of the street. This was getting ridiculous.

Although my sports jacket fit like a glove, I had an old raincoat in the closet that was loose, a remnant from heavier times. I encircled my waist with the bubble-wrap, put on the coat and buttoned it. Then, I applied the beard and moustache, topped off with the gray wig, grabbed the cane, and ran downstairs carrying my gray plaid suitcase. Outside, I bent over and limped away in the opposite direction from Tino, praying that once again I could fool him. My disguise worked. On the bus uptown, I yanked off the hot raincoat, folded up the padding, and unglued the beard. Whew! Sure, I received a few odd looks from the other passengers, but this is New York, home of the seriously strange.

I rushed into Le Bernadin, crossing the restaurant's august portal and immediately drawing some odd stares, though I thought my appearance was acceptable. Joanne was sitting at a table and wore a fuchsia dress with a turquoise silk scarf limping over her shoulder.

"Hi, Joanne," I said.

She turned and gave me a horrified look, then burst out laughing.

"What's so funny?"

Her laughter was so loud that other patrons turned in their seats. I sat down quickly, ditching my cane and suitcase under the table.

"What's wrong?" I whispered.

"Derek, your hair! And that moustache!" She grabbed a napkin to dab her eyes.

I reached up and felt the gray fright wig and then the hair applied over my upper lip. Oops. "Sorry, Joanne," I said. "Just a little joke."

She was still chuckling when the waiter came to take our drink order. I asked for a double vodka on the rocks.

CHAPTER THIRTEEN

Jealousy

Dinner was perfection—at least the food part. Lovely raw oysters and a delicious halibut. And, as straight dates go, Joanne was fun. She had a good sense of humor, told outlandish and dishy stories, and, yes, paid the bill, which I admit was somewhat embarrassing. I also didn't like the idea that I owed her anything, or her father, for that matter. As we were strolling out of the restaurant, I steered the conversation toward Howard, hoping to ascertain why La Donna was blowing a gasket about him.

"I know your father is a businessman," I began, "but what does he sell?"

"He imports products from Asia. Clothes, jewelry, electronics. Whatever he thinks will net a profit and that he has an outlet for."

"An outlet for? Does that mean he has stores in New York?"

"Mmm. Several."

"Any I might frequent?" This came out sounding like Guilia or Kiri. I quickly returned to my Derek voice. "I mean, just curious."

"Dad's main office is in Brooklyn, but he has a fur emporium on Lexington Avenue."

"Oh, too bad! I'm not into furs."

"And two diamond exchanges and an electronics outlet on Sixth Avenue. The diamond stores just opened."

Electronics, diamonds, furs, jewelry—all possible La Donna territory. "He must have quite a bit of competition in that neighborhood."

"Yeah, but he's selling at prices the other dealers can't match."

Sounded like sizzling hot goods to me, I thought but didn't say.

"Actually, my mother is running some of the business," Joanne continued. "She deals with the advertising and the accountants. My father hires most of the employees, handles security, and purchases the merchandise."

"A family affair."

"Yeah. I guess you could say that."

I was wondering whether Joanne's mother knew La Donna. Maybe the problem was a family affair, too. "What's your mother like?"

Joanne smiled at me, assuming my question about her mother indicated interest in herself. "Oh, she's got red hair like I do. We look quite a bit alike except she's prettier—"

"Oh, I doubt that." I felt like this was a necessary insert.

She blushed. "No, it's true. Well, I mean, she was pretty when she worked on Broadway. She had the lead in a musical called *Jungle Fever*."

Even though my knowledge of show music was encyclopedic, I'd never heard of this dog. Probably it had opened on the matinee and closed that night. "Wow! Who else was in the cast?"

Joanne consulted her memory and told me who the tenor was. "And there was a second woman—a singer—she was very good. I can't remember her name, though. Let me think. Hmm . . . it was Italian."

Bingo. "How did your mother get on with this woman?" I asked, as I flagged down a cab.

Joanne gave me a funny look. "I don't know. I guess okay."

As I held the car door for her, she patted me on the arm. "No, wait, Derek! I do remember. The woman who played my mother's rival in the play, she was originally supposed to be the star. Then, my father bought into the production and switched the two parts."

I joined Joanne in the back seat of the taxi, and she gave her address to the cabbie. "Really?"

"I'm a little hazy—I was only twelve—but I recall the show opened, and Mom got great reviews. She was so happy!" She smiled at the memory, but, in an instant, the smile turned into a frown. "And then it happened. Mom broke her leg."

"An accident?" I knew I was being too persistent, but I had to find out.

"She fell backstage. Daddy went crazy. He blamed that Italian lady and threatened revenge."

"What happened with the show?"

"My father closed it."

"So he never gave the other woman a chance to sing the lead?"

"No, he didn't. Daddy was furious. And besides the other singer couldn't do it," Joanne said. "There was something weird . . . oh, yes. I think she drank something in her coffee that damaged her vocal chords."

"I hate to ask, Joanne, but doesn't that sound a little suspicious? I mean, after your mother broke her leg."

"Yeah, I guess so." Joanne shrugged.

We were arriving at 71st and Broadway where Joanne lived. I had plenty of questions, but I sensed that either Joanne wouldn't confide anything more or else she knew nothing more about the feud, which apparently had been instigated by the double "accidents" during *Jungle Fever*.

Joanne snuggled against my arm. "Would you like to come up for a drink?"

"I would love to, Joanne, but we have *Rigoletto* rehearsal tomorrow, and I need to study."

"Oh, come on, Derek. I bet you know that role perfectly."

I opened the cab door and escorted her to the entrance of the building. "Even so, this is a big chance for me. I want to do well." I gave her a peck on the cheek. "Thank you so much for dinner, Joanne. I really enjoyed the evening."

"You did?" Her eyes grew large and happy. "Great! So I'll see you again?"

"Absolutely." Since the cab was waiting for me, I had a good excuse to leave.

—

I changed into my Amish disguise in the car and had the driver drop me off in front of my building. No Tino, or at least not that I could see, although there was a suspicious cardboard refrigerator box three doors down in which he might ensconce himself. Maybe he was taking a page from my tricky playbook, and this was the only disguise he could fit in.

As I took the stairs two at a time, I chortled with laughter. I was a clever rogue indeed with all my various outfits! Maybe the Duke was rubbing off on me? I was humming "La donna è mobile" when I saw that my door was open a crack. One thing about me—I always lock everything. Scared and yet curious, I gave it a little shove. The room was dark, but I sensed a presence. Carefully, I stepped inside and turned on the light. There, lying on my bed, was Gal Friday. She had picked the locks, one of her many skills.

Gal sat up when she saw me. "Hi, Gil. Or who should I address you as?"

I pulled off the beard, moustache, and wig and unwound the padding. "Don't be funny. I'm not in the mood."

"I'm not in the mood, either. You're in some serious shit."

"I realize that, *girlfriend*," I said sarcastically. "I can't believe you got me mixed up in all this!"

Gal sighed. "Me? Hey, it's not my fault. I didn't want to involve you, but La Donna knew we were friends and found out that you were an opera singer. That's how it started. Then, she liked you and your singing. Everything was fine until she heard you were hired by Lowenbaum and Company. After that, there wasn't a damned thing I could do."

"But surely she realizes I didn't audition for Howard with the intention of upsetting her? How was I to know they were enemies?"

Gal shrugged. "La Donna doesn't care what your intentions were. She looks at the bottom line, Gil. And the bottom line is that you ignored her warning and went to rehearsal."

I sat down, feeling defeated. "What do I do now? How do I fix this?"

"Maybe if you cancel your arrangement with Lowenbaum—"

"But he's already paid me a retainer! You even helped get it!"

Gal winced. "Yeah, and I don't think La Donna would like that very much if she found out. Good thing I went in disguise as your agent."

I considered the leverage I had over Gal. She would be in more hot water than I was if I let her employer know of her disloyalty, despite the fact that all of this happened before either of us knew the Lowenbaums and La Donna were arch enemies.

"So maybe we better work together to solve this," I suggested.

Gal walked fore and aft in front of my bed, arms crossed behind her back like a captain on a foredeck. "Right. Guess we better. Do you have any more of that soda pop?"

I looked at her blankly. She shook her head and went over to my cabinet and withdrew the crème de menthe bottle.

—

When I left as Guilia Hancock for my *Così* rehearsal, Tino was not around. I presumed that Gal had sent him on an errand, or else La

Donna needed him for a more important task. Just in case, I carried my disguise in my overnight bag.

The doughnuts and Joanne had already arrived by the time I did, as had the rest of the cast. Ivan was standing near the conductor, Cavendish MacDougal, who was sniffing the air and trying to place the foul smell. Gareth Kerr made a beeline for me and began chatting away without preamble.

"Oh, Guilia, ith tho good to thee you!" he exclaimed.

I hoped his lisp wasn't contagious. It was undoubtedly the worst I'd ever heard, and let me tell you, I've heard some beauts. "Hi, Gareth."

His rubbed his hands in happy anticipation. "I can't wait to thing today. I mean, thith ith very exthiting, don't you think?"

This little conversation was happily interrupted by Nate Lowenstein, the bass-baritone, who asked us all to gather in front of the music stands. Howard Lowenbaum, who was slouched in a front row seat, called to the maestro to begin. We started with warm-up scales.

After we finished, I was a trifle more encouraged about the production's potential and was feeling relatively pleased with the cast until Gareth took my arm.

"My, you are *tho* wonderful! I am honored to thing with you. Abtholutely honored!"

Gushing was usually fine with me, but Gareth was not my type, not by a long stretch. Still, as with Joanne, we had to work together. "You were wonderful, too, Gareth." No lie, he really wasn't a bad singer. His acting, however, was another matter entirely. In this arena, Gareth was seriously deficient, as he was in other areas we won't mention. (I always check these things out.)

"Thank you! That'th tho nith of you to thay." He drew close and whispered confidentially, "That Ruthian really thmellth, doethn't he? Oh, my god!" Gareth's eyes rolled merrily. "I don't mean to be a backthabber or anything, but really!"

I allowed him his amusement and nodded my head. "He is pretty awful."

Joanne, not one to be ignored, circled around my other side. "Gareth, could you excuse Guilia and me for a moment?"

Gareth was not happy about this interruption but wasn't about to cross the boss' daughter. He backed away with a disappointed expression on his face.

"What's up?" I asked Joanne, suspecting what was.

"Oh, Guilia! Your brother Derek is absolutely dreamy! We had such a great time last night."

"He said the same thing."

"Did he?" she asked.

"Yes."

"What else did he say?" Her eyes glowed.

"Er, not much. That the dinner at Le Bernadin was fantastic . . . that you had a great sense of humor—"

She giggled. "He's so funny! He showed up wearing a gray wig and a moustache!"

"He did? Well, he does like his little pranks."

"Did he say anything . . . you know . . . more personal?"

"Just that he really likes you. Derek is shy about expressing his feelings."

"Does he need encouragement?"

"Sometimes." I didn't like where this was heading.

"I understand." She gave me a knowing grin. "Yes, I understand entirely."

—

I took a chance on my Guilia Hancock disguise and didn't change into Mr. Amish. After a few errands, I arrived home to find the street free and clear of old Bulging Head, which was a good thing because I needed to prepare for my date. During the afternoon, Hank had sent a brief email confirming our dinner and the restaurant. "I look forward to seeing you," he wrote. Wow! And was I ever looking forward to seeing him! Tonight there would be no cosmetics, wigs, or nail polish, but I did prepare with a long, luxurious shower. Instead of my Mr. Republican clothes, I decided on a tan linen shirt and chocolate brown linen slacks. Very European, very chic, even if they had been bought in a consignment shop.

No Tino to block my getaway. I sailed to Osteria Dando on wings of joy.

CHAPTER FOURTEEN

A Fabulous Dinner

My heart was beating like I'd run ten miles uphill in a stiff head-wind. Oh, dear. I had it bad. I was ten minutes early!

The restaurant was all dark wood and green plants and little alcoves stacked with opaque glass bottles in pale pink, aqua, and lavender. Lighting was minimal—candles on the tables, along the teak bar, and between the bottles on the walls. I stood on one foot and then the other, trying to calm down my runaway nerves. Finally, I made myself sit on a chair by the reception desk. At exactly six, Hank Braylock came through the glass doors and gave me a radiant smile. I could feel its warmth down to my toes.

"Hi, Gil."

"Hi."

"I made reservations for us."

"Great!" *Us.* Oh, my god!

We were shown to a corner table near the window. The evening light fell on Hank's face and illuminated his green eyes. I was mesmerized.

We ordered vodka tonics and agreed on sardines, Caesar salads with anchovies, and a pasta with scallops and langoustines, amused that all the food we liked had once been underwater. Hank chose a Muscadet to accompany dinner.

After our drinks arrived, I apologized for the mix-up at the Purple Plum, saying I had been waiting for him but had to leave after my second act.

"A command performance, so to speak." I said.

Hank raised his eyebrows, probably wondering if that involved singing or some other activity that was best left unmentioned. He sipped his vodka and skipped the inquisition, for which I was grateful, not wishing to explain my convoluted dealings with La Donna. I then told him more about my two operas. He showed genuine interest, laughing when I described Gareth, Ivan, and

Maestro Cavendish MacDougal, a deep rich laugh that I adored, and inquired about the *Rigoletto* cast. In turn, I asked him about his work and learned that his special interest was genetic, familial, and sociological causes of determining sexual orientation.

"With the way my life has been the last few weeks, I would be a case study for you. I am totally confused about who I am most of the time." I listed my various *dramatis personae.*

"Sounds like you need a little consolidation of your characters." He sat back and studied me with a calm, analytic expression that made me feel like the center of the universe.

"Can you help, doctor?" I grinned at him, eating a sardine.

"Tell me more."

I did. Hank Braylock was the easiest guy to talk to. Words flooded out of me. I told him all about my childhood in Atlantic City, my escape into theater and music, and every hope and dream I'd ever harbored. Throughout, he listened attentively, asking questions, smiling with amusement, frowning with concern. I have always been a superb raconteur, mind you, but I've never had such an audience. He was with me from start to finish, the smoothest verbal partner with whom it's been my pleasure to converse. When the Muscadet and our salads arrived, after we clicked glasses, I kept talking.

I negotiated a large leaf of romaine into my mouth. As I did, I realized I'd been monopolizing the conversation and apologized.

Hank shook his head. "I love stories . . . the experiences people have."

"Yes, but it must get boring after while . . . listening so much."

"Not at all." He wiped his napkin on perfectly shaped lips. "I learn a great deal—not just about the other person but also about myself. Your story is, in many ways, my story."

"You're my brother and I'm yours?"

He laughed. "Well, sort of. I don't mean to sound like one of those guys who leads men's workshops in sweat lodges."

"I'm glad to hear that. So, what about you? You said you've been dealing with some family issues."

"Yeah." He paused, causing me to wonder if he would say more.

"Are you comfortable telling me about what's going on?" I sounded like a therapist, but I was sincere in my interest.

"It's my brother, Kenny." Hank cut an anchovy in half. "He's two years younger than I am. Gay, like me, only he knew about himself before I did. I was kind of slow to figure things out." He paused to eat some salad. "While I was in my junior year at Princeton, he started studying at the Fashion Institute here in New York. It turned out he had talent, but after his second year, during the summer, he apprenticed to a designer as an intern. Next thing I know, Kenny was doing drugs and about every guy he met." He drank some wine. "My life at Princeton was completely different. Sheltered. Even when I moved to New York, I kept to myself, studied, went home on weekends. Kenny asked me to parties, but I didn't go, or at least not after the first two, which were too wild. We argued and finally I told him I didn't want anything to do with him." Hank laid down his fork and looked sad. "I don't know whether my behavior put Kenny over the edge, but he overdosed the day after. Although he recovered, during the same period, my father was dying from asbestos poisoning. I decided to take care of Dad rather than Kenny."

"Was your brother estranged from your parents?"

Hank nodded. "Then, yes. My mother was exhausted from nursing my father, and Kenny's behavior and drug use scared her. He was stealing money from them."

The main course arrived. The scallops and langoustines were swimming in a rich cream sauce on top of a snowy pile of risotto.

"That's understandable."

"Mmm. Yeah, but being disconnected from the family was a disaster for Kenny. Made him feel untethered, more adrift. After the overdose, he transferred from the hospital into rehab, then returned to school but started the drugs again. And that's been the pattern ever since except for a few months when he stayed off the stuff, when my mother developed ovarian cancer. He moved back home to be with her until she died. Afterward, Kenny returned to the city and the scene. He's HIV positive and not doing well, mostly because he doesn't take his meds consistently, or at least not the right drugs. He never forgets to take cocaine."

"I'm so sorry to hear that," I told him. "How can he afford to keep going? Is he working?"

"Here and there. Like I said, he's really talented."

"That's a heartbreaking story. And about your parents, too."

Hank stared at me and nodded.

"So where is your brother now, Hank?"

"In rehab. It won't last," he replied sadly. "And I think he's developed full-blown AIDS. Even though I'm his only close relative—his brother—he won't tell me."

"Can't you ask the doctors?"

"Kenny has forbidden them to speak to me. There really isn't much I can do, even though I try to help when he allows it, which is usually when he gets into serious trouble. Mostly, I worry that he doesn't care what happens. If my brother continues like this, he won't live long."

I reached over and touched his hand. Hank looked up, tears rimming his eyes. He swiped at them and smiled sadly. "My apologies. I didn't mean to go on like this."

"That's okay. I'm glad you told me, Hank."

We ate in silence for a few minutes while he composed himself. Then, he sat back and gave me a searching look. "You know, I haven't told anyone about Kenny. I don't know why."

I was unexpectedly moved by this admission. "Thanks for confiding in me."

"Well, I think it's time to change the subject. We should laugh and make merry."

"That's what I'm good at." As I said this, I realized it was true, but I wasn't altogether happy about these limits. Something about Hank made me wish for deeper communication, a communication I'd avoided all my life.

—

When we left the restaurant, I gave Hank tickets to my operas and then invited him to the Purple Plum for my revue. I hoped that he would come, but despite the upbeat ending to our dinner, I sensed he hadn't shaken off the effects of his melancholy from earlier.

"Gil, thanks for a great evening," he began, "but I think I'll pass on the show tonight."

I felt my hopes sink. "Oh, that's too bad."

He took my hand. "Please understand, I want to see you again."

My hopes did a U-turn. I couldn't help but smile. "Great! When?"

"I'm not sure. Family comes first, I'm afraid. Or at least right now."

My family had never put me first. This awareness suddenly ignited my old childhood sadness. I went quiet and then chided myself for feeling moody, worried Hank would misinterpret my reaction.

When he noticed my expression, he added, "Hey, let me deal with Kenny and get my head together, okay?"

"Sure."

"I promise to call you."

I looked into his serene eyes and hoped I could believe him.

—

Pink feathers and fancy gowns suddenly seemed frivolous, nevertheless I dressed and put on the wig and makeup, preferring to be anyone other than Gilbert Eugene Rose, even though I wasn't completely sure who he was. The feelings from the evening did find an outlet in my singing, however, as I dedicated the opera arias to Hank, telling the audience, "This is for a friend who is hurting."

At the end of the second half, I retreated to my dressing room, realizing that I hadn't focused on anyone in the audience. I was startled, therefore, when someone knocked on my door.

"Who is it?" I called out in my Kiri voice.

"It's Joanne."

I sunk my head into my hands and felt like singing "Ridi, Pagliacco." Then, I smartened up. Joanne had seen me perform as Kiri, who was pretty damned close to looking like Guilia, but who was supposed to be Derek.

"Joanne, I'm sorry," I answered in Derek's timbre. "I'm not dressed."

"Oh. Well, maybe when you're finished?"

"Okay, but it will be awhile. Why don't I call you tomorrow?"

"I don't mind waiting."

Of course she didn't. I was stuck, stuck, stuck. "All right."

As I scrubbed at my face, I muttered imprecations. At least I had Gilbert's, I mean, Derek's clothes. I combed my hair, changed outfits, and opened the door.

Joanne was sitting on a stool and turned. "Derek, hi." She looked a little shook up, like she'd seen a ghost. The question was which of my ghosts had she seen? Derek as Kiri or Guilia as Kiri? Or Derek as Guilia and then Kiri? Maybe I should just tell her Guilia was actually Derek or, rather, that there was no Derek, only Guilia pretending to be Derek, who was pretending to be Kiri? If I was a

106

woman impersonating a bisexual male and singing a tenor role and also singing as a drag queen, was that any more unbelievable than twins, one of whom sang tenor and also performed in drag shows? My head felt like a boiling cauldron. "Hi," I replied after a pause that was very pregnant.

"Can I come in?"

"Oh, sure." I'd hung up my dress, hidden my wigs, and neatened the room. The less of Kiri showing the better. "Would you like a glass of water or something?" Unlike classier acts, I did not sport a bucket of champagne in my dressing area, unless a beau brought one.

"No, thanks."

Joanne was definitely subdued.

I rubbed my forehead to gain extra thinking time. "What did you think of the show?"

"You have a great voice, but I have to say," she began, "well, I'm confused."

Honey, you're not alone. "About what?"

"I don't know how to say this, but you look so much like Guilia on stage. It's really shocking. You're wearing a lot of makeup and everything . . ." Here, she pointed at my chest. "But I don't know if I could tell the two of you apart."

Neither, my sweet, could I. "It must seem very strange to you," I said. "Guilia actually helped me with my first cosmetics application."

"She did?"

"Yeah."

"But don't you feel funny looking like your sister?" She scrunched up her nose. "It is a little incestuous, isn't it?"

Was she visualizing the one bed in the apartment? And did she think I was having incestuous relations with my twin? In fact, I wasn't having relations, incestuous or non-incestuous, with anyone, sorry to say. "I know it appears rather . . . degenerate . . . but it isn't. I'm doing the show because I couldn't get a job singing as a tenor. A friend told me that this club needed a drag entertainer, and, well, with some coaching from Guilia, here I am."

She moved closer. "So your sister helped? Oh, I'm so relieved. You can't imagine what I've been thinking."

And that's probably only half of what you should be thinking. I let her put her arms around my neck, although I wanted to run for the hinterlands, wherever the hell those are.

"Derek, you're really special." She leaned against me.

Was she trying to see if I had male parts? I leaned in so she could, figuring that might clarify the situation. "Thanks. I had a really good time the other night. That was so nice of you to take me to dinner. One of these days maybe I'll be able to afford restaurants like that."

"Guilia told me you enjoyed our evening."

I had her back believing in fairies . . . or maybe not in fairies exactly. "Mmm. Guilia told me she told you." Why did I talk this way? I gently disengaged and sighed. "Now, I am sorry, Joanne, but I'm totally beat." Fake yawn. "Can I call you a cab or something?"

"That's okay. Daddy is sending the driver down whenever I call."

Great. Daddy knows Derek does a drag show. "Did you tell your father? About my cabaret act?"

Joanne shook her head. "No, I just said I was meeting you in the Village." She was obviously embarrassed by what I was doing. I was becoming embarrassed by it, too.

"I see."

"Just between us, Daddy gets a little overly protective some-times. You know what I mean? But I don't tell him everything." Here, she batted her eyelashes.

Great. Howard is overly protective. I shuddered to think what he'd do if I rejected Joanne. "That's good." I started to wink and then changed the movement into an eye twitch. "Okay, well, we should probably leave."

I walked her to the street and watched as she pulled out her cell phone. I knew she was hoping I'd invite her somewhere for a drink, but I didn't. Considering the fact that Guilia was ostensibly sharing my tiny apartment, Joanne couldn't suggest we go there. Home free. Well, almost. As I said goodbye to Joanne and trotted back to my place thinking of Hank, I saw the Pink Caddie gurgling its tailpipe and Gal leaning against its door.

Nervously, I crossed over to the sidewalk by the car, worried that Tino or another one of La Donna's goons was tucked in the back seat. The Caddie was empty, but Gal looked gaunt, like she hadn't slept for days or like she'd spied the Guilia ghost Joanne Lowenstein-Lowenbaum had seen.

"What's up?" I asked.

"You tell me, Gil."

"What do you mean? Look, I'm bushed. Can't we talk in the morning?"

Gal shook her head. "I got word that Lowenbaum's daughter was at the Plum tonight."

"How did you find that out so fast?" The cat was out of the burlap.

"The Lowenbaum family chauffeur gets a few bucks now and then."

"For information?"

"What do you think?"

"And Joanne was chatting with him about me?"

Gal nodded solemnly. "I don't mean to mess up whatever the hell you got going on here, Gil, but I can't help you out if you keep dumping gas on the fire. Get my point?"

I hung my head. "Yeah, but I didn't invite her to the show. I didn't even know she was in the audience until she came backstage. Believe me, I wasn't happy about the whole thing." I sat down on the Caddie's front fender, feeling like a hulking hood ornament.

"Doesn't matter. La Donna is going ballistic. Bad enough you're singing with Lowenbaum. Worse that you're humping his daughter."

I was outraged. "I am doing no such thing!"

Gal smirked. "You know that. I know that. La Donna was told by the limo guy that Joanne Lowenstein-Lowenbaum said you were hot stuff. Now in this day and age, Gil, old buddy, wouldn't you assume that you were—"

"No, I wouldn't! I just pecked her on the cheek. Once."

"Well, how're you gonna get out of this mess?"

I thought for a few minutes, but my brain battery was low. Then, old Thomas Edison switched on the light. "What if you tell La Donna that Howard is forcing me to see his daughter? That he's threatened me physically. Said I was going to get snuffed or something . . . and, you know, that we started with the opera before La Donna told me to quit, but I was already in too deep." I liked this plan until I realized it might incite La Donna into further violence against Howard and even against Joanne, whom I liked despite her Saran-Wrap personality. "On second thought, I don't want to make things worse for the Lowenbaums."

Gal Friday mulled this idea over. "Very noble of you, but what you don't get is that La Donna's on the warpath, with or without you in the mix. There isn't anything you can do to stop her, Gil. The only thing we can do is to save your neck."

"There must be some way of resolving the situation."

Gal shook her head. "La Donna isn't going to resolve a god-damned thing until the Lowenbaums are resolved."

I felt awful and guilty and said so.

Gal placed her hand on my arm. "Look, I'll tell La Donna that your involvement with Howard was an accident and that Joanne fell for you big time. I don't think anything'll happen to your *girl-friend*," Gal said with undisguised irony. "La Donna is after the parents, not her."

"Are you sure?"

"No, but maybe it'll turn down the heat on you at least."

I sat in silence for a few minutes. "Would it be okay to go to rehearsals?"

"Probably really stupid." She slipped off the fender, dusted off her black chinos, and jangled her keys. "But you're going anyhow, aren't you?"

I nodded. "What about Tino? Where is he?"

Gal chuckled. "Oh, he's busy righting a slight."

I looked a question.

Gal put up her hands. "Don't ask."

CHAPTER FIFTEEN

Madame Clara Revisited

Friday dawned cool and clear with autumn on its dewy breath. No, I have not been reading Lord Byron again, although I'm sure I would have loved the guy, and he would have loved me. Maybe I'm waxing poetic because I was pining for Hank? The more I thought about how our date ended, the more I worried that he wasn't going to call. This distressed the hell out of me. I decided, therefore, to consult the stars. Madame Clara had a session available at ten o'clock.

Her place is spiderweb-ish. Weird orange lights, hanging Spanish fringy shawls, crawling green ivy grayed with dust, New Age smoothie music glissading around the room. I adore the place. It's cozy.

Madame Clara gave me a little kiss and showed me in. She was round and jolly, decked out in a black Gypsy outfit and covered in drippy jewelry, such as a carnelian necklace composed of chunks resembling throat lozenges and an assortment of rings, the most prominent of which was a huge cat's eye oval carved with a female goddess' head. I always have an urge to kiss the ring when I enter. I think Madame Clara would approve.

I sat at the round table and waited while she handed me a mug of herbal tea, or that's what I hoped the evil-smelling brew was. She then hunched in her chair and smiled as the gold pillar candle between us raked shadows across her face.

"Now, *cher Gilbert* . . ." Madame Clara pronounced my name like it was French, a language she affected whenever she remembered. "What would you ask zee spirit today?"

My spirit guide was called Bob. I thought this was a rather pedantic name, but that's what the Ouija board had spelled out several visits back, perhaps because of laziness and disinterest in slogging around for a longer moniker (see previous mention of his indolence regarding the year: 009 for 2009). However, this had not perturbed Madame Clara, who counseled me to go with the protoplasmic flow and I had.

"Guess," I replied. We played these little psychic games. They delighted Madame Clara.

"Ah, it is zee *amour, oui*?" She gave me a wicked grin. "I see zee signs in your eyes."

Well, she is good, isn't she? I nodded but didn't provide details, choosing to be as mum as King Tut.

Madame Clara licked her red, lush lips and laid aging hands on the glass globe surrounding the candle. "*C'est un homme*," she announced. "He is tall and handsome."

Now, I know this description is obvious given my own stature and attractiveness, but she wasn't finished.

"I see zee *colour vert*," she whispered. "His eyes are green. Ah, *magnifique*! Such beautiful eyes!"

"Yes, he does have green eyes. What else can you tell me about him?" I asked eagerly.

She cogitated in psychic space. "I see *une tragédie*." She lifted a hand to her brow and said we must consult the spirit guide for more information.

I knew this was my clue to switch off the dim lights and return to my seat. I closed my eyes as Madame Clara called out to Bob for assistance. Being a dutiful spirit, he arrived a minute later but complained about being interrupted in the middle of a seduction. Bob, you see, is an amorous rake of the heterosexual variety and isn't always pleased at mortal requests. Nevertheless, his voice came through Madame Clara's, minus the French accent.

"I am here," he said in a booming baritone.

"*Bonjour*, Bob," Madame Clara answered in a sprightly soprano.

"What do you want?" he asked.

"*Gilbert*," (the French version again), ". . . he wants to know about zee special man."

I was silent while a few thumps could be heard in various parts of the room and a small draft wafted about. These phenomena made me nervous so I opened my eyes.

"This special man is not in danger," Bob said, "but someone close to him is in peril."

"Who?" asked the psychic.

Bob demurred, rapping and tapping and shaking the table. "A man who is younger."

Kenny, Hank's brother? That must be the man Bob meant. I wanted to ask, but Madame Clara had instructed me never to interfere in celestial communication.

The candle flickered as she asked if there was romance in my future.

"I see romance, but first it is cloudy and dark. There will be trials and difficulties." Bob paused, apparently trying to see through the psychic veil. "Then, it is just a matter of time . . ."

Exactly what Madame Clara had told me two weeks ago! My spiritual path was opening before me, and Hank and I would live happily ever after. After, of course, my star was blazed in the opera firmament, and we resolved the peril problem, whatever it was.

Madame Clara lifted her head. "He is gone." She fluttered her lashes a few times as if waking from a deep sleep. "Did he tell you zee anzer you wanted?"

"I think so," I replied.

"*Bon*. I believe whatever is meant to happen will happen soon."

—

I was so excited that I wanted to run home and send Hank an e-mail, but I restrained myself. I had to be patient and wait for Kenny's situation to be resolved, hopefully for the better, because that needed to occur before Hank could freely pursue our relationship. Feeling uplifted, I decided to lift spirits at the AIDS center. There, I found four guys, who I gathered around the battered upright piano. I asked them what they wanted to sing, and one answered, "Hello, Dolly," which was always rousing. We did several choruses, and I took requests for a while. Later, I went into the kitchen to peel some potatoes and stir a pot before going wig shopping for my Fiordiligi role. As I was coming out of the Wigwam with a purchase in hand, I ran into Luis.

He slapped his chest in surprise. "Why, girlfriend, how're you doing?"

"Fine, Luis. And you?"

"Oh, peaches and cream . . . I'm in peaches and cream." He rolled his eyes in ecstasy.

"Who's the lucky guy?"

"An absolutely fabulous gym instructor. I mean, we're talking Hunk of Hunks, Stud of Studs, God of all Gods."

I laughed. "What's his name?"

Luis lowered his voice to a whisper, "I have no idea."

I laughed again and whispered back, "But you're sure he's interested?"

Luis looked at me as if I were nuts. "Like, do diamonds sparkle, honey? You betcha I'm sure. In fact, I am sashaying over there right now, just so he can get a glimmer of my glamour."

"Has he asked you out? Or maybe, you know . . ." I shrugged my shoulders to imply a little exchange of nooky.

Luis took my arm. "Gil, you know how these things are. They're *sensitive*." He tucked in his chin and batted long false eyelashes at me. "I am sure I'll have more to report later. Now, how 'bout you, girl? What's happening? Tell Mama."

So I filled him in on Hank Braylock but omitted mention of his name and where he lived. I figured there was no point in advertising that such a handsome man was in the vicinity. Luis probably wasn't Hank's type, but why take chances?

"Oh, my, Gil, sounds like you have it bad!" He grinned at me. "Maybe we'll both be tying the knot by Halloween. I can see it now—an orange and black theme although I must confess I always expected to wear white, virgin that I am."

"If you're a virgin, Luis, I guess that makes me extra-virgin!"

We laughed and I gave him two tickets for my two operas. "A great first date."

I then trotted home with Fiordiligi's wig, a mass of long blond curls, and ran upstairs to model it in the mirror. I sang through my arias, the wig providing inspiration for my acting. When it came time to gaze lovingly at my lover's portrait, however, I took one look at William's photo and tossed it in the trash. Mid-afternoon, I rushed uptown to my first *Rigoletto* rehearsal, which went well and lasted long, until early evening.

—

No e-mails or calls from Hank. I was now positive that my momentary upset about families coming first had turned him off, even if I hadn't explained the cause of my brief change in mood and that I had been thinking of my own family and not about his. On Saturday, I chewed on this relentlessly and didn't leave the apartment. It wasn't that I had nowhere to go, but my get up and go had, well, got up and went. I watched QVC and drooled over some chandelier earrings that Kiri needed and a mandarin collar, doupioni silk jacket that was perfect for Guilia. Then, there was a new corkscrew for Gil (wink) and a pair of running shoes for Derek that of course Gil could wear, too. I felt like I had gone Christmas shopping by the time I'd finished ordering. It was so wonderful buying for all my friends and family! For good measure, I even watched a little CNN, though I must say the wars and bombs and terrorist plots weren't fine frolics for a fun afternoon.

After forcing myself to do laundry, I composed a short note to my mother, listing my two opening nights, the addresses of the theaters, and enclosing tickets. I finished by saying that if she couldn't make it into the city, I would understand. This was just self-protection. I wouldn't understand, but I didn't expect her to come. I'd send the letter and try not to feel rejected when she reached for alcoholic solace instead of supporting me.

I made a pork chop and salad for dinner, then moseyed over to the Purple Plum for my performance, which was good but not great. The audience was noisy and inattentive, although they quieted down for my act and applauded loudly. When I returned to my dressing room, I saw a note taped to the mirror. Hank! Had he come? Thrilled, I snatched the paper and flipped it open. Written in a thick scrawl: "Don't do Howard's opera or his daughter."

I little shiver slalomed down my spine. No signature. None necessary. Gal.

—

In the morning, after my shower, I found a phone message from Joanne: "Derek, something terrible has happened. Call me as soon as you can."

I feared that La Donna had been busy, or perhaps Tino had finished righting his slight, and the slight had to do with Howard. I dialed Joanne and she answered immediately.

"Oh, Derek! Thank god!"

"What's happened?"

"It's the theater. It caught fire!"

"No! Was anyone hurt?"

"It was empty, which was really lucky. The damage is mostly in the stage area. Fly curtains, some sets, and the piano. The seats

115

are okay, but the upholstery smells of smoke and will have to be replaced."

"When did it happen?"

"Last night."

"That's odd if no one was around. Must have been a wiring problem or something."

Joanne sighed unhappily. "Oh, Derek, I'm afraid not. The fire chief says it's arson. They think Daddy torched his own theater."

"That's crazy. Why would they think that?"

"He went to the theater around ten o'clock to check that all the lights were off. Sometimes he gets worried. Anyhow, Ronald—that's our driver—drove him. Ronald told the police he'd taken Daddy there."

"Well, why didn't he tell them when he picked your father up?"

"That's just it. Ronald didn't pick him up. He said the car got a flat tire. Daddy had to take a cab home."

La Donna's signature was writ large. I didn't say anything to Joanne about my vindictive employer or their double-agent chauffeur because I wasn't sure if Joanne was toe deep in the family business or up to her neck. Despite my anxiety, I liked Howard and was upset about the theater.

"So your father is really under suspicion?"

"Yeah, especially since the theater is losing money."

"What? They think he burned the place for the insurance?"

"Yeah. The fire began on one of the paper flats. It was started by a cigar, which the police found a few feet away. The same brand Daddy smokes."

Ronald had passed Howie's stogie preferences to La Donna along with Howie's schedule or used that knowledge to do the deed himself. "It doesn't sound good, Joanne."

She surprised me with her sudden vehemence. "Don't you see, Gil? He was set up! The whole arson thing is a goddamned frame job!" She blew out an angry gust of air. "If my father ever gets his hands on who did this . . . oh, boy!"

Oh, boy, indeed! Even if I had nothing to do with the fire, I was leashed to the woman who had ordered it. I began cataloguing the ways her father would take revenge on La Donna or possibly me, picturing fiery demises like in the last act of Wagner's *Götterdämmerung*, the Immolation Scene.

Joanne had a full head of steam worked up. "But my father won't quit! He's going to rent another theater."

"He is?"

"Yes. And he's getting some of his boys to keep an eye on things at the new place. Says he can't let me down." At this mention of paternal caring, her tone softened, and she began sniffling. "He's such a dear. Daddy will do anything for me. Absolutely anything."

I groaned inside. The decision to continue the production would effect La Donna like shaking a stick at a rattlesnake. Increasing the number of troops—presumably the Russkies—could create a bigger conflagration.

Suddenly, I became angry. Very angry. I didn't want anyone hurt. I didn't want Joanne to lose her chance to sing or for me to lose mine. No! I would go and talk with the opera-loving mobsterette. She had no right to behave like this over a rusty old grudge that happened years ago.

"Joanne, I'm so sorry," I said, trying to sound calm. "I'm sure everything will be all right." Okay, well, I am allowed to speak inanities every once in a while.

"Oh, Derek, do you really think so?"

Mad as I was, I couldn't help myself from envisioning Joanne looking up at me, tears glistening in her eyes, just like in old movies. I had to snap myself out of my reverie. I wasn't Clark Gable, and Joanne was no Vivian Leigh, nor the other way round. "Yeah, I'm sure. Just watch. Your father will fix everything. That's what he's good at, isn't he?"

"Yes," she replied tentatively. "He is. Oh, and I guess I better tell Guilia. Is she there?"

"Er, yeah. I think I hear her coming up the stairs. She went out for . . . doughnuts," I added quickly. "Just a minute."

I opened and closed the door, rattled a paper bag, and said in my Derek voice that Joanne was on the phone. Then, humming a high note so that I'd think high voice, I answered as Guilia.

"Joanne, what's the matter?"

Joanne reprised her story while Guilia made sympathetic noises and asked the occasional question. At the end of the recounting, Joanne said that the planned ten o'clock rehearsal on Monday would be at the Lowenbaum home.

"We'll meet there until Daddy finds a new theater."

"Okay, well, again, I'm really sorry, Joanne. Please tell your father, too."

"Thanks. I'll see you Monday. Oh, could I speak with Derek again?"

"He just left."

"But you just brought—"

"Er, bagels."

"I thought you were getting doughnuts?"

"I did. For me. Derek took his bagel and went to his voice lesson."

Joanne accepted this confection and hung up.

I knew I had to do what a man has to do, though I wasn't sure I was the man to do it.

CHAPTER SIXTEEN

Confrontation

I walked briskly over to Mott and Spring Streets, clenching and unclenching my fists. I'll fix that pernicious gangsterette, I exhorted myself as I approached La Donna's building. Who does she think she is? I hit the buzzer with force. I was a man, after all, and it was time to stand up for my woman. Hold it. Turn off the movie. I had no woman, didn't want one, and was closer to being one than . . . well, this was too complicated for my overheated mind. All I knew was that La Donna was in the wrong, and my allegiance was not with her regardless of her fat fifty-dollar packets. That said, threatening such a dangerous woman might be suicidal. She could have my head stuck on a platter like Salome did with John the Baptist's.

A woman's voice came through the intercom. I gave my name, relieved that the voice didn't belong to Bulging Head. The door opened, and I stomped toward the elevator, squaring my shoulders, working myself up to my full height, and trying to regain my confidence. But then I thought of the last fight I'd been in. Senior year in high school. A painful disaster and a bad thing to remember on the cusp of being upchucked from the Otis elevator I was standing in.

The big steel doors slid apart like a sideways guillotine, and I crossed to the door, which opened before I could knock. My pal Tino blocked my entrance, arms crossed over his chest like Mr. What's-his-name, the all-purpose cleaner. He looked like he intended to stuff me in a bucket and mop the black-and-white checkerboard floor with me.

Bravado, I thought to myself, is just a few letters longer than *brava*, a word I was used to hearing. I set my jaw and ventured forth.

—

Tino thunked a meaty hand on my chest, a thunk that thunked down to my toes. His steely little eyes appraised me with anger.

"Hey! Whatcha doin' up here?" He thunked me again. "We been lookin' for you."

The elevator door closed, cutting off my retreat. I stood up straight, my slender six-foot-one stacked against his bulky five-foot-ten. "I want to talk with La Donna."

He snorted like a bull spying a red cape. "Ha! That's pretty funny. You think you can just walk in here and ask to see the boss?" He shook his massive head and snorted again.

"Yeah, I do."

My stubbornness surprised him but not enough. "Well, think again, pervert."

I thought I looked very classy and not at all like a pervert, which, in turn led me to wonder if his boss appreciated anti-gay remarks in her domicile. "I wish to speak with La Donna," I repeated. "Right now."

Tino rubbed a whiskery chin and squinted at me like maybe I wasn't the person he thought I was. I tended to agree with him. Just then his desk phone rang. He ambled over to it, keeping a wary eye on me as if I might cut and run, which if I had any sense I would have. In fact, I realized I had no plan, no strategy, no brains, and my courage was leaking out like air from a tire pierced by a pick axe.

He answered, listened, and hung up. "I don't like this none, but you got the okay."

I started to take a step and was thunked again.

"Remember, no funny stuff," he growled.

I was allowed passage, escorted by Bulging Head. My suspicion about the place having bugs and cameras seemed credible because of the approval granted unseen, though the woman who buzzed me in may have used a second intercom, one not by the elevator, and knew that I was the visitor.

Upon entering the Potted Palm Room, which suddenly resembled a funeral parlor, I wondered if I was about to be stuffed in a coffin. Anxiously, I peered through the greenery for the petite Handel lover and finally located her sprawled on a chaise by a large window. She was reading the newspaper, half-glasses perched on her diminutive nose. When she saw me, she smiled.

"Gil, so nice of you to stop by!"

This was not the greeting I expected. I forcibly kept my mouth from falling open, mumbled hello, and was told to sit, which I did on a tufted ottoman across from her.

"To what do I owe the pleasure?" Her voice was low, with a faint rasp. Damage from decades back, when someone had contaminated her coffee?

I decided to submerge any trace of anger and match her tone until the lay of the land became clear. "I hate to bother you, but I have a problem that's difficult to resolve."

"Really? Can I be of any help?"

Why was she being friendly? "Yes, I think so. You see, it's like this. I finally have this great opportunity to sing a lead in a Mozart opera. To launch my career and realize my dreams."

"Mmm," she said noncommittally.

"Well, it's a soprano role. Sooner or later I'll be found out, but so far I haven't been."

"And what has this to do with me?"

"You've already warned me about Howard Lowenbaum."

Her eyes narrowed almost imperceptibly. "Yes, I did."

I hesitated, then lunged ahead. "Perhaps you know him from an old show, *Jungle Fever*?"

La Donna folded the newspaper with exquisite care. "Yes. He's a first-class bastard," she said in a whisper thick with vehemence. "He's no one you can trust, Gil. No one you should be involved with."

"I agree with you, but I've already promised to do the part. It's really important to me."

La Donna was silent, as if she had told me all I needed to know. I couldn't let it go, however, although a tiny tic was twitching the corner of her mouth.

"First, one of the singers was attacked, and last night someone torched Howard Lowenbaum's theater."

"Pity. It's always sad to hear about a theater fire."

The warm current turned cool. I had to be careful. I was swimming with a barracuda. "Yes, it is a pity." My sarcasm was subtle. I paused, weighing what to say next. "But I'm in a real mess. Howard thinks I'm the twin brother of Guilia Hancock, who is the soprano I'm pretending to be in his show. His daughter, Joanne, is also in the production—in fact that's why he mounted it in the first place—for her. She's got a great voice, by the way."

"I've heard that." The neutrality of her words didn't match the intensity of her stare.

I continued. "Joanne is attracted to me—as Guilia's twin, Derek. She's told her father all about our relationship, even though there is no relationship. Howard has communicated that my well-being and my sister's well-being are dependent on my perfect behavior with Joanne." This was the story line that I hoped Gal had already fed La Donna. Despite this logical explanation for why I was stuck, I rued having to rely on the truth rather than a brilliant concoction of lies; lies usually being more persuasive than honesty.

"In other words, he's threatened you?"

"Yes, in so many words."

"I see."

"What should I do?"

She gave a short bark of laughter, placed her elbow on the arm of the chaise, and propped her chin in the vee of her hand. Her smile disappeared. She said nothing.

The "take pity" angle wasn't working. I felt a flash of renewed anger, and, without considering the consequences, I foolishly dove into deep water. "Well, I can see you aren't going to help. Maybe because you burned his theater?"

La Donna closed her eyes and exhaled a long breath. "I didn't do any such thing, Gilbert."

I knew she was lying; she knew I knew she was lying. We were quiet for a few minutes, testing how the silence felt.

"I've already given you my advice," she continued, staring at me again. "Terminate your relationship with the Lowenbaums. All of them. At once."

"But what about Joanne? If I reject her, Howard will be furious."

"That's your problem." La Donna said this dismissively, as if the conversation were at an end.

I didn't let it go. "So you don't care what Howard does to me?"

She sat on her chaise like a fifth carved head on Mount Rushmore. Mute as stone.

Unsure what to do, I stood to leave. "By the way, Lowenbaum intends to continue with the *Così* production." I shouldn't have said this and instantly regretted it. Quickly, I added, "I'm telling you this because I hope you're done and the score is even."

But she didn't appear satisfied with the score. Suddenly, her synapses seemed to be short-circuiting with fury overload. "I'm sorry to hear that," La Donna said in an ominous voice.

I had erred big time and needed to skedaddle to avoid losing my kneecaps. Before I did, I held out an olive branch and asked her if she wanted me to sing some Handel. She stiffly informed me that there were matters requiring her attention. Tino ushered me to the elevator, his big mitts tightening into fists of frustration. I could tell he'd like nothing better than to pound me into Gilbertburger.

When I was on the street at last, I was flooded with relief, although I was not out of the woods. In fact, if anything, I was more *Into the Woods* than ever. What a disaster! If I suddenly cancelled with Howard, he would think my behavior was suspicious, and, if I also broke off with Joanne, he would believe I was acting dishonorably toward his beloved daughter. Both actions would set him hot on my heels, along with La Donna, who might be so perturbed with yours truly as to sign my death warrant. Of course, if she intended to kill or maim me, why hadn't she just done it while I was in her clutches? Maybe she didn't want to bloody her pristine black-and-white floors? Or perhaps she wanted to see what I would do. If I quit the opera and ruined the production, was that her primary goal? And if I achieved that, would everything be okay? Tomorrow was a *Così* rehearsal. I considered a fast trip to Madame Clara but decided I'd better save my money in case I had to return the retainer to Howard, if Howard was alive to receive it.

Feeling miserable, I walked over to Washington Square, removed my shoes, and dangled my feet in the fountain, hoping that answers would wick up through my bare feet to my brain. And, too, there was always the possibility that Hank would be there. It would be such a help to talk with him about everything.

Sunday in the Park with George, I mean Gilbert, was not successful. No Hank, no brilliant solutions, a bunch of screaming kids trying to dent my head with flying Frisbees. I left and went home after a stop at the grocery store.

—

I arose with the roosters and the commuters, and, against my better judgment, I dressed for the rehearsal, wearing the blue dress, the griffin scarf, and navy low-heeled shoes that were quietly stylish.

123

Tucking my wallet and lipstick in a red purse, I took a bus uptown to the Howard Lowenbaum residence. Outside, a few feet from the landing, was a guy with high cheekbones, tiny eyes, and a huge chest. Very much in the mold of Tino, except I was sure the man was Russian. He wore a black suit, smoked a brown cigarette, and was scanning everyone who entered the building.

I swallowed hard and adopted a purposeful air as I strode forward. Luckily, Fiona O'Sullivan was coming down the street. I waved and called out a cheery hello. Together, we climbed the steps and escaped inside the building. Fiona began talking about the fire, her freckled face turning alternately red with anger and pale with concern. She, too, had heard about the police questioning Howard and wondered if he was capable of burning his own theater. I offered an opinion that he hadn't, which seemed to relieve Fiona. As we entered the elevator, we both started to laugh. We knew who had been its occupant before us: Ivan.

The Lowenbaums owned the ninth floor, a spacious pre-war flat that was knickknack-kitsch heaven. On every inch of wall were family photos and folksy paintings, and on every table, chest, and bookcase were Venetian glass animals, porcelain figurines, mounted butterflies, silver candy bowls filled with peppermints, chocolates, jellybeans, and trail mix. The overall effect was colorful and crowded, even more so with the six cast members and conductor stuffed in the room.

A stout woman with piled-high red hair and a commanding presence welcomed us. Mrs. Lowenstein-Lowenbaum had most likely been attractive in her prime, fine for scrutiny on stage but not on screen. However, those happy days were well behind her. She led Fiona and I to the piano, where Maestro MacDougal was warming up Nate Lowenstein and Ivan. Gareth Kerr sashayed in, trailing a long silk red-and-black scarf that I envied. He gave me a coy smile.

"Good morning, Guilia," he said. "I'th tho nice to thee you!"

"Hi, Gareth. How are you?"

"Juth fine, though I wonder at the goingth on!"

"You mean about the fire?"

He rolled his eyes toward Howard, who had walked in from the kitchen, then nodded and whispered behind his hand, "We're all wondering did he or didn't he."

"I'm sure he didn't."

Joanne entered. She looked a bit wan as did her father. Howard announced that the set designer was painting drops and constructing some new flats. He asked us to begin rehearsal.

Halfway through, Maestro MacDougal tipped his Irish cap and stared at me. "You have such an interesting voice, Guilia. I mean, 'tis a strong sound and secure, but I've never heard a soprano like you."

"Thank you," I said quickly, not wanting to encourage more commentary. Although I was delighted to be singled out for praise, I didn't want my wee charade to be found out before opening night, or better yet, ever.

"I think her voithe ith thimply gloriouth!" Gareth winked a shiny brown eye at me.

"So do I," Joanne added, not to be outdone by Gareth.

These raves settled our curious conductor, who resumed the rehearsal until 11:15, when Mrs. Lowenstein-Lowenbaum, or Doris, as she asked to be called, issued forth from the dining room with invitations for coffee and refreshments. The singers were eager to partake.

For once, Howard remembered who I was—perhaps because he was wearing his glasses. "Guilia, you really got volume."

"Thank you so much."

"Hey, I gotta ask you something." He led me to the far side of the table. "The missus and I, well, we want you to come to supper. You know, kinda a family shindig. The wife makes a helluva brisket."

"That's very nice of you to ask, Mr. Lowenbaum."

"Call me Howard, okay? And maybe you could invite your brother, too? Joanne says he might have a great voice like yours. I'd like to meet him. Maybe offer him a job or something."

"Derek has a wonderful talent, Howard, and I'm positive he would love to come for your wife's brisket, which I am sure is out of this world." I was going on like this in the hope that I could connive my way out of being at the same place, at the same time, as two different people.

Then that little mischievous tenor edged himself into the conversation. "Oh, Guilia, you muth tathte Dorith' brithket! I'th abtholutely divine!"

I had no notion as to why the Lowenbaums had been socializing with Gareth, but I was not pleased he was setting my buns to the fire by pushing the invitation. He gave me a self-satisfied grin that bordered on sly. I grinned back at him, hoping to convey a *soupçon* of malice.

"We would be delighted to come," I told Howard, "but let me check with Derek."

"How about Friday at 6:30?" Howard asked. "We'll send Ronald to pick you both up."

Super duper, I thought. La Donna's spy would report me as soon as my heels touched down on the limo's carpet.

—

I sprinted out of rehearsal when it concluded. The last thing I wanted to do was chat with that lisping little serpent, Gareth, or be pressured by Joanne. I rushed downtown to change my duds, gobble a turkey sandwich *sans* mayo (so as not to crud up my throat), and dress as Christopher Gilbert Rose-Wren, *tenore suprimo*. Then, I took the subway uptown and arrived with a second to spare for the two o'clock *Rigoletto* rehearsal. Here, at least, I could breathe easier since I was who I was supposed to be, more or less, except that I wasn't quite Gilbert Rose. My voice, however, was perched for mountain-climbing soprano range from this morning and had required some practice on the street and subway to coerce it into a tenor sound.

Malcolm Earl was standing in the rear of the theater, urbane in a dove gray suit and charcoal silk tie. He said hello and escorted me to the piano, where Oletha Svenson, Chester Boone, and the rest of the cast were standing next to a woman with her back turned to me.

"Maestra Della Vigna," Malcolm said, "this is your Duke, Christopher Rose-Wren."

The woman turned and gave me a warm smile. It was La Donna's pianist, Raffaella.

CHAPTER SEVENTEEN

Raffaella Della Vigna

I shook Raffaella's hand and tried to disguise my shock. Raffaella smiled, her beautiful brown eyes shining with good humor.

"Christopher, is it?" she asked.

"Yes, *Christopher*. Nice to meet you."

I was desperate to know how she'd been hired and what had happened to the original conductor, but Malcolm Earl was in a hurry to begin rehearsal. Raffaella gathered everyone around and played the music with impressive dash and precision, which garnered appreciation from the cast. Although I, too, was glad that Malcolm Earl had signed her because she was an excellent musician, I was unnerved by the unhappy possibility that La Donna had dipped her poisonous spatula in yet another of my operatic cakes. There was no chance to ask questions until we took our break.

After filling a cup with coffee, Raffaella whispered, "Gil, I bet you're wondering what happened."

"I'm happy to have you on board, but you bet I'm wondering."

"Well, the conductor got sick. Appendicitis or something. He's in the hospital. Our mutual employer heard about it and suggested I should call Mr. Earl. She knew you were involved and wanted to help out."

Could I count the ways La Donna might help out? "I didn't know you conducted."

"I don't have a lot of experience, but Verdi is my favorite. I know the *Rigoletto* score very well. It's a great opportunity for me, just like it is for you."

We chatted about a few points on the score, and then I inquired about her relationship with La Donna.

"No different than yours. She whistles. I come."

I nodded but there was something about the expression on Raffaella's face that made me question her veracity. Were La Donna and Raffaella lovers? It was hard to picture the two of them together.

Raffaella was tall, beautiful, twenty years younger, and sexy. La Donna was short, beautiful, twenty years older, and scary, though I supposed the line between scary and sexy might be permeable in some cases.

"That's how it is with me, too," I agreed, pondering the likelihood that La Donna had sent Raffaella to spy on me or for some other nefarious purpose. "Do you think our musical relationship with her will last long?"

"I don't know," Raffaella shrugged, "but I hope so. It's lucrative." She finished her coffee. "Hey, I guess we better get back to work."

Was she avoiding more questions? I studied her as she walked with liquid elegance toward the piano, her head carried high and proudly. If I weren't of my special persuasion, I'd be attracted to her. With a start, I realized I was. Okay, just a little.

—

After we finished, Raffaella offered to share a taxi downtown. I thanked her, explained I had errands to run, and said I'd see her on Wednesday for the next rehearsal.

"Are you sure? It's no problem for me to drop you off somewhere."

If I didn't know better, I'd swear she was flirting. That was probably her way. Cover all bases with all sexes and orientations. But even so, I felt a twinge of nervousness.

"No, thanks. Catch you later." I observed her as she left, studying her stride and erect carriage and thinking that my character Fiordiligi might move similarly. Then, I returned to the piano to go over a few sections of two arias. Chester Boone, the baritone, hung around with me, offering some helpful suggestions. Afterward, we walked out together, and as we did, I had the weird feeling someone was watching me. I searched the street and the cars but didn't recognize anyone.

—

After a stint at the department store, I arrived on my block after midnight and cautiously looked around before heading for my door. I had no idea what La Donna would do once she learned I had attended the rehearsal at the Lowenbaums' residence. I hoped she was content with destroying the theater—if she was the culprit, a fact she hadn't confirmed—and piercing the singer's eardrum, which Gal had implied, and would forego destroying me. Upstairs, I popped open a soda and looked at my e-mail. My pulse raced faster than the Daytona 500. Hank.

Dear Gil,

Sorry that I haven't written or called. Things have been worse with my brother. It's really late otherwise I'd phone, but it's been a long day, and I think I better pack it in.

I enjoyed dinner with you and hope we can do it again very soon when my life calms down. There's a chance I can get to your Saturday performance, but I am not sure.

How are the two operas coming?

Best, Hank

The e-mail had arrived at 11:05. Why hadn't he called? I wouldn't have been home, but at least I could have heard his voice message. I sat down and answered his note, explaining about the rehearsals, aching to say more but afraid and shy, as the *Carousel* song goes. Of course, I could always call him tomorrow, but his e-mail implied that I should be patient. I drank my soda and thought of all the people who were attracted to me, now and in the recent past. It was just my luck that the one man I wanted wasn't hot on my trail. At least, I had shed dippy Douglas, but I had gained Joanne and, I feared, Gareth, the wily little beast who could unmask my Guilia disguise.

—

My hand edged toward the cell phone about twenty-nine times the next morning. I wanted to talk to Hank in the worst way. I needed reassurance and despised myself for needing it. Finally, I girded my loins and called Joanne.

"Hi, Joanne, this is Derek."

"Oh, Derek . . . how nice of you to call!"

"Thanks. I spoke with my sister, and she said your father invited us to dinner on Friday. Would you mind if I came by myself?" I knew she wouldn't mind at all and was not surprised to hear her voice do cartwheels.

"Oh, sure! That's great!" she replied. "But what's up with Guilia? Is she okay?"

"Yeah, she's fine but my mother . . . our mother fell in her house. I mean, my mother's house . . . and Guilia is away to help."

"That's a shame. Did you mother break anything?"

"No, she just sprained her ankle."

"I hope she's better soon," Joanne replied. "Will Guilia miss the Wednesday rehearsal?"

"No, no. She said she planned to be back for that—the opera is so important to her—but then she's returning home afterward."

"Your family does seem to suffer a lot of maladies," she said. "Well, I'm sorry she can't join us, but I am very pleased you'll be there. Ronald will drive down—"

"No, that's okay. I'll come on my own. Thanks, though." The last thing I wanted was for Ronald to provide a comprehensive report to La Donna.

After we ended the conversation, I felt slightly ill. I didn't know why I was persisting with my connections to the Lowenbaums. That's not true, I did. Stupid stubbornness for one thing. And then there was money and fame and a career and a new apartment. As I made myself a cup of coffee, I wondered how La Donna was interpreting the news bulletins on my activities. I decided to call Gal for an update.

She answered after a few rings, yawning in an unladylike manner. "Yeah? What's up?"

I explained about Raffaella's new conducting job. "So, Gal, what gives? Is she there to spy on me?"

"Oh, Gil, relax. Why do you think she's there?"

"I just told you what I think. She's a spy. A beautiful spy . . ."

Gal chuckled. "Ha! So you got the hots for Raffaella now?"

I could feel a little blush coming on and was thoroughly glad Gal couldn't see it. "Not at all," I insisted. "How about you?"

"Nah, she's too glam for me."

Even though she denied it, I could tell Gal was flattered by my suggestion. "No, she isn't," I protested, even though I agreed with Gal's opinion.

She snorted, reminding me unpleasantly of Tino. "Yeah, she is."

I gave up on Avenue B and returned to Avenue A. "You didn't answer me about the spying stuff. What's going on?"

"Don't know. Probably La Donna was trying to help you out by sending Raffaella over and at the same time helping Raffaella by finding her some work."

"Killing two birds with one stone?"

Gal didn't laugh. This unnerved me. I continued as if I hadn't said anything sassy about killing birds. "So La Donna is just playing patron?"

"Could be."

I considered this possibility and asked if Gal had told La Donna about Howard threatening me if I didn't play nice with his daughter.

"I told her. Yeah."

"And?"

Gal could be infuriatingly terse.

"And she's declared war on him. There's history between them for years. Lots of skirmishes and retaliations. You just got in between. And you better get out of *in between* before you get in between a coffin and its lid."

"What a lucky guy I am," I said sarcastically.

"Or gal, as the case may be," Gal replied with equal sarcasm.

I sipped some coffee. "So, if I have this right, Raffaella is a gift from La Donna, but if I continue with Howard and the opera and his daughter, I'm in no-man's land without a white flag."

"You got it, Gil. More or less."

She let me bluster for a few minutes, then added, "And La Donna wants an hour of you-know-what tomorrow night."

"No."

"I think that was a yes?"

I groaned and we disconnected. A second later, the phone rang. Loretta, asking me to fill in for a salesman in the jewelry department who was out for an afternoon doctor's appointment. I agreed to do it because money is money, and I never had enough of it. Besides, I do enjoy perusing the golden goodies at Oscar's.

As I walked to the subway stop, I replayed the conversation with Gal. Something about her reaction to Raffaella didn't lie flat or else she was flat out lying. I was pretty sure that someone was sleeping with my conductor, and it wasn't Tino. I had a well-honed instinct for these things. Gay boys do, you know, especially gay boys that cross-dress.

Oscar's was busy selling to the procrastinating crowd, those parents whose kiddies were not yet properly rigged for school, which had started a few days ago. This meant that my counter was relatively quiet since most attentions were glued to the little squirmy ones and their need for cute wooly outfits. I polished the glass countertops and adjusted lights and thought about Hank. I also sang my Fiordiligi and Duke arias in my head, confirming that I really did know all the words. Lucky for me I had a grand gift for memorization.

CHAPTER EIGHTEEN

Trouble in River City

So far, my two rehearsal schedules hadn't coincided. Today, Howard Lowenbaum threw a king-sized wrench into this fabulous felicity. He called at eight o'clock to say that Gareth, who had arranged for a West Side theater rental through his uncle, could only reserve time from 12:00 to 2:30. My *Rigoletto* rehearsal was planned for 2:00 to 4:30 on the other side of town. I smelled a rat. One with a speech impediment.

I explained to Howard that I had to leave early for a dentist appointment. He wasn't pleased, so I promised to see what I could arrange. Figuring that perhaps Raffaella might smooth the waters on the East Side, I called Gal for her number, which Gal gave me after some grunts and groans and complaints about having a bad back. Since every lesbian has a bad back—it is a *maladie de rigueur*—I was used to this and made the appropriate sympathetic noises. Then, I heard some scuffling and whispering that confirmed Gal was not flying solo. Although I was tempted to tease, I didn't.

"But don't call her yet, Gil. Maybe around 10:30."

This made me wonder if perhaps the lady in question was occupying the other half of Gal's bed. Again, I minded my manners, particularly since I had a favor to ask.

"Any chance you and the Caddie are free this afternoon around 1:45?"

"What the hell! Do you think I'm your personal chauffeur?" Here, I heard muffled sounds, as if Gal had covered the phone. Then, she came back on the line. "What are you up to?"

"I'm up to being in two places at the same time."

"I thought you'd perfected that."

"Nearly. But I desperately, desperately need a ride between west and east. Nothing else . . . no waiting around or anything."

"I got a helluva lot of better things to do than cart you and your wigs around town."

"Please?"

Gal mumbled something that sounded like an okay.

"You're a dreamboat!"

At 10:30, I called Raffaella and left a message asking her to delay rehearsal a few minutes on some pretense because I would be late.

—

The theater was on West 79th. Mingy, dingy, dusty, with about four hundred seats, it was fine for an intimate opera like *Così. Rigoletto*, with its large chorus and cast, would have required fold-out stages. As I walked in, cleaners were vacuuming the velvet seats, several artists were painting flats, and one guy was nailing together a wooden trellis for the garden scene. More ominously, five black-clad figures were scattered in the darkest areas of the orchestra and balcony. Guys with high Slavic cheekbones and tiny eyes; guys that drank vodka like water and ate too much Stroganoff and Pirozhki. Though they all wore suits, I suspected their jackets concealed weapons. Howard wasn't underestimating La Donna. I just hoped that his little Russkie army could protect us if Ronald had tipped off the mobsterette about our rehearsal and our new digs.

This thought made my heart do a loud thud-thud in my chest. I forced myself to stroll down the aisle cool as a cucumber all the while my gut felt like I'd gorged on six hot chile peppers doused with jalapeño sauce. Joanne was warming up with Maestro Mac-Dougal as were Ivan and Gareth. Seeing the stolid bass, I wondered if he had lumbered out of the same Brooklyn den as the Russians hulking around the theater. I decided he might be a relative of one of them, recommended to Howard, but I doubted Ivan was a card-carrying mob member himself. He didn't seem to have a malicious bone in his body.

Everyone said hello, and, as I stepped onto the stage, Gareth grinned at me and patted a stool next to him.

"Hi, Guilia. Why don't you thit here, dear."

So now I was a *dear*? Yuck. Since it was the only stool left, I was forced to take it, much to Gareth's delight.

"You're looking fabuluth today. I like what you've done to your hair."

For a second I panicked. Had I donned one of the Kiri wigs instead of the more demure Guilia wig? I touched it to check, as a lady would, and then smiled at the compliment. "Why, thank you. How nice of you to notice."

"Oh, I notith a lot about you," he replied, arching one eyebrow.

I thumbed through the musical score as if it were a movie magazine and said casually, "I'm sure you do."

Gareth wanted to play and wasn't happy that I was ignoring him. He leaned over and whispered in my ear, "Your curvatheuth legth, your full breath . . ." Here, I assumed he meant *breasts*, though it was possible he was referring to my extraordinary lung capacity.

I took my nose almost literally in hand and edged closer to Ivan. Since the Russian was unaccustomed to anyone moving nearer to him, he gave me a surprised look that quickly changed to oh-too-pleased. Out of the fat, into the fire, or perhaps it was the other way round.

"Ah, my little Fiordiligi!" Ivan whispered, placing a heavy hand on my shoulder.

I sat up straighter and stared from Gareth to Ivan and fervently wished I had two eject buttons. "Er, Ivan, do you think we should practice a little?"

"I would be honored," he replied, hitting the "h" on "honored" with a gust of garlic and vodka breath and giving my knee a mighty squeeze. The ampleness of my joint must have impressed him, so he squeezed again, his eyes bright with delight.

"Maestro MacDougal?" I slipped off my stool and ran over to the conductor with Ivan in tow like a fevered bloodhound. "Could we run through 'Sento, o dio' once?'" This was the first act scene in which the two pairs of lovers sing their farewells.

"Yes, let's," Joanne agreed. "Come over here, Gareth."

Since at this stage of the opera I was supposedly in love with Guglielmo, Ivan came up next to me and took my hand, far too possessively for my comfort. Gareth followed suit with Joanne, although he was looking puppy eyes in my direction.

We began singing the farewells, and I swear Ivan teared up, pressing my hands to his massive chest and working himself into the depths of drama. The odor emanating from his body—a combination of raw beef and mothballs, the latter from a wool blazer freshly released from its summertime closet home and the former, well, from Ivan himself—was so overpowering as to make my stomach heave. I managed to sing on despite this offense to my nostrils, which in turn emboldened the basso to embrace me and then, horror of horrors, kiss me! His aforementioned breath, now experienced upfront and personal, caused me to step backward, which gave the Russian an opportunity to pull me close, quite the opposite of what I desired most—a half mile of space.

Maestro Cavendish MacDougal came to the rescue. He forwarded us to Act II and the switch of partners. Unfortunately, this paired me with Gareth as Ferrando and created an opportunity for more flirtation, causing me to wonder why I was so magnetic to the same sex, the opposite sex, and the indeterminate sex.

Gareth grasped the hand so recently held by Ivan and moved toward my *décolletage*, which was about on level with his eyes. I suspect the Lisping Lamb had a maternal fixation since he nestled into my padded bosom with zestful glee.

"Oh, my, Guilia," he whispered, looking up at me with adoration. "I thimply love thith thene, don't you?"

I backed His Royal Stickiness off my well-endowed fakery and sang my lines with hand to brow, my face turned toward the audience of two, Howard and his wife, Doris. After I finished, I heard clapping from them both, which was appropriate for my fine rendition. Gareth, however, was not to be separated from his beloved.

"I know what you're up to," he whispered in my ear. "The thlimey Duke of Mantua thith afternoon?" He chortled merrily. "Thall I tell Howard that you're no thoprano?"

A threat? I guided him stage left as Joanne and Ivan worked with MacDougal. "Gareth," I began, "keep your mouth shut, do you hear me?"

This pleased him, as did any attention paid. "I think we need to thpend time together. I have a nith thparkling wine at my plathe. All nith and cool, unlike mythelf." He tossed me a wink. "I could thee you after *Rigoletto* . . ."

I had time before my presence was requested at La Donna's, but I wasn't going to waste it on Gareth. "I'm sorry, but I have a singing engagement tonight."

"Not at the Purple Plum."

This took me aback. Did he know about Kiri De Uwana, Christopher Rose-Wren, and Gilbert? Had he been following me around? Was he another of La Donna's plants, but, if so, why would he arrange for the theater rental if La Donna was trying to shut down our production?

"I don't sing at the Purple Plum. My brother, Derek, does."

He laughed, hand splayed across his mouth. "You are tho funny! There'th no Derek!"

That flimsy fabrication demolished, I had to retreat and regroup. "Maybe we can get together tomorrow or the day after."

"It better be thoon," he replied. "I am in thuch a hurry." His eyes roamed over me with predatory interest.

Joanne walked over, bless her heart. "Guilia, I'm so sad to hear about your mother. Is she all right?"

I went blank. My mother? What was wrong with my mother? "Yes, I think so."

"How is her sprain?"

Oh, yeah, the fall. "Thanks for asking, Joanne. Mother is a bit better, but she also bruised her knee and hurt her back. She's got one of those tricky backs, you know—"

"Tho do I," Gareth inserted, "Thometimeth I require thome at-tithance getting out of bed . . ." He drifted off provocatively.

I ignored him and turned to Joanne. "She'll be fine in a few days, but she needs help. I hope you understand about Friday night."

Gareth's pointy little ears rose. "Friday night?"

Joanne stared at him and then did the unthinkable. She asked the tenacious tenor to dinner. My heart stopped.

Gareth tossed me an exultant glance, took Joanne's hand, and accepted the invitation.

—

I waited until Gareth, Joanne, and Ivan were engaged, made my excuses, and bolted out of the theater. Gal was tapping thick fingers on the top of the Caddie's rearview mirror. I hauled the bag full of disguises and myself into the back seat and began changing identities.

"Hey, no hello or anything?" Gal asked.

"Sorry. This morning's been beastly . . . or rather, the beasts have been beastly."

"That little squirt tenor?" Gal knew about Gareth.

"Yeah," I replied, pulling off my flouncy blouse. "And the stinky bass has developed an attachment, too."

Gal laughed. "Everyone loves you, Gil. You're one popular guy."

"Thanks." I slimed my face with cold cream and dabbed at it with a wad of Kleenex.

The big car surfed through the traffic as I frantically donned slacks and socks over my pantyhose. I was going to be hot, but I didn't have time to completely strip away all remnants of Guilia Hancock. As the Caddie swooned toward the curb, I combed my damp hair into place and then mussed it slightly for the casual look Christopher Rose-Wren favored.

"Am I okay?" I asked.

Gal turned around in her seat, her leather jacket creaking. "Earrings, Gil."

—

I was twenty-five minutes late, but Raffaella had started with the chorus, to give me some time. She was at the piano, looking ravishing in black pants and a tight, black, short-sleeved sweater. I observed the gentle curve of her biceps, the long line of her neck, whether with envy or interest I wasn't sure. After stowing my bag, I sallied up to the stage, remembering in the nick of time not to undulate my hips. If I'd forgotten, they would have sunk my ship. Or was that lips sinking ships?

"Hi," I said to everyone, opening my score and sitting between Chester Boone and a guy whose belly looked like he'd swallowed a stuffed Santa's sack. I introduced myself to him again, since we'd only met briefly at the last rehearsal. Edgar Noonan from Abilene, Texas. He was in his early sixties, dressed in polyester—need I say more? However, his voice was fine for Count Monterone, and when he laid a curse in Act I, he appeared suitably apoplectic.

We worked hard and did well. My voice was a little stressed, but no one seemed to notice. Or so I thought, until Raffaella mentioned it during our coffee break.

"Singing soprano earlier?"

I nodded, glad that we were standing apart from the cast. "Yes, but please don't mention it to La Donna, okay?"

Raffaella gave me a partners-in-crime look. "I wouldn't think of it."

As she said this, I wondered if Gal or our employer had told Raffaella about the rehearsal.

Raffaella took a sip of coffee. "Hey, are you seeing La Donna tonight?"

"Yeah, if I have any voice left."

"Don't worry. La Donna knows opera, but I think she feels more than she hears."

"I doubt it. I think it's the other way round," I replied.

—

As we were walking out of the theater, Raffaella invited me to her place for a quick stir-fry dinner. Since it was already 4:40 and we had to be at La Donna's at 8:00, I accepted. My refrigerator was an echo chamber, and I figured her cooking trumped mine any day.

"I'll see you in a few minutes," I told her. I needed to change for the evening and drop off my Guilia clothes.

—

I showered, donned a polo shirt, khaki pants, and my navy sports jacket, then checked my e-mails, but there was no word from Hank Braylock. For some reason, I felt like I was cheating on him by going to Raffaella's, which I knew was crazy. She was a gay girl, and I was a gay boy.

On my way over to her place, I bought a bottle of chardonnay. I shouldn't drink and sing, but I shouldn't sing soprano, tenor, and mezzo in one day, either. As I walked along, despite all the worries I could be worrying about, I was chiefly upset about not hearing from Hank.

CHAPTER NINETEEN

Into the Stir-fry

Raffaella answered on the first ring and greeted me in a scarlet toreador jacket, low-cut black silk blouse, black slinky slacks, and red sandals. She looked regal and yet very sexy. As I passed by, I could smell her perfume hovering in the air. It was some kind of sprightly oriental scent that was intoxicating.

I sat in a tan leather chair and was served a glass of wine. Suddenly, I felt quite chipper. I loved being treated like a rajah, eating cheese, and being attended to by a beautiful woman. She half-reclined on the sofa and asked all kinds of questions. Without hesitation, I answered, enjoying her company, and thinking she was wonderful. We ate a perfectly prepared beef stir-fry, and before I knew it, it was twenty to eight. We flew around the apartment, tidying up and laughing like old friends, and bolted downstairs and into—you guessed it—Bulging Head.

I applied the brakes but not fast enough. His arms were around my chest before I could yell to Raffaella to run. But surprisingly, she didn't run. Instead, she regarded me with cool professionalism and indicated that Tino should stuff me in the Cadillac, which regrettably was not driven by Gal Friday. As Tino lifted me up and carried me forth, my screams drew a few glances from passersby but nothing more since Raffaella waved everyone away, saying we were filming a movie. Of course, no cameras were present.

Finding myself in the backseat, I kicked and yelled, but old Tino whacked me with his trusty blackjack, ending my evening with one fell swoop.

—

When I awoke, I had a ferocious headache and was lying on sand. A waning half-moon reflected in an oil-slicked creek to my right, and sea gulls swirled above, fat and eager like vultures. A noxious garbage stench filled the air. Nearby were suspicious bulldozed lumps in the earth. Was I in a landfill? In New Jersey?

Just then, I heard voices. Through waving tall grasses, I saw Tino and Raffaella arguing—Raffaella who had just wined and dined me and who I thought was a new friend.

"We can't leave him alive," Raffaella was saying.

"La Donna didn't say nothin' about no snuff job," Tino shot back.

I felt like hugging Tino, except my hands were tied in front with white laundry line.

"He knows too much," the traitor, Raffaella, insisted. "Just because she didn't spell it out for you, use your head."

Tino thought this last comment bordered on an insult. He put his hands on his hips, which would have frightened me into acquiescence, but it seemed to have little effect on Raffaella.

"You'll do what I tell you, Tino, or else," she said firmly before withdrawing a long screwdriver from behind her jacket.

So she had done the eardrum job on Ben! Now I was really scared. I rolled over, tucked my feet under me, and took off through the marsh. Although I was no match for Tino physically, I could run. I had learned just how fast in high school when the boys would try to corral me behind the football stadium. No one could catch me then, and I prayed no one could now.

Since the wind was blowing and the sea gulls were making a racket, my two assassins didn't hear me escape. I was forty yards away before I heard Raffaella shout. I kept sprinting, aiming to beat the minute mile. Soon enough, even my operatic lungs were straining, but I kept going, especially when I turned around and saw Raffaella and Tino slicing through the high grasses. I dodged a rusted washing machine and jumped over a hillock, wondering what was underneath. Was this Tino's private burying ground? Did he bring all his bodies here like some kind of deranged dog hiding bones? This thought spurred me on past a pair of red baby Keds, several picked-apart fish, a trio of steel drums oozing toxic-looking puddles, and all sorts of plastic jugs and bottles. As the ground rose, I tripped on a rotten tree trunk and fell into a thicket of briars, palm first. "Damn!" But there was no time to pull out the thorns. I rolled down a small mound of sand and stood up. My pursuers were yelling at me and at each other. Raffaella was well behind Tino, probably because her footwear wasn't appropriate for speed.

Tino was considerably closer but looked about to explode with fury and lack of oxygen. I took off again.

Despite my huffing and puffing, I suddenly heard a whirring hum. Traffic? I climbed on top of a knoll and saw the blessed Garden State Parkway. I ran for it as fast as I could. After scrambling up to the roadside, I scissored over the silver guard rail and looked north. To my immense relief, two cars were parked on the shoulder: a car with a flat tire and, in front of it, a New Jersey State Trooper patrol car. Prettiest thing I'd seen in years.

"Help!" I shouted. "Help!"

The two troopers saw me and hesitated, then began to walk in my direction.

"Hurry!" I tried to run toward them, but I could only manage a slow trot.

As they approached, I jerked my head toward Tino and Raffaella. "Officers," I gasped, "please . . . those two following me . . . they're trying to kill me . . . mob . . ." I practically fell on one of the troopers. "You've got to catch them."

He eased me to the pavement and drew his gun.

—

Late that night, I called William, who was with Douglas. We decamped to William's old apartment, where they heard my tale and settled me with sheets and towels before leaving for Douglas' condo. After using tweezers to remove the thorns and bandaging my gouges, I crawled into bed, feeling exhausted and frightened. The New Jersey police had caught Raffaella and Tino, taken my statement, and driven me to the Fifth Precinct so I could explain what I knew about La Donna's operation. I hadn't mentioned Gal, though I wasn't sure my loyalty was deserved since she may have communicated all my activities to her employer, even if she'd felt terrible about doing so. The loss of our friendship depressed the hell out of me. I was also worried that I'd misjudged Hank's interest. Like I'd misjudged Raffaella's near-fatal flirtation.

Then Madame Clara's last words—or were they Bob's?—came floating back. Something about the younger man close to Hank was in peril. With a start, I realized I was younger than Hank, and, sure enough, I'd nearly been pushing up posies with my toesies. Even so, Bob's/Clara's clairvoyance was impressive. It also heartened

142

me to think that the directive about it being "just a matter of time" would also be correct, although maybe I had it wrong and it was just a matter of time before my death. But, no, I told myself, this couldn't be true. My career was going full speed ahead: starring roles in two operas, continued success as Kiri De Uwana, and even some much-needed cash for singing Handel, though I wouldn't be performing George Frideric again. I had money in my pocket and would have more, especially because the police would inform Howard Lowenbaum who set fire to his theater, thus removing him from suspicion of arson and allowing our production to continue, hopefully without further interference from La Donna. I prayed the police wouldn't mention the male source of their information to Howard, or that I would have to testify in public, at least not until after the *Così* performances.

When I finally fell asleep, I dreamed about Hank Braylock.

I slept until eleven o'clock and woke with a crushing headache and welts on my palms, especially the left. I rummaged around the bathroom for some salve, which I applied before microwaving a frosty-looking bagel and making instant coffee—that's all that was left in the bare kitchen. William had also removed most of his clothes from the closet, but I found a shirt and pants, both a little loose. After scraping marsh muck off my shoes, I shined them and took two aspirins. That was the best I could do.

I ran downstairs and bought a newspaper to look through the apartment listings. One of the policeman at the precinct, Sergeant Alcott, had suggested that I move and had offered to meet me later so I could pack some things at my place. No one was underestimating La Donna.

After ten calls to landlords and landladies without success, I phoned Luis, who explained he had a friend, Myra, who was leaving on Friday for a month in Trieste and was frantically searching for someone to housesit her plants and tropical fish while she was away. I called and told Myra I was her man and promptly arrived at her doorstep fifteen minutes later. We hit it off, and she said I could use her bed because she planned to sleep at her boyfriend's place until her departure. I was delighted and thanked her a gazillion times, promised to keep everything neat and the fish stuffed to the gills. Then, I called Sergeant Alcott, who met me at 2:30, helped me fill boxes I'd saved from my last move, and drove me and all my things to Myra's. The policeman was so nice, and, yes, he was one of the lads.

Even though I was achy, tired, and my head and hands hurt, I went to Oscar's because my usual Thursday night Purple Plum performance was cancelled due to a stage renovation. I was taking a chance going to the department store because La Donna probably knew I was employed there, but my schedule was extremely irregular, especially this evening, when I wasn't supposed to be at work.

Loretta was filing her nails and chewing gum. I didn't tell her about my near-death experience but gave her two tickets to *Rigoletto* before going upstairs to fix my seesaw display. Some rogue had replaced the kiddie mannequin with an adult male, bent the body into a provocative position, and lowered his pants. Although I was amused, I was too tired to laugh.

The night edged past twelve o'clock. I walked to the empty service department and exited through the back door, keeping an eye out for any gangster goons who might be lurking. Then, I returned to Myra's and quietly let myself in.

—

The *Così* rehearsal began promptly at ten. The guys in black had beefed up their number to seven, which did nothing to reassure me that we were safe. Joanne seemed unconcerned by their presence and was acting like her usual breezy self, passing out doughnuts as usual, and everyone was devouring them as usual. Gareth observed my entrance with appreciation; Ivan did the same, although he was less subtle about it. As I approached the piano, the Russian took my hand and kissed it before I had a chance to avoid him.

"Oh, Guilia," he whispered in a voice thick with emotion, "it is so wonderful to see you."

Gareth came up on my other side, giving Ivan the rolled-eye treatment, which the bass didn't notice. "Yeth, it ith nith. What a pretty thuit that ith, Guilia!"

"Thank you both," I gave them a flap of eyelashes, since, after all, I did have to sing with the two gentlemen. "You're looking very dapper this morning, Gareth," I said, fingering his newest silk scarf. "Italian?"

144

Gareth nodded, pleased.

"And Ivan, what a great tie!" Or at least it had been a great tie once, before it had been subjected to a blitzkrieg of borscht.

"Thank you," Ivan replied, expanding his chest like a hot-air balloon.

Joanne came up and took my arm. "Good morning. Maestro MacDougal wants us to work with Fiona. Will you excuse us for a few minutes?"

Thrilled to be rescued from my predicament, I gladly went off to sing with the girls.

At the break, I asked Joanne if Derek could bring anything to the dinner party. Unfortunately, as I did, Gareth swooped in behind me and overheard.

"What'th the matter, Guilia, aren't you coming tonight?"

"No, I can't . . . my mother needs some help."

"And Derek ithn't going with you?" He treated me to a catty look.

"There's no need for both of us to miss the Lowenbaums' dinner," I replied.

He giggled, which Joanne found irritating. "If you ever thought of anyone but yourself, Gareth, you would understand these things. Family commitments are very important."

Gareth walked away, refusing to be chastised. In his stead came Ivan, twisting his big hands together.

"Guilia, I would like to ask you something."

"Oh?"

He nodded gravely. "Yes. Yes, I would."

"What?"

"Er, well, would you like to go to dinner Saturday night?"

Poor Ivan. "Saturday night? I'm sorry but I have plans for the weekend. My mother fell, and I'm needed at home."

He tried to arrange his face to correspond with his emotions but only managed to sort them out into a split mask, half tragedy/half comedy. He was dejected that I had turned him down and happy I had a good reason.

"Ivan, I would be delighted to have dinner with you at some later time, however I must explain that I have a boyfriend. He often travels for business, but we are in a very committed, very close relationship." You can say that again since we're the same person.

Ivan's brow creased. "Okay. I understand."

Joanne grabbed my arm. "Guilia! I didn't know you were seeing someone?"

"Oh, yes, for the last . . . six months, since Christmas."

"That's nearly nine months," Joanne corrected.

"Mmm . . . well, it feels like six months. You know how it is."

At this serendipitous point, Maestro MacDougal tapped his baton for us to start Act II.

CHAPTER TWENTY

Din-Din with the Lowenbaums

I brought a bouquet of yellow and white snapdragons, a bottle of French burgundy, and a large box of chocolates for the Lowenbaums. Well, what did you expect? I was nervous. I felt like I was surfing a gigantic wave, one that would either be a thrilling ride or dash me on the rocks. In addition to the above, at the consignment shop, I purchased another navy blazer, since the previous jacket bit the dust or, shall we say, the sand. With this, I paired a bright purple and blue tie, charcoal gray slacks, and, black tie shoes—you know, the kind the Wall Street boys wear?

I splurged on a cab and arrived two minutes early. Joanne opened the door and threw her arms around me. "Congratulations!"

I squeezed past her into the overdeveloped bosom of her mother, Doris, who followed suit in the huge hugs department.

"Welcome to our house, Derek," she said. "I'm Doris."

"Nice to meet you."

"The pleasure is all mine," she enthused. "And congratulations are in order, aren't they?"

I was out to sea without a paddle. "Congratulations?"

Doris whacked her daughter's arm. "Oh, he's so modest! I love that in a man! And my, so good-looking, too."

Joanne picked up a newspaper from a side table and showed me an article featuring a photograph of yours truly, my Christopher Rose-Wren head shot, used to advertise the *Rigoletto* production. "I knew it was you because you said you were singing the Duke. But why the different name?"

For a second my nimble brain froze. Then, *presto*, it defrosted. "Oh, that. I use Christopher Rose-Wren for the stage. Derek is so, well, Yankees baseball." I took a few steps toward the living room, since I had been at the Lowenbaums' before, for the rehearsal, and then remembered I'd been here as Guilia and came to a halt.

Howard walked in from the living room, wearing his glasses. A stogie was clamped between his teeth.

"Daddy, this is Derek," Joanne said.

We shook hands. I was careful to add a little heft to the shake, so he'd get the right idea or rather the wrong idea. I handed the flowers and chocolates to Doris, who blushed with pleasure, and the wine to Howard, who checked out the label and approved with a manly wink.

"Thanks for inviting me," I replied, the very model of a well-mannered young man.

"Come and park yourself," Howard offered, steering me toward an overstuffed high-back chair that reminded me of an inquisition seat. "Hope the cigar doesn't bother you, son."

This was not a question, and, yes, it did. Thankfully, Joanne told her father to put it out, that it was disturbing her. Mr. Lowenbaum shrugged, tossed a glance at his wife for support, got none, and tamped the smoldering log in an extra-wide ashtray.

"Sorry. Gotta remember about you opera singers," he muttered.

Doris was eager to play flattering hostess. "Now, Derek, tell us about the *Rigoletto*. We're so proud of you and so excited!" She clasped her hands together like a teenager, which she most decidedly wasn't.

"Well, it's running about the same schedule as ours . . . I mean, Guilia's and Joanne's." I slapped my forehead lightly. "I can't keep her life separate from mine!"

Everyone laughed, me a little too heartily.

"And you're playing the Duke?" Doris asked. "My, my!" She did the handclasp again and shook her head in amazement. "And you're so young to have the lead . . ."

"I'm as old as Guilia," I pointed out reasonably. This strange statement about my twin produced no frowns, so I continued. "It's a small company, otherwise I'm sure I wouldn't have been considered for the part."

"Oh, so handsome and so humble," Doris commented, looking at her daughter and nodding approvingly. "He's gonna make some gal a great hubby."

I swallowed hard, a Pavlovian reaction to the mention of marriage.

On his way to the bar, Howard grabbed my shoulder. "Don't listen to a thing those girls say, Derek. They're always tryin' to trap us guys, and they aren't happy 'til they do."

I smiled at him. "I know what you mean, Mr. Lowenbaum."

"Howard. You gotta call me Howard. Hey, name your poison." Thankfully, he was gesturing at the liquor.

"A vodka tonic would be fine, if you have it." I looked around the room, pretending I'd never been here before. "My, what a nice place you have, Mrs. Lowenstein-Lowenbaum."

"Thanks, Derek. And, please, I'm Doris to my friends."

Just then, the door bell sounded. Joanne jumped up and escorted Gareth into the room, or rather she presaged his entrance. Gareth was decked out in a blue-and-white seersucker suit, pink shirt, and an oversized paisley bowtie. His Truman Capote imitation was spot on.

"Good evening one and all," he announced grandly, as he went to shake hands with the Lowenbaums. When he arrived in front of me, his eyes crinkled with amusement. "And Guilia, I mean, Derek, it'th a plethure meeting you. My, my! You do rethemble your thith-ter, although Guilia ith a little prettier." He giggled naughtily.

I knew I had to be careful. For some reason, Gareth intended to push my identity to the edge of disclosure. As Howard fussed with the bottles, ice, and glasses, and the two women fetched two groaning trays of hors d'oeuvres, I whispered to Gareth, "If you behave yourself tonight, we might go for a drink afterward."

He brought his forefinger to his lips and tapped demurely. "And if I don't?"

I glowered at him. "Just don't mess around, Gareth."

He tossed his head and then rushed over to assist Doris. "May I help? Pleath, thith ith too heavy for you."

I found this display rather nauseating especially since Doris was taller and broader than Gareth. It made me wonder about his role in this little dinner party comedy. The fool? I decided not to be outdone by the scamp.

"Doris," I said, after accepting a cocktail. "I understand you have a musical career." Notice the present tense—always sure to flatter.

"Why, yes, Derek. But not for many, many years."

"Oh, it couldn't have been long ago."

"Yes, it was." She was pleased as punch. "I was in several productions."

149

"I remember reading about *Jungle Fever*," I said, giving Gareth a quick glance that indicated he was losing in the flattery contest.

"My goodness!" Doris exclaimed. "That was way back."

"I never did see the show, but I'm sure it was my loss. It was supposed to be first rate."

Howard beamed at me. "Yes, it was. Old Doris here was quite the foxy lady then—"

"And thtill ith," Gareth piped up, with a smarmy smile.

I sipped my vodka tonic and thought of a suitable rejoinder. "If I recall, Doris was the lead, wasn't she?" I asked Howard. It was always important to spread the attention around.

"She was and a dandy, too. Unfortunately, there was an accident, and she only did one performance."

"How thad," Gareth sympathized, "but I gueth your daughter inherited your talent."

"Yes, Joanne is marvelous as Dorabella!" I said.

Gareth turned a *gotcha* look at me. "You've heard Joanne thing Dorabella?"

"No," I replied, "but my sister says she's great. Guilia always talks about her when she comes back from rehearsal."

Joanne passed the tray heaped with cheeses, grapes, pâté, stuffed grape leaves, figs, and melon wrapped in prosciutto. As she did, she displayed her ample cleavage for my perusal. Her gold knit dress was scooped low in the front and fitted her form far too well, leaving very little to the imagination. "Try the figs, sweetie," she said to me.

I did, stuffing one in my mouth to avoid the necessity of a return endearment.

Gareth crossed his legs precisely, observing the perfect crease of his trousers. "I think the girlth are the thtarth of our thow. Abtholutely. Guilia ith tho good ath Fiordiligi. I mean, what femininity the hath, but with thuch a thtrong voithe." He stared at the piano sitting in the corner of the large room. It was draped with black and red shawls, the decoration much like at Madame Clara's. "I have a thuper idea!" he exclaimed. "Why don't we thing for a bit? I bet Derek can do the thoprano part, can't you? Joanne and I can do our own roleth."

Before I could swallow the fig, Joanne jumped up. "Great idea! I even have the music here," she announced, walking toward the piano.

I took a large gulp of vodka. "Oh, I couldn't do Fiordiligi, Joanne. Why don't the two of you sing? I'd love to hear you."

"Oh, come on, Derek," Joanne said, "this'll be fun."

"Yeth, Derek, pleath do," Gareth begged.

Indiana Jones never faced a more dangerous trap. "I really can't. I worked with my voice coach this morning, and we have all those rehearsals this weekend." Although I was thinking of *Così*, I luckily didn't mess up and say so.

Joanne looked disappointed, and Gareth looked nixed in his Trix. They went to the piano and began to sing. I offered to assist Doris in the kitchen, thus resurrecting myself as a good guest, but she told me to sit and enjoy the music.

—

The brisket was fantastic as advertised, though Doris piled too many slabs on my plate along with an Alps-sized mountain of mashed potatoes and a stack of asparagus that any lumberjack would have been hard-pressed to demolish. This was followed by poppy seed cake and coffee, and then Howard asked me to join him in the library, presumably because I was eligible for his daughter and Gareth was not. Gareth appeared mildly miffed at this snub, but after removing his seersucker sports jacket to reveal pink suspenders decorated with dark green and blue frogs, he helped Doris and Joanne clean up.

Howard escorted me to the book-lined room, poured two hefty tots of brandy, and winked at me as we clinked glasses. "To your future."

I hoped he meant this as a positive toast rather than as a subtle warning that my days were numbered. "To you and Doris and Joanne!"

He liked that. I liked that he liked that.

"So, Derek, how're you makin' out with Malcolm Earl? That's the guy that's producin' the opera you're in, right?"

I nodded. "Very well. He's doing a very professional production."

"I bet it's gonna be great." He began to remove a cigar from a humidor, remembered that he shouldn't light up, and gave me a comradely grin and took a slug of brandy instead. "You know, Derek, I've been thinkin' about what I should do after this opera. I kinda like bein' in the biz. Of course, it depends on our gate, but I might try another production. Nothin' too big like *Aida*. Small cast stuff. Got any ideas?"

I considered this, visualizing myself as Butterfly or Tosca, but my voice was not dramatic, although I, myself, was. Fine to do those arias at the Purple Plum but not as a serious endeavor. "What about *The Barber of Seville?*"

"That might be interesting," he said. "You could sing the Count, and Guilia could sing Rosina."

Whoops! Not on the same night I couldn't. "That's very kind of you, Howard, but don't you think Joanne would make a wonderful Rosina?" This wasn't necessarily true since Joanne's voice might be a tad heavy for the role, even if Marilyn Horne had once performed it.

"Well, nice of you to think of my daughter. You're probably right, though it'd be kinda hot to feature twins," he replied. "Sorta different. Good for PR."

"Yeah, I'm sure it would be, Howard, but you might want more contrast in the sound. Guilia's voice is much like mine . . . only lighter, of course. And besides, didn't you start the opera productions for your daughter? Why not ask her what she'd like to do?"

Howard appraised me and sipped some brandy. "Good point. I'll talk to Joanne. And speaking of her, I kinda think she likes you."

"I like her, too."

"Well, that's good because anyone who dates my daughter better treat her real nice. You know what I mean? I get pretty perturbed when a guy tries to take advantage of my little princess." Howard gave me a hard look. His avuncular expression had vanished.

"I understand completely."

I drank a large gulp of liquor as beads of perspiration broke out on my forehead. Luckily, Howard didn't notice because he had turned to the bottle of brandy and was topping off his glass.

———

After we rejoined the ladies (yes, including Gareth), I was feeling the effects of vodka, wine, and brandy. I realized that I needed to exercise caution, especially with Gareth present. He sidled over to me almost immediately.

"Oh, there you are! We mithed you. Did you two boyth have brandy?"

I nodded and reminded him to behave. Unfortunately, Gareth loved to be scolded, took my arm like a beau, and raised himself on tiptoe to whisper in my ear.

"I think you're tho thexthy."

I subdued a shudder and disengaged his hand. Howard and Doris were looking on with concern, no doubt wondering if their potential son-in-law was a bit bent. Without a moment of hesitation, I gave Gareth's back a solid slap that made his eyes bug out.

"Good idea!" I told him before turning to Joanne. "Gareth just suggested the three of us go for a nightcap." I looked at my watch and at the Lowenbaums. "We shouldn't keep you two up . . ."

Howard agreed. "Yeah, you youngsters should go out and have a ball. It's kinda late for the missus and me anyway. We're early birdies, aren't we Doris?"

Doris nodded dutifully, although I could tell she would have been happy to go another round with something alcoholic.

Joanne was observing me with confusion. While she wanted us to have fun, having fun with Gareth was quite another matter. "Oh, Derek, honey," she began, "that would be fine, but I thought that maybe you and I could spend a little time together." She stepped across the room and took Gareth's hand. "I hope you'll understand just this once."

This put old Gareth on the spot, got me off the hook with him, and onto the hook with Joanne. He treated me to a peeved look but graciously told Joanne that perhaps he was tired. We both thanked the Lowenbaums for a wonderful evening and made end-of-night chat while Joanne went to get a sweater. When she returned, I helped her put on the cardigan, and the three of us left. Gareth was silent until we were outside.

"Now you mutht take good care of our Derek," he explained to Joanne.

She kissed Gareth on the cheek and said she would.

"Tho long," he said to me, "and remember your promith."

After he left, Joanne asked me what promise he meant.

"Oh, nothing really. I told him we might practice sometime, but I was just being polite." I started to say "he wasn't my type" but realized no man should be my type so long as I was out with Joanne.

"He is a little much." She laughed and took my hand. "So, where should we go?" Her voice turned suggestive, giving me the impression that I should offer my apartment as the destination because

Guilia was out of town tending to our ailing mother and Joanne's place was being painted. Not only did I want to avoid a potential sexual encounter, I was also worried about any search-and-destroy missions assigned by La Donna that might ensnare us. However, since I wasn't familiar with many straight bars, I didn't know of an alternative location. We crossed over Broadway, and I espied a little jivey dive called "Late, Late Night." Perfect.

I pointed it out to Joanne. "Ever been there?"

"Yeah, once. It's not bad."

Her enthusiasm was faint, but because she had offered no overt criticism, I steered her toward the bar. Inside, we were shown to a booth built for two midgets rather than for Joanne and myself. Its curve thrust us together like yins and yangs. I laid my arm on the top of the banquette and well above her shoulders. Unfortunately, she placed her hand on my thigh, nearly causing me to leap in the air with panic, and pressed her considerable battlements into my chest. Giving me a meaningful smile, she said, "Oh, Derek, I guess this isn't too bad after all."

"No, I suppose it isn't." I looked around for a waitress, desperately hoping for an interruption. Finally, a girl appeared, her hair twitched up like it had been electrocuted and then dipped in purple dye.

"What would you like, Joanne?" I asked.

"An apple-tini," she said.

"A Coors Light," I told the frizzy apparition.

After the waitress left, Joanne snuggled in closer, forcing me to move my arm down around her shoulders. "I think Daddy and Mother really liked you."

"I liked them."

"They could tell that."

"Very good brisket, too."

"Mmm." She was a bit disconcerted at this food fork in the conversational road. "So Daddy might do another opera?"

"He mentioned it to me."

"Well, I would love to have you sing with me, Derek." Her hand crept up my leg like the itsy-bitsy spider. "You really are leading-man material."

While this was true, so, too, was the opposite. I was definitely leading-lady material as well, though with my recent success as a tenor, I might stand a chance at a serious career playing it straight.

I had no intention of letting this affliction (playing it straight) creep into my personal life, however.

"Well, thanks," I replied, pulling myself back to the present. "That's nice of you to say."

Our drinks arrived, which gave me the excuse to withdraw my arm. Joanne picked up her martini with her left hand and kept the other planted, much to my chagrin. Even more to my chagrin was who I spied taking seats at the table across from us: two hunky gay guys. One, in particular, was really built. He checked me out, raised his chin an inch to indicate interest, and gave me a small smile. What with Joanne's ministrations and the beauties across the way, a physiological response occurred, one that Joanne interpreted as being created by her.

"Oh, Derek," she whispered, "maybe we should do something about that."

Joanne hadn't witnessed any of the table-to-table transactions. I stirred in my seat, taking her hand off my leg. "I really think we should wait."

"We could go to your apartment . . ."

"Can't. The AC is broken."

"Well, if there's nowhere else and you don't mind paint fumes, my place is close by."

"But I don't have any, er, protection."

"Doesn't matter," she replied, fingering my jacket collar. "I'm on the pill."

Damn. Think, you fool. "Yeah, but I'd feel better with . . . well, I think it's always wise."

She sipped her drink and stared at me, moving her hand under the table. "But you are so, so ready."

This was true from my perspective but not true in regard to her.

Joanne gave me a little squeeze that made me gulp. "Besides, there's a 24-hour pharmacy open two blocks away. We could buy some condoms, and we wouldn't have to worry."

I smiled at her, pretending to be Cary Grant—debonair and charming. Then, I knocked the remains of my beer in my lap, splashing some on Joanne. I jumped up, grabbed cocktail napkins, and began dabbing at my trousers and at her dress.

"Oh, god, how clumsy of me! I am so sorry, Joanne."

She stood and blotted with her cocktail napkin. Across the way, the two gay lads put their heads together and giggled over their cocktail straws.

CHAPTER TWENTY-ONE

Hope Dashed and the Threat

This intentional accident crashed the curtain on our evening. As I escorted Joanne to her apartment, I knew she was disappointed and suspicious that I had deliberately sabotaged the sexual stage of our relationship, which, of course, I had. I regretted ruining her dress, dashing her romantic hopes, and stringing her along in order to stay in the Lowenbaums' good graces so I could sing Fiordiligi. To put it bluntly, I felt like a giant rat.

"Are you sure I can't pay for your dress to be cleaned?" I offered.

"No, thanks. I'll wash it by hand."

"I'm really sorry." I was, too. Should I confess the truth about Derek and Guilia? Doing the honorable thing was tempting, but I hadn't thought through the ramifications of such honesty. My impulsiveness had already landed me in hot water, not to mention the swampy wilds of New Jersey. "Well, Joanne, please thank your parents again for dinner. And thank you, too, for such a lovely evening. I'll call you very soon." I leaned down to peck her on the cheek, but she surprised me by grabbing onto my lapels and kissing me hard.

"You'd better." She smiled to indicate that I was forgiven for my clumsiness and that hope stirred again in her ample breast.

"I promise."

With this we parted. I took the subway to Myra's place, did my own hand-washing, and went to bed thinking of Hank and hoping that I would see him at the Purple Plum.

—

I trotted uptown the next day for my *Rigoletto* rehearsal. Malcolm Earl greeted me at the door and asked if I'd seen the publicity story

157

in the newspaper. I said I had and thanked him for supplying my head shot to accompany the article.

"No, problem, Christopher. Like I said before, we're going places together."

His interest in my tenor career was heartening, which meant other male roles would be forthcoming from him. Howard had also promised parts to Derek, so my days singing soprano seemed numbered. Perhaps it was just as well. As I recalled Hank's comment about preferring to go to bed with a man who looked like a man, my love of lipstick was fading fast.

"I hope I don't disappoint you, Malcolm. I'll try my best," I told him.

"I'm sure you will. And by the way, I'm changing the schedule a little."

I held my breath because the final dress of the Lowenbaum production was on Tuesday. "Oh?"

"Yes. We're shortening Monday's rehearsal since we're practicing today. The final dress will be Wednesday and opening night on Friday, of course."

I was relieved. "Oh, good because I have to take my mother to the doctor's on Tuesday." Relatives—existing or not—were proving useful components in my intricate fabrications.

"Nothing serious, I hope?"

"No, just some tests."

He nodded. "Well, let's get this show on the road." Malcolm Earl guided me down the aisle to introduce the new conductor. "I hope you like him," he said. "I have no idea what happened to Raffaella. She just disappeared. I seem to have terrible luck with conductors."

We approached the piano. On its bench sat an elderly man with a bright white mane of hair. He was wearing a double-breasted black suit over a silk shirt with French cuffs. Large gold cufflinks glinted whenever his wrists popped out from his jacket, which seemed to occur without the slightest provocation.

"Maestro Zanbini, this is your tenor, Christopher Rose-Wren."

The conductor took my hand and gave it a limp, slightly disinterested shake. He smiled in my direction but not exactly at me. "Pleased."

"Nice to meet you, too."

"Christopher," Oletha Svenson said, "come sit by me."

I was happy to do so, thankful that this cast was normal compared to the West Side crew.

"Nice shot of you," she remarked.

"Thanks, but I wish your photo was used. After all, you're Gilda."

"It doesn't matter."

"I bet Malcolm will have a production photographer at the dress. You'll be featured in the paper after that."

"I hope so." She stared at the man behind the piano. "What do you think of our new conductor?"

"I don't know. Never heard of him."

As I said this, Chester Boone came up behind me. "I have. He has an orchestra that plays for mafia weddings and confirmations. You know, like when the godfather throws a party you can't refuse to attend?"

My head snapped around to stare at Zanbini. Was he another La Donna employee? Did she have an inexhaustible supply of conductors? As I studied the man, he obliged by standing so I had a better view. He was all large head and skinny body. Not intimidating.

"*Primo atto*," he said to us, tapping his fingers loudly on the top of the piano.

—

The rehearsal went relatively well, although I wasn't impressed with Zanbini's slow *tempi*, nor with his personality, which was downright haughty. All in all, however, he didn't seem like the kind of guy that La Donna would favor. The more I thought about this, the more I doubted there was any connection.

This led me to Gal Friday. I hadn't heard a peep out of her since Wednesday, which was not surprising under the circumstances. My traitorous behavior—as viewed by La Donna—might have placed Gal in jeopardy, though I believed in her ability to withstand any weather. Even so, I worried that our vindictive employer would do her harm or, at the least, terminate her services. I decided to call Gal after lunch.

I took a bus downtown to Greenwich Village. Four blocks from my stop, I saw a man who looked like Hank Braylock. In fact, it was Hank Braylock. He was walking along with a dark-haired, slim guy who glided beside him as if they belonged together. When the bus was abreast of the two men, I watched in horror as the brunette turned toward Hank and embraced him, an embrace which Hank returned and held. I flew to my feet and yanked the cord to stop the bus, but by the time I got off and rushed back to where I'd seen the two men, they were gone.

Oh, god! That was the reason Hank hadn't called. He had a lover!

—

I slumped upstairs to Myra's apartment, feeling miserable. I fed the fish in the tank and ate lunch. The afternoon slipped past while I imagined Hank and his lover in bed, kissing and hugging. The more I pictured this, the more I doubted Hank would attend my show at the Purple Plum, though it occurred to me that he might arrive with the brunette in tow, as William had done with Douglas. This thought was excruciating. I would cancel my performance. But if I did, I'd never know if Hank had come and if he'd been alone. No! I would sing and sing with fire—a lady spurned.

—

The new lighting at the theater wasn't properly modulated and was far too bright, blinding the performers. I could see very little of the audience, which was rotten since this was one night I desperately wanted to see who was out there. Only at the end of my first half was there a moment when the stage lights dimmed, and the house lights were raised a third. I scoured the room as quickly as I could and still take bows. Several blond heads dotted the darkness, but I was unable to determine if any of them belonged to Hank.

I returned to my tiny dressing room and wished for a sign. Where was my spirit guide when I needed him? With eyes tightly closed, I prayed to Bob for guidance. Then, I changed gowns, freshened my makeup, and waited, still hoping Bob would come through or, better yet, Hank would arrive. When I heard my two-minute call, I sighed and opened the door. Jason, a stagehand, was outside. He handed me a single red rose, whose long stem was snapped.

"Sorry, Gil. Didn't have time to deliver this earlier," he apologized and left.

I stared at the rose. Was red a color Hank would select? I didn't think so. Too obvious. Probably some stage door Johnny or maybe

Douglas or William was rebounding again, although William would never send a damaged flower, unless Jason broke the stem.

Somewhat encouraged by this turn of events, I walked on for the second half and blazed like a comet across the firmament. When I finished, a roar of applause greeted me. I took my time absorbing the love, hoping that someone was loving me more than all the rest. After repairing to my dressing room, I quickly changed into Gilbert clothes. And waited. And waited. Silence. Twenty minutes later, after checking the inside of the house, I walked out of the Purple Plum. Maybe Hank sent the rose because he couldn't come? But why hadn't he left a message?

I started to walk toward Myra's but then sensed someone following me. I spun around and searched the dark street. Was it one of La Donna's hired guns? No one was there. I suddenly realized that my operatic and romantic preoccupations had prevented me from calling the police to check on La Donna's status. Even though they had impounded her Cadillac and jailed her two cohorts, it was possible that La Donna had avoided arrest, or failing that, had made bail. The detective assigned to my case had warned me that she had escaped charges many times before. For that matter, La Donna may have bailed out her two minions.

I hurried my pace, seeking out a brighter street. Behind me, I now heard heavy footsteps, the kind made by engineer boots.

I pivoted around. "Gal?"

The footsteps stopped as a black figure emerged from the shadows. "What?"

I walked toward her cautiously. "I was going to call you."

"Yeah, right. When?"

"This afternoon."

"But you didn't." She joined me under a streetlight.

"No," I replied. "I didn't know what to think . . . whose side you're on . . ."

"Have the same problem myself. Let's go for a drink. You're buying."

We went to the Marlene D. and wedged into a tiny table that reminded me unpleasantly of my tight encounter with Joanne. We ordered a pitcher of beer and two bags of peanuts.

"Did you send the rose?" I asked her after I poured our drinks.

"Uh-huh."

"Bent stem and all?"

"Yeah. Thought you'd understand." Gal took a hefty swallow of brew and tossed down a handful of peanuts.

"I didn't until now," I admitted. "I was hoping it was from Hank."

"Still stuck on him, huh?"

I nodded. "He said he might come to hear me tonight. He must have changed his mind."

Gal was silent, her eyes cruising around the lesbian bar. "Too bad."

"Mmm." I didn't feel like talking about Hank any more. He was probably off with his lover . . . maybe a fall weekend in Provincetown? "So why were you following me?"

Gal turned in my direction and sipped her drink. "Conflict of interest. Yours, mine, hers."

Succinct as usual. "What's going on?"

"First of all, sorry about the jaunt to Jersey. I didn't know about it."

"What would you have done if you had known?"

She shrugged and crunched some nuts. "Might've warned you."

"And might've not warned me?" I swallowed some beer, feeling my temper rise.

"Gil, if I'd helped you, La Donna would've had my neck in a noose. She told me not to see you, talk to you, or think about you until she'd taken care of unfinished business."

"My extermination."

"Didn't say that exactly, but I guess you gave her the slip by changing digs?"

I nodded.

"And from what I hear, the police are trying to work up charges against her, as you know since you probably coughed up a bunch of things about La Donna. Anyway, she's keeping her nose clean for a few days."

"Letting the sand settle?" I asked sarcastically.

"Hey, no need to get mad at me. I told her you were a dumb drag queen who wants to sing opera. That the deal with the Lowenbaums was just you being an idiot. Problem is, see, La Donna doesn't like her people to be independent."

"I noticed that."

"And she doesn't forget or forgive."

"Meaning I'm still on her list." I ripped open my bag of peanuts and chewed on a handful. "So who's after me? Anyone I know?"

"Yeah."

"Who?"

"Me."

I sat up straight in my chair and stared at Gal. "What?" For a moment, I thought she was kidding, but her expression was serious—deadly serious. "As of when?"

"Soon. Like Wednesday."

"Right before the *Così* opening on Thursday?"

Gal nodded. "Double bang. She screws Lowenbaum and Company and fixes your wagon for ignoring her wishes."

"And how the hell are you going to accomplish this?"

"Depends on circumstances."

I was shocked at Gal's matter-of-fact tone. "You mean you intend to go through with it?"

She was silent.

"I can't believe this," I began. "I thought we were friends."

"We are."

"But?"

"Yeah. But."

"But it's either kill me or be killed?"

Gal shrugged. "More or less."

"Would La Donna murder her lover?" I threw this dart into the blackness of the Marlene D. and watched as Gal's head came up.

"Off limits, Gil."

I finished my beer, though it suddenly tasted bitter. "I don't think there's anything off limits in this conversation. You've just told me you're going to kill me because some lunatic mobster asks you to, regardless of how you feel about it. Don't you think I might be upset?"

"Yeah." She diddled with the bag of peanuts.

"Is that all you're going to say?" I was angry.

"Probably."

"Probably? This is crazy!" I scanned the room without taking it in. "Have you ever killed anyone before?"

Gal squinted, as if the memory were painful, but didn't answer.

"I can't believe you! Are you insane? What kind of bad mafia movie is this?" I stood and reached for my wallet. "Well, I don't want to be in it." I threw down a twenty on the table. "Our friend-ship is over."

Gal looked genuinely alarmed. "Gil, come on—"

"No, I'm done. You can tell your employer that I intend to sing on Thursday night. I'm giving the police a report of our conversation so that if anything happens to me, they'll know who's responsible."

Gal groaned. "Don't do that!" Her head dropped into her hands. "You'll make her furious! She'll kill you for sure then."

"Well, what options do I have?"

She pondered my question. "Maybe if you call in sick and don't go on that'll satisfy La Donna." Immediately after saying this, Gal shook her head. "Oh, hell, that won't work." She let out a long sigh and thought some more. "How about leaving town? Move to Hollywood or something? You know, disappear. Force Howard to cancel the show. La Donna isn't going to send her boys on a cross-country manhunt. You're not that important."

I started to say I was that important and stopped, making do with a frown. "Not many opera opportunities in Hollywood."

"Wherever! Jesus, Gil! You're being an idiot!"

I hadn't ever seen Gal lose her cool before, but at the moment her radiator was boiling over. "Look, I'm scared, and I should be. I got that," I said. "But I made a commitment to Howard and to Malcolm Earl, and I'm not going to break my word and vamoose. And, besides, if I stiff Howard, he might turn me into a stiff, rolled up in a carpet like a Russian blini and dumped dead in Brighton Beach. So the answer is no. The show must go on."

She groaned again and rolled her eyes. "Okay, but it might not be me coming for you." She rose to her feet, her leather jacket creak-ing. Just be careful, Gil . . . and I'm sorry."

I left the Marlene D. and ran to Myra's apartment at top speed, checking every few blocks to be sure Gal, or someone else, wasn't following me. By the time I was safe in Myra's bedroom, I was drenched in sweat.

CHAPTER TWENTY-TWO

Blackmail at Lunch

Although I had a ten o'clock rehearsal, I awoke early to call Detective Morris, who had been assigned to my case. He had just arrived at the precinct after a late-night surveillance, but he became alert when I told him about Gal Friday's warning.

"What's her real name?" he asked.

"Gal's? Sharon something." I gave him her phone number, though I felt guilty about doing it. "I don't know where she lives, but she might be staying with La Donna." I didn't suggest the possibility that they were lovers.

"Okay, we'll track her down. Don't worry."

"Don't worry? That's easier said than done." I explained about today's practice, the final dress on Tuesday, and the opening night on Thursday.

He excused himself for a second and called to someone. When he returned, he told me that an officer would drive me uptown. "I can't promise chauffeur service everywhere, but it won't be necessary if we keep La Donna Gabrielli busy until we nail her on charges."

I'd almost forgotten La Donna's last name. "I hope so. Thanks."

"Yeah, and we got that Tino character locked up tight. He won't be visiting you anytime soon. Raffaella Della Vigna, too."

—

When the police car came, I realized I hadn't mentioned that I would be dressed as Guilia Hancock. This involved some overwrought explaining, but finally the cop drove me uptown, stifling a snort or two whenever he looked in the rearview mirror. When I stepped out of the car, he said, "Break a leg" and chuckled.

Since I was late, I sprinted across the street to the theater, forgetting to do so as a woman. As I was stepping up on the curb, I saw

Gareth's nose pressed against the lobby window like a Dickensian waif. As he held the door for me, his brown eyes sparkled with mischief.

"My, my, Guilia, you do run like a Pitthburgh Thteeler."

"I'm in a hurry." I wanted none of his silliness, especially his affected lisp.

"I can thee that, dear, but after rehearthal, we'll have a bite to eat."

I halted on my two-inch heels. "Why are you being so persistent?"

"Becauthe I'm thimply mad for you, darling!" He laughed.

I continued to walk toward the hall. "I doubt it."

"Oh, but it'th true! It wath love at firth thight."

"Okay, a quick lunch and that's it. And don't get any ideas."

"*Moi?*" Gareth rolled innocent eyes in my direction.

I glared at him and let him hold the second door.

Everyone was gathered on stage. Doris, who apparently had assigned herself the task of director, stood in the first row tut-tutting to get the cast's attention. I took my place and wondered where the original hiree was—a retired San Francisco Opera director.

Ivan and Gareth stepped forward for "La mia Dorabella" while Nate Lowenstein stood by. Everything went fine as we passed from one scene to the next. The problem came when Gareth, as Ferrando, switched affections to me, as Fiordiligi. We began singing and then dear Doris said, "No, no. That's all wrong."

Gareth and I were several feet apart, but not as far apart as I would have preferred.

"Gareth," Doris instructed, "please move in tight to Guilia. We need a little sex in this to make it sell."

Now, I have told you before that *divas* do not like being touched, but *divos* are quite another matter. And though this *divo* had no *machismo*, Gareth shared lecherous traits with his more manly counterparts. Thus, Gareth was delighted with Doris' stage direction. I was not.

"But, Doris, Fiordiligi isn't sure she wants to break her vow of fidelity to Guglielmo," I explained politely.

"Well, wait a minute or two longer, but I definitely want a kiss."

Oh, god! Damn Doris to hell! Any operatic director knows better than to ask a soprano to come within two feet of any tenor. It just isn't done. Those boys sweat and spit too much, except for yours truly.

After Doris' remark, Ivan glanced at me with adoration, obviously considering how he might revise our scene in the first act, when I had been his. Although earlier he had maintained proper distance while declaring his love, I was less sanguine about his behavior next time round.

"I know juth how to play it, Dorith," Gareth assured her. "Like thith."

And before I could fend the little weasel off, he grabbed me tight and thrust his lower body against mine. After he did so, his eyes popped open, and his hand flew to his mouth in surprise.

"Oh, my!" he exclaimed.

Everyone stared at us with curiosity. I glared at him in fury, realizing I'd forgotten to pivot in order to disguise certain southern districts of my anatomy. If ever there was a tricky moment, this was it.

Gareth's face turned pink. "I am *tho* thorry, Guilia." He did a little wiggle, hitched up his trousers, and turned to Doris. "I think my privaeth got carried away."

After a second of stunned silence, this announcement was greeted with hilarity by the cast. Gareth grinned at everyone, enjoying his moment in clown heaven. Then, Doris told us to continue but with a space between us.

"However, on opening night I want a kiss. Got that?" she said.

Gareth gave me his naughty-boy smile and nodded.

—

After the rehearsal, I went to Sunday lunch with Gareth, fearing that if I didn't, he'd pull another stunt in public. He selected a French bistro and ordered a bottle of pinot blanc, which we nearly demolished before we finished eating the mixed green salad with warm chèvre.

"Okay, Gareth, why are you so intent on giving me a hard time?"

He rolled a black olive around in his mouth and daintily removed the pit. "Becauth it amutheth me. You thee, Guilia, I thaw your thow at the Purple Plum awhile ago and wath thmitten. You were tho good! At our firth rehearthal, I recognithed you right away."

"Are you going to tell Howard?" I asked, spearing a leaf of arugula.

"I'm not thure. It dependth on our relathionthip."

"We don't have a relationship, Gareth."

"Prethithly."

I deciphered his meaning. Gareth was blackmailing me. "If I have this correct, you want me to go to bed with you or else you will out Guilia?"

He drank a sip of wine and smiled. "Yeth. In a nutthell."

I sighed and was thankful that the waiter was delivering my sole meunière, thus affording me an opportunity to cogitate, but after two bites of fish, I couldn't think of a solution.

"Gareth, I realize this is a big opportunity for you as well as for me. The opera, I mean."

"Yeth, it ith."

"And I understand you have, er, certain fond feelings for me."

He nodded, hovering a forkful of salmon a few inches above his plate.

"But isn't the production more important than our personal situation?" I thought I was channeling a diplomat very well.

His eyes grew large. "No."

"Come on, you're a professional. We need to honor our careers and the tradition of carrying on."

He wagged his head from side to side. "Oh, I'm thure we can do both. After all, think of how many thtage romantheth there've been. It would add thparkle to our performanth."

There was something about Gareth's stubborn obliqueness that reminded me of La Donna. It was possible that he was one of her employees, although it didn't make sense that he was. I decided to investigate, just in case.

"You wouldn't know anyone by the name of Gabrielli, would you? A woman?"

"No. Why?"

I scrutinized his face for dishonesty and saw none. "Oh, just wondered."

"Tho will you?" He reached across the table and placed his hand on mine.

"If you tell Howard, then the opera won't go on. Furthermore, I might not go on, either. Howard is affiliated with the Russian mob. If he thought I'd treated him unfairly—or worse yet—Joanne unfairly, I probably would be swimming with the sturgeon."

"Thturgeon?"

"Yeah, you know, like in caviar? *Russian* caviar? Do you want that to happen?"

"No."

"Then don't say anything to Howard."

"Only if you thleep with me."

I groaned. "I can't do that, Gareth. I'm not in love with you."

"You probably have thexth with loth of men, whether you love them or not."

This was not true, at least not recently. I told him this, but I wasn't making any progress with the little mule. I leaned back in my chair. "Would you want me to do something I didn't want to do? If you care about me, you wouldn't."

He shrugged his narrow shoulders. "I'm thure you'd like it." He tried on a weak smile.

"And I'm thure I wouldn't," I mimicked. "You have some nerve, Gareth, blackmailing me like this. I haven't done anything to hurt you. All I want is to sing. Is that so much to ask?" I spoke with heartfelt emotion. "I guess you'll have to decide if you'd rather have the opera cancelled and me dead, or whether you can accept my response like a gentleman." I finished my rice and my wine. "And how do you think Howard will react if you tell him something so upsetting? Ever hear of the blame falling on the bearer of bad news? I doubt you'll be in his good graces for long. In fact, your days would probably be numbered."

This argument seemed to penetrate. Although I knew my hand was a two-pair compared to his flush, Gareth wasn't willing to risk the gamble.

"Okay, I won't mentthion your thexthuality," he replied.

The waiter returned to ask about dessert and coffee. I said I wasn't interested in either, pulled out sufficient cash for my lunch and the tip, and came to my feet with the slow dignity of Joan Crawford. "Goodbye, Gareth. I'll see you on Tuesday."

With this, I grabbed my suitcase and made a grand exit.

—

I trudged home. On the way, I deposited my Purple Plum check in the ATM and bought some groceries, thinking the second saddest night of the week to be alone was Sunday—Saturday being the hands-down winner.

CHAPTER TWENTY-THREE

Howard in Hot Water

On Monday morning, my voice was fatigued and so was I. The last thing I wanted to do was to drag myself to *Rigoletto* rehearsal, but at least I didn't have to get myself got up as Guilia today or later in the week as Kiri—I'd cancelled her two Purple Plum performances. With full final dresses the next two days and Thursday and Friday opening nights, I decided to mark my singing to avoid more strain.

Besides worrying about vocal difficulties, I also had to worry about Gal when Wednesday rolled around. Although it was hard to believe she would make an attempt on my life because of our friendship, La Donna was a friend of hers, too. And an employer and maybe a lover. Most importantly, La Donna wouldn't tolerate betrayal, which Gal knew, and she was extremely dangerous, which Gal also knew. When push came to shove, I'd get the shove.

I arrived early, grateful for the relative safety of Malcolm Earl's beautiful jewel box theater. Maestro Zanbini was present as was our stage director, Clotilda Bailey, who was a renowned floater among third-and-fourth tier opera companies. She was a great old gal—breezy, buxom, with blondish gray hair that wisped around her head like a seriously disturbed halo. Her laughter boomed as did her voice.

"Let's start with Rigoletto and Sparafucile," she announced.

Chester Boone and Liberio Lazarre, who made a first-rate skulking Sparafucile, took their places, me waiting offstage, which afforded an opportunity to observe Maestro Zanbini, whose mesmerizing cufflinks popped in and out of view with amazing rapidity. His style of conducting reminded me of Leonard Bernstein: all flying hair and agony. Although Zanbini was not in Raffaella's league, he elicited some dramatic sounds from the orchestra, who were joining our rehearsal for the first time.

About four minutes before my entrance, someone tapped me on the shoulder. A crew member whispered that I had an emergency call in Malcolm Earl's office. I followed him down a long inside corridor and picked up the phone, wondering who it was, what the hell was so urgent, and which voice to use.

"Hello?"

"Oh, Derek!"

"Joanne?"

"Derek, it's Daddy . . . he's been arrested."

"Why? For the fire?"

"No."

"What then?"

"For selling stolen diamonds. I can't believe it! There was a burglary on Park Place. The cops got a tip that Daddy ordered the break-in and was selling the hot merchandise in two of his stores. Since the owners had provided identification photos of the pieces, the police found the jewelry right away. In the window showcases! Who would be so stupid as to do that? Daddy has no idea how they got there and told them he was being framed. But the cops got warrants, closed our businesses, and are checking the inventory and books."

"That's terrible! I'm sorry, Joanne. I really am."

"This is so upsetting! I don't know what to do."

I didn't either. "I wish I could be there to help."

"Oh, could you? I mean, come?"

A chorus member opened the door and told me I was on. "Joanne, I wish I could, but I'm in rehearsal. Can I call you after two o'clock, and we can talk about all of this?"

"Okay, but why don't I meet you for a drink. Where's the theater?"

With some misgivings, I agreed and she suggested a restaurant several blocks south.

—

While I was changing out of my emerald velvet Duke's costume, I reflected on Howard's trouble about the burglary. The timing of his incarceration was extremely coincidental—tomorrow was the final dress for *Così*, and the opera opened on Thursday. Even with La Donna's police problems, taking down Howard and his production would be terrifically appealing. Ronald, the spy, had undoubtedly played some part, such as calling in the tip, but he may also have moved the hidden jewelry to the showcases or told La Donna's boys how to do it. As I combed my hair and tied my shoes, I hoped her thirst for revenge had been quenched by this latest coup and would distract her from pursuing me. I didn't think the little sidewinder would give up, however.

Since the stalwart Edgar Noonan, our Count Monterone, was leaving the theater at the same time, I struck up a conversation about the positive attributes of his home state, Texas, in the hope that he would provide some cover until I could slip away to the restaurant. As we exited the lobby, I scanned the street, wishing that Gal was still driving the very visible pink Caddie, but it was cooling its tailpipe in police custody. A much more subtle car—something in basic black—was more likely to house my assassin. While I kept nattering on about Abilene and Dallas and El Paso and every Texas town I knew, I checked for thugs who might plug me. I was so nervous that I almost reached for Edgar's arm for protection but caught myself just in time. I was Christopher, after all, and soon to become Derek.

At the corner of East 72st Street, Edgar said goodbye, and I continued downtown, anxiety tightening my chest. I didn't want to run the last two blocks, but I wasn't thrilled at being so exposed on the street. I took to my heels.

—

Joanne looked slumpy and glum. I slid into the seat across from her and ordered a coffee, even though she was drinking gin. The last thing I needed was to pour alcohol down my sensitive throat, though my sensitive brain could have used a double, nay, a triple.

"Hi," I said, fighting the urge to squeeze her hand and losing. She seemed so sad.

"Hi. Thank you for coming, Derek. I'm sorry for calling during your rehearsal, but I've been out of my mind since this morning when my mother called. The police woke them up at six a.m."

"How is your father? Is he still at the police station?"

"Yeah, he is, but I don't know much more than that."

Should I tell Joanne about the La Donna-Howard war? If I did, Howard's hoodlums would go after La Donna's gang, if they weren't doing so already, which would endanger Gal, though she might be endangering me very soon. And, if I confessed about my

172

relationship with La Donna, this would automatically classify me as an enemy of the Lowenbaums. Or maybe not, if I could induce Joanne to vouch for me, unless she then saw me as the enemy, too.

"Can his lawyer get him out of jail?" I asked, as my coffee arrived.

"Probably, but it may take until this evening or perhaps tomorrow."

"Does he have an experienced attorney?"

"The best."

"That's good." I stirred two heaping teaspoons of sugar into my cup. "Has this kind of thing happened before?"

"Yeah, but not this serious."

"Do you think someone who works for your father . . . well, maybe sold him out?"

Joanne stared at me with hardened eyes, and suddenly I saw the resemblance to her father. Being examined in this fashion was chilling. I wanted to gulp my coffee and run.

"It's possible," she admitted.

"I'm sorry, Joanne. I guess I've been watching too many police shows on television. I'm sure that it's all a misunderstanding of some kind."

We both knew this wasn't true, but Joanne relaxed a little and chased her lime wedge around her glass. "Derek, one other thing. I don't know if my mother is up to running tomorrow's rehearsal. She's an old pro, but this is a big shock. Besides, she might need to be with my father."

"I can imagine."

"Hey, I've got a great idea!"

Joanne's great ideas usually gave me wicked heartburn, plus it was clear that this one hadn't been spontaneously hatched. "What?"

"You're off tomorrow, right?"

I sipped my coffee. "Mmm."

"Maybe you could come and help—or at least be with my mother as support if she's able to be at the rehearsal. I mean, she adores you . . . and that would make me feel better. And if she can't attend, we could really use someone to keep the cast on track and organized."

"Whoa," I said, raising both hands. "I don't know the opera at all."

"I bet you do."

"No, seriously, I'm like out to lunch when it comes to Mozart." This wasn't true, and Joanne didn't believe me for a second.

"You don't want to help. That's it!" she accused. "I can't believe it! You won't help me, my father, my mother, or your own sister. I didn't realize you're so selfish!"

Joanne was in high drama. I racked my mind for some excuse, but every one I thought up had already been used or was too flimsy. "I really would like to be there . . ." I drifted off in search of a shaft of brilliance.

"Well, you would be there unless you can't be there."

I stared at her. "What do you mean?"

"Maybe it's because you're part of this whole plot to get my father. You know, first burn his theater and now get him charged by the police. Everything has gone wrong since he's known you and Guilia. Maybe you're in it together."

"But Joanne . . . I had nothing to do with any of this. And my god, Guilia didn't, either!"

"Then come to the theater tomorrow. Prove your loyalty."

It was my turn to slump. I was hoisted on my own petard. "Joanne, I guess I better explain why I can't come tomorrow."

Her jaws tightened like a steel vise, but she listened.

"It's a long story. It began with a friend of mine—a woman friend."

Joanne's eyes flashed. "I don't want to hear about—"

"No, not a girlfriend. Far from it. The woman's a lesbian. Anyhow, she works for another woman, who is also a lesbian, who, well, has a grudge against your father. I didn't know about this until after my friend arranged for me to sing for her employer. Before I knew it, she expected me to be her private singer. To come whenever she wanted. When she found out about my connection to you and your father and, er, my sister's participation with his opera production, she was furious. She's sent her guys to kill me."

"You're kidding!"

"No, I'm not. Well, they're in jail, but she's not. Or not at the moment. I think it was this woman who hurt Ben Silverman and had your theater burned and also tipped the police about the diamonds or maybe even set the whole thing up. The timing is too perfect. Just before opening night."

"What's this woman's name?" Joanne asked, as that flinty look came over her face again.

"La Donna Giovanna Milana Gabrielli."

As I uttered this, Joanne went dead still and her florid cheeks went white. "Her."

I nodded.

Joanne clenched her cocktail napkin into a hard ball. "That's the woman who tried to kill my mother."

"Really?"

"Yeah. Really." She was staring at the space above my right shoulder. "I think my parents will be very interested to hear about this."

"That's why I've been acting kind of strange, Joanne. I was being followed and threatened and told not to see you or your family. In fact, your chauffeur is spying for La Donna—that's what everyone calls her."

"You're kidding? Ronald? Damn him! Wait until my father learns that!"

"That's probably why the driver didn't show up the night the theater burned."

"Or else maybe he set the fire after Daddy left."

I nodded and finished my coffee. "The thought crossed my mind."

"Why didn't you tell me all this before?" Joanne was back in accusatory mode.

I held up my hands. "I should have, I know, but La Donna was trying to murder me. If I told your father, I thought he would be mad at me, too. Then, I'd have two people after me, and Guilia's big opera chance would be ruined. I was hoping that the police would stop La Donna, and everything would be fine."

"Well, everything isn't fine, Derek! Not by a long shot." She finished her drink and slammed the glass on the table. "I'll be honest. I don't know what to do. Let me talk to my father."

I started to ask how she felt about my admission but didn't. While I could feel myself slipping into melodrama, I needed to avoid making the situation worse. "Okay," I said, "but please tell him how sorry I am. And also that Guilia knows nothing about any of this."

"What? How could that be? I mean, you two are so close and live together. And wouldn't she be in danger, too, if this gangster is trying to ruin our production?"

"Yes, but La Donna was focused on me first since I was singing for her. When I realized what was going on, I suggested Guilia stay at a friend's place. Luckily, the air conditioning broke at the same time, so I had a good excuse." I was relieved at my mental agility and added, "And, of course, she's been helping my mother."

"So where've you been living?"

"I beg your pardon?"

"Where are you staying?"

All of a sudden I became anxious again. "I really can't say, Joanne. I promised I wouldn't. It's just a short-term house-sitting arrangement."

"No women involved?"

I shook my head. "Absolutely none."

Somewhat appeased, Joanne called for the check.

—

We left the restaurant together, arm in arm like lovers. I wasn't comfortable about this, but Joanne needed reassurance, even if she was made of the same stern stuff as Papa Lowenbaum. As I raised my hand to flag a taxi, a black Ford Explorer skittered up to the curb instead. Inside were two very unattractive people.

CHAPTER TWENTY-FOUR

Singing to Hit Men

The SUV's door popped open and whacked Joanne. I pulled her away and stared at the two men who bolted out of the car, both of whom looked like Tino's kith and kin, perhaps a bit older, no wiser, definitely rough trade. The one with slicked-back silver hair grabbed Joanne and tried to haul her toward the Ford. I kept hold of her other arm and attempted to free myself from the grasp of the second thug, a pockmarked, greasy-looking guy with jet black hair and a moustache worthy of an Albanian in *Così*.

Joanne, who was being tugged in opposing directions, was a fighter. She aimed a solid kick at Mr. Silver Hair, landing her pointed shoe in his privates. I thought this was an exceedingly nifty move and did the same thing to Mr. Black Hair, though I rued not being shod in my stilettos. Both goons let go of us and grabbed their smarting parts. With surprising speed, Joanne took off. Obviously, her father had counseled her in the fine art of fight and flee. Mine, however, had not. I hesitated for a split second too long. Mr. Black Hair recovered, and, as I began to dash, he tackled me.

While fleet of foot, I am no footballer and fell on the sidewalk. As I came to my knees, the other guy glued himself to my back like a barnacle.

"Give it up!" he growled. "Get in the fuckin' car."

He lay a knife blade by my ear. I stopped struggling and followed orders. Mr. Silver Hair shoved in beside me on the back seat and slammed the door. Mr. Black Hair took the wheel and rushed off with a screech, heading down Lexington Avenue, driving like Mario Andretti, or even faster, like a Paki cabbie.

After the car swooped to avoid a delivery truck and I was thrown to the side, I righted myself and asked my seatmate who he worked for, though I knew.

"Nonna your beeswax," said the erudite thug.

"La Donna?"

177

Mr. Silver Hair squinted so that his tiny brown eyes disappeared altogether. "Hey, whaddya got a problem wit your hearing? We're just goin' for a little ride, is all. Chill."

This amused the driver. "Hey, Eddie, that's good. Chill. Like in the Big Chill, huh?"

Eddie laughed. "Yeah, you're right, Gino. On ice, so to speak."

They both did a little heh-heh-heh chuckle.

We slipped around two cars, nearly sideswiping both. Behind us, I heard police sirens, but the cars were probably chasing someone else. Even so, Gino shot ahead through a yellow light and swerved in and out of traffic. The coffee I'd just imbibed sloshed around, making my stomach feel like an overloaded cappuccino machine. Thereafter, we bogged down at every stoplight, until, at last, he circumvented Gramercy Park and continued south, undoubtedly aiming for La Donna's domicile.

"Where are we going?" I asked, more to fill up the silence than anything else.

"Hey, Eddie, tell the guy to zip it."

Eddie nodded his head. "Yeah, shut your trap."

The car careened around a knot of people, causing pedestrians to shake their fists in anger. Gino ignored them and lit a cigarette, which made me cough.

"This guy's a regular prima donna," Eddie said, thrusting a thick thumb in my direction. "I don't think he likes your cigarette."

"Too bad, Tiger Lily," Gino said to me. "Hey, from what I hear tell, you're like some kinda opera singer or somethin'."

"Watch it, there, Gino," Eddie interrupted. "I got a soft spot in my heart for opera. My mama loved it, god rest her soul." He crossed himself reverently.

"Yeah, mine, too, may she rest in peace." Gino made the sign of the cross.

Just my luck to get two opera-loving, motherless louts. "I'm singing Verdi," I said.

"Hey, like that's some serious stuff," Eddie mused. "I love *Traviata*. Gets me all sentimental."

"I'm more of a Puccini man myself," Gino chimed in. "Maybe you know some of that?" he asked me.

The thought of singing to these hit men was beyond macabre. My voice was also tattered, and Puccini was always tough. "I couldn't."

"Hey, yeah, you could," Eddie crowded my shoulder. "Whatcha got to lose?"

This was regrettably true so I began "Un bel dì, vedremo" from *Butterfly*, really pouring on the pathos. As I sang, Gino slowed the car a bit, and Eddie seemed to relax. Channeling every dramatic soprano I'd ever seen or heard, I outdid all my Purple Plum performances and my most impassioned renderings in front of the mirror. Eddie's eyes stared into space, his eyes rimmed with tears, no doubt seeing the image of his dear departed mother.

We came to a light as I approached the high B flat at the end of the aria. I let it rip with excruciatingly shrill volume and proved once again that too much of a good thing is, well, too much of a good thing. Gino took both hands off the steering wheel to muffle his ears, and Eddie slapped his palms against his head. I stiff-armed Eddie and grabbed the door handle on my left. Less than a second later, I was rolling on the street, praying that I hadn't broken my shoulder. I came upright, ran for the sidewalk, and careened into a hot dog vendor's cart, causing its owner to scream expletives as the hot, briny water splashed all over. The big car pulled into a "No Parking" spot, with Eddie and Gino loudly cursing Puccini. Although I wasn't sure where my feet were, I finally found them and took off.

Luckily for me, the boys had been smoking too many cancer sticks. Their breathing resources, as a result, were soon severely taxed because of the world-class pace I was setting. As I turned a corner, I patted my breast pocket for my cell phone in order to call Detective Morris, only to note that the phone was smashed into my chest like a black heart transplant. I slowed and plunged into a clot of tourists, ducking my head so I wouldn't be visible, and then zipped into a store that sold, of all things, light bulbs. I rushed toward the counter at the rear, wondering who in their right mind would devote an entire business to selling bare bulbs, spotlights, and some designer lights that dripped from their sockets.

The proprietor was standing behind an old-style silver cash register. When he saw me, his mouth opened in astonishment, as if he were surprised to have a customer. I was just considering how strange the place was, when he put up two meaty hands.

"Hey, we're closed," he said. His voice was similar to Eddie's and Gino's, and his appearance was, too. Brown hair plastered to a humongous skull, shaggy eyebrows that could use a comb, and a Fu Manchu beard that looked scrawny on his pudgy face.

I halted on the proverbial dime. "What do you mean you're closed?" I asked, my head swiveling around as I took in the hundreds of bright lights.

"Like I said, buddy, we ain't sellin' nothin' today."

I tried to disguise the fact that I had used up my oxygen allotment for the week. "Oh, okay," I said, taking a step backward toward the front door. I didn't know what kind of establishment this was, but I could tell I was in the wrong place at the wrong time.

Just then, the door chimes tinkled. I turned and saw Gino and Eddie. They began to guffaw.

"Hey, Frankie," Eddie said, "good catch."

"Whaddya mean?" the proprietor asked.

"We've been after this guy," Gino explained.

I didn't like the fact that the three lads were acquainted. Without hesitation, I ran around the counter and threw open the rear door. There, to my surprise, I saw a whole nest of Tinos, Eddies, Ginos, and Frankies. To a man, they swiveled their heads on thick necks and regarded me without the slightest shred of bonhomie.

I stared at the guys wearing black shirts and white ties, at the cash and cards on the table, the wineglasses filled with chianti, and froze in my tracks.

"Shit," said one, after removing a cigar from his mouth. "Who the hell are you?"

"He must be a light bulb salesman," the guy across from him said. They all chuckled.

Frankie and Gino and Eddie fanned out behind me, blocking my retreat. I dashed past the table, parted a dark red curtain, and rushed into the storehouse, which was swarming with men loading huge brown boxes of TVs and computers onto the rear end of a truck. Beside it stood a large van whose contents were being stacked. The doors to the garage were closed, so my escape route was sealed. I could either try another round of Puccini arias or give up.

The guy with the cigar grabbed my forearm. "Come on, light-foot. Time to go for a ride."

Since the place was replete with packing materials, it took no time for the boys to truss me up with duct tape. The only information I ascertained was that the guy with the cigar, Little Larry, was related to La Donna, or so I surmised since one of the lugs

180

called him Mr. Gabrielli, and he bore a faint resemblance to my ex-employer, despite about two-hundred extra pounds of pasta padding.

Eddie explained the situation to Little Larry, who took it all in with grunts, head nods, and belabored sighs. Clearly, he wasn't happy to have his poker game interrupted.

"Okay. I guess I gotta call Sis," Little Larry said in a ponderous voice remarkably different than La Donna's fine elocution. She must have attended a finishing school, I thought, learning demeanor, speech, and her special kind of "finishing." He flipped open his phone and speed-dialed. "Hi, how are ya?" he began. "Yeah, good . . . good. The missus, too. Yeah. Yours?"

This meager communication confirmed that Little Larry was comfortable with his sister's sexual orientation, and that La Donna possessed a significant other. Gal Friday? Or Raffaella, who I hoped was still incarcerated?

As I was pondering this, Little Larry began to relate the circumstances of my capture. In turn, he listened, grunted, and nodded, sounding palsy-walsy and a shade deferential, the latter seeming to go against the goodfellas' macho grain. When he glanced in my direction, I noted that he was sweating up a storm, which supported my supposition that La Donna was a vindictive and feared woman, regardless of her size and sex.

"Yeah, okay. Will do," he promised. "You sure I can't take care of it? It's no trouble." Little Larry listened for another minute. "Got it. In a few." He pocketed his phone.

"Hey, it's your lucky day," he said to me. "You're invited for cocktails." He laughed at this. "Get it, fairy? Cock-tails?" Everyone chortled on cue. "Now, stow this guy."

I was promptly grasped by Eddie, and my mouth was duct-taped to mute the screams emanating from my lips. They dumped me in an empty washing machine box, taped the flaps, angled the box, lifted it into the van, and off we went for a jolly ride to La Donna's place.

—

After about ten minutes of bumping and banging, the box and I were loaded on a hand truck and carted into an elevator, which rose to what was probably La Donna's penthouse. I heard the elevator and entrance doors open, and the box and I were wheeled forward, to the right, and then came to an abrupt stop, falling sideways, and hitting the floor. My head popped the flaps, and I wiggled through, smelling like *eau de cardboard* and perspiring mightily from my stuffy confinement. My coming-out location was appropriate—right across from the Yamaha piano. Indeed, I felt rather like the White Rabbit—more Jefferson Airplane's version than *Alice in Wonderland*'s. As I sorted out my legs and stood, I was flanked by Eddie and Gino, who were armed with guns. Gino ripped the gray duct tape from my mouth, taking half my lips with it, unraveled the tape from around my shoulders and hands, and turned me to face the queen of gangsters.

"Gil, it's so nice of you to pop up," La Donna said, observing me with her usual serenity.

This brought hoots of laughter from the guys.

"Hey, pop up—get it?" Gino dug an elbow in Eddie's ribs. "Outta the box!"

"Thanks," I told her, dusting off my jacket. "It's great to be here."

"Better to be here than nowhere," Gino warned.

I gave him an annoyed look. "As a matter of fact, I'd rather not be here at all."

"That'd be easy to arrange," Eddie retorted.

"Gino, Eddie . . ." La Donna raised an eyebrow, a gesture which sent the two men scurrying for chairs like chastised puppies. La Donna then patted the ottoman in front of her. I got the message and sat.

"Now, Gil, we have a problem, don't we?"

I wasn't sure whether this was a rhetorical question or one I was supposed to answer, so I simply said yes.

"You know about my former relationship with the Lowenbaums, so there's no need to discuss their despicable behavior except to say that some of their past conduct has been rewarded. But since you were just socializing with their daughter, I'm sure you know all about what's happened to her father."

"I do."

"Good. Well, what has not been rectified is how you've behaved. I told you not to hobnob with Howard and his ilk. Still, you continued to rehearse, to see his daughter, and in every conceivable manner throw your disdain in my face."

"It wasn't like that," I began. "You know I auditioned for How-ard before I heard about your history with him. I made a commit-ment which I needed to honor. In your business, you respect when someone gives his word, don't you?"

She went dead still and glared at me like a viper spying a bare foot. "I pay attention to what people do. No one crosses me, espe-cially over the Lowenbaums." After she said this, La Donna's face suddenly darkened, revealing a boiling fury underneath, a fury fed by years of hatred.

Turning to Gino, she snapped her fingers. "We're done. Take him—"

"No, please! I didn't mean to make you angry. Give me another chance!" I cried. "Think of Handel!" To anyone else, this plea would fall upon deaf ears. Well, they would have to be deaf not to appreciate Handel.

The crazed look on La Donna's face slowly eased, a frightening Hyde-to-Jekyll transformation. I shivered, aware that I'd briefly peered into the abyss of a malignant soul.

I waited a moment, hoping she would be moved, and then pressed her hot button again. "No more *Serse, Rodelinda, Guilio Ce-sare,* or *Ariodante*! Who can sing all these parts for you? Only me." Not that I knew the operas well, but I'd learn every note if my life would be spared.

At the mention of her favorite music, her forehead relaxed, and she seemed to return to a semblance of sanity. The room was quiet except for a wheeze from Gino. I kept my eyes fixed on La Donna, mentally urging her to relent. Finally, she leaned forward, coughed, and spoke in a rough whisper. "I must maintain my reputation or else I won't have one. It's not smart to get sloppy about an opera singer, no matter how talented."

"But all I want to do is sing!" I pleaded. "Tomorrow is the final dress, and the next day is the one for *Rigoletto*. Please, La Donna, you've had your revenge on Howard and his wife. Can't we just go on as before? I'll come and sing for you whenever you want."

La Donna stared at me. In a cold voice, she said, "No. You were warned. Gino, put him in the bathtub. I want to do this myself."

Gino jumped to attention and clutched my arm.

"Wait! Think of *Ariodante*? That's your favorite, isn't it?"

"There's nothing I can do." She shook her head and crossed her arms. "Nothing."

"Please!"

"Nothing . . . unless . . ." A cunning look sharpened her gaze.

"Unless?"

La Donna scrutinized my face and saw my pain—or at least that's what I hoped. "Unless you are willing to act as my agent." She traced her thin lips with a tiny finger. "I'll make a bargain with you—which is very generous of me since I never bargain."

"Whatever you want," I replied eagerly.

"You open your Mozart opera . . ."

"Yes?"

"I'll give you the opening night's first act."

"And then?"

"And in the next act you will reveal your true gender. On stage, in a manner that is overtly sexual. I don't care how you do it, but I want it to shock the audience into leaving."

I thought of Gareth, my Act II lover, and groaned. "But my career will be finished!"

La Donna made no response.

"I'll be humiliated!"

"You should have considered that when you decided to impersonate a soprano. Look on the bright side, the music critics will probably know you're a male anyway."

This was the secret anxiety I'd harbored ever since my Fiordiligi audition. What was surprising was that no one in the cast had questioned my voice except Maestro MacDougal and, of course, Gareth.

"Can I still sing in *Rigoletto*?" I asked her.

She hesitated, struggling with her operatic sensibilities versus her dyed-in-the-wool vengefulness. "Only if you ruin Howard's production and close the show."

I could see her emotional logic. The opera would end, thereby evening things up with Howard, and I would embarrass myself and ruin my career. It wouldn't take long for the voracious New York City press to connect the dots and determine my identity—there were too many Kiri photos floating around and portraits of Christopher Rose-Wren publicizing *Rigoletto*. When the risk to my operatic future was weighed against my death, however, what choice did I have? I quickly agreed to her plan.

"On your honor?" she asked, staring at me with unwavering intensity.

"Yes."

184

La Donna offered her hand and sealed my doom with a surprisingly powerful handshake. "And remember, I'll be in the audience on Thursday night. So, don't try anything. If you do, you'll be dead. And so will your mother in Atlantic City."

—

I wasn't allowed home. The boys took Myra's apartment keys, a list of necessary items, and went on a treasure hunt. I was remanded to an interior guest room, which was decorated in shades of purple and lavender: restful under most circumstances but not these since I was frantically worried about my Faustian arrangement with La Donna. I sat on the bed and imagined when and how I would fulfill her demand. It would definitely involve Gareth, who I prayed would react with comic improvisation. If he was successful, perhaps the scene would appear intentional. *Così* was an *opera buffa*, a humorous, madcap spoof. What better way to modernize it than by inserting a gender twist? If the critics approved of this interpretation, my career might be salvaged, but then La Donna wouldn't achieve her goal, and I would pay the price.

Besides being scared for myself, I hated the thought that I was going to harm Howard and Joanne more than I already had. They'd been nice to me. And as for Joanne, I was sure she was worried about my capture. Had she called the police after the kidnapping? Her family was not exactly police-friendly. Or would she tell her father what happened and ask for his help? With the news of my trouble with La Donna, this last possibility was the most likely. It also meant that I was in the middle of their escalating war, caught behind enemy lines.

And I wasn't the only one at risk. La Donna had made threats against my mother and seemed to know where she lived. Unless Gal told La Donna about Hank, he wasn't in jeopardy, but if he attended *Così*, he might be, depending on what else La Donna was planning. At the least, he would witness my humiliation. How could I explain why I was making a mockery of the opera and of myself? On the other hand, he probably was off with his boyfriend and had forgotten all about me. I bunched up the pillow and held it, wishing that it was Hank.

CHAPTER TWENTY-FIVE

La Donna's Most Unhappy Fella

La Donna's boys carted my stuff into the room several hours later, grumbling about the wig boxes, costumes, and diva clothes. After I settled everything in the closet, I was allowed to practice at the piano, but I was so tired and tense that I feared vocal strain. Thankfully, my hostess didn't insist that I sing for my supper, which was composed of four courses of finely prepared food. I ate, though my appetite was nonexistent, and passed on the wine.

After a poor night's sleep, I donned my ecru suit, flowing chiffon scarf, and Guilia wig, and then awaited my escort to the final dress rehearsal, feeling foolish decked out in women's clothes. When the bedroom door opened, I was relieved to see Gal Friday (wearing her Sol outfit); less pleased to see that Gino was standing behind her.

"Gil," Gal said by way of greeting.

"Gal," I answered. "Thank god it's you."

She didn't smile. Maybe her men's gabardine suit pinched. "This is business. Remember that."

I ignored her chilly demeanor, sensing that it was mostly for Gino's benefit and possibly for her employer's, if my theory about bugged rooms was correct. "Hey, as my agent, maybe you can negotiate a raise for me."

"Gil, cut the crap. I figured it'd be easier to sit in the theater if I had a reason to be there. Besides, aren't we supposed to get a check today?"

I had forgotten. "Yes."

Gal and I carried my costumes, Fiordiligi wig, undergarments, and pump shoes into the hall. Gino ogled me as I passed by.

"Hey, not a bad lookin' dame," he said. "A little broad in the beam maybe—"

I wheeled on him. "I am not!"

He caught the end of my scarf and gave it a tug. "Hey, but I like my girls with some meat."

I grabbed the scarf from his fingers, gave him the cold shoulder, and refused to speak to either of them in the car. While we drove uptown, Gino whistled twice at women on the street. Gal might have done the same had she been in a chipper mood.

—

At the theater, Gino parked near the stage door, thus blocking any exit. He remained in the car, which was a short-lived relief until I noticed a suspicious bulge under Gal's suit jacket when she held the door for me. If I didn't behave, trouble could brew faster than instant coffee.

We walked down the long hall to my dressing room and hung my blouses and gowns and stored the other items. My makeup was already in place in front of the three-paneled mirror. Then Gal escorted me toward the stage and slipped out the emergency door to take a seat in the rear of the theater, presumably ready for action if anything went amiss.

When I saw Joanne in the wings, I beckoned for her to come to me. For a second, I forgot I was Guilia and almost blew everything, although why I was being so careful to maintain my false identity was anyone's guess since it would do a Vesuvius in two days.

"Oh, my god, Guilia! Is Derek all right?" She grabbed me by the forearms, too distracted to register the shape of my biceps.

"Yes, he is. Luckily, he got away from those two mobsters."

She exhaled an exceedingly long sigh, the kind dramatic mezzos often do. "I'm very glad he's okay!"

"Me, too," I said. "It's so hard being a twin. Everything he feels, I feel, and vice versa." This was especially true in my case.

"Oh, I can imagine. You must be so worried about him."

"He's explained the situation to me, and, yes, I am worried," I replied. "Joanne, in addition to reassuring you that Derek's okay, he also wanted me to send his apologies. Under the circumstances, he can't come today. He's really sorry, but between us, it just isn't safe."

"La Donna?"

I nodded. "The same. She was behind the attempted kidnapping of both of you. In fact, I hope you're being careful. Derek believes he's the main target, but you and I could be ones, too."

"So he's hiding out somewhere?"

"Yes."

"Where?"

"I'm sworn to secrecy." Here, I crossed my lips with two fingers.

"Guilia, you must tell me where he is! I've been calling his cell phone—"

"His phone was smashed yesterday. There isn't any way to call Derek at the moment."

Joanne looked dismayed. "I have a message for him from my father."

"Is Howard here?"

"No. Neither is my mother." She sat on a stool. "My father intends to put La Donna out of business. He's cooperating with the police, although there isn't much hard evidence against her. That's why it's so important to find Derek. Did Derek report yesterday's attack?"

I considered my answer. "No, he was too concerned about retaliation. Did you report it?"

"I wanted to see what Daddy planned to do first. Now that I've talked with him, I'll go to the police after our rehearsal, but I really think Derek should be with me."

"Joanne, he can't yet. You've got to call Detective Morris on your own." I recited his phone number. Of course, I could have explained that Derek hadn't escaped, was being held captive, and needed to be rescued by the police, but if I did this, it would reveal my impersonation, betray my agreement with La Donna, and generally bollocks up my relationship with everyone. And, too, it was entirely possible that I might die if a battle ensued between the police and La Donna's household worthies. "Believe me. This is the only way it can work."

Before I could say more, Maestro MacDougal instructed us to don costumes for Act I. As I stepped away from Joanne, Gareth sidled up to me, attempting a swagger that fell far short of dashing. He was dressed in a scarlet military outfit, with a swallowtail coat that made him look like a little boy playing dress-up because its proportions were designed for a taller and more robust figure. Gareth also sported a big sword that nearly scraped the floor despite the inches of height added by elevator heels on his black boots.

"Well, Guilia, long time no thee."

"Oh, Gareth. Hi. Listen, I have to change."

"Tho thoon?"

His flirtation made me queasy. I gave him a toodle-loo wave and dashed to my dressing room, thankful for the lock on the door. There, I applied theatrical makeup over Guilia's modest cosmetics, transferred my falsies, donned the pale blue crinolined high-necked blouse and the darker blue gown, then swapped my wig for the long, curly blond wig. When I was ready, I looked stunning. My skin was creamy white, my lips luscious red, and my eyes glittering violet.

In the hallway, I encountered Ivan and Gareth, whereupon I witnessed Cupid's arrow pierce Ivan's fulsome chest and Gareth's mouth open like a stunned fish. I eluded them and hurried onstage, noting that a photographer was planted in the second row. I would need to avert my face from him in order to avoid any revealing shots of Guilia.

—

After the rehearsal was over and we were once again in street clothes, I approached Joanne, who had acted as stage director, and thanked her—girl to girl, diva to diva—for not enforcing her mother's edict about kisses and tight embraces. In fact, though both Ivan and Gareth had zoomed in for the squeeze, Joanne had warned them off, telling them to hold the romance for opening night. This produced disappointment on the lads' countenances, but they cheered up when Joanne announced she had checks. These she dispensed like a mother bird handing out worms.

As I accepted mine, I saw Gal stand. It was time to leave.

"When is your father coming home?" I whispered to Joanne.

"Sometime today. Bail is being arranged."

"That's good. Tell Howard what happened but for god's sake remember to call Detective Morris." I repeated his precinct and telephone number.

As I hurried up the aisle, I wanted to sprint out the backstage door, but Gino was parked there, and Gal was blocking the entrance to the lobby. Besides, the warning about my mother tipped the scales in favor of compliant behavior.

Outside the theater, Gal made me walk halfway around the block, where Gino was supposed to meet us.

"Can I deposit my check?" I asked, pointing to a nearby ATM.

"Yeah, but remember our deal." Gal's taciturn manner was whittled to minimal.

"Okay. You get your cut in cash, but I can only take out $500." I stood in front of the machine and inserted the envelope. After the receipt squeezed through the ATM's silver lips, I punched in the amount for withdrawal. As I did, I surveyed the street, once again considering a run for the gold.

Anticipating this, Gal grabbed my elbow. "You know what I have under my coat, Gil. Don't make me use it."

"I guess things have progressed past screwdrivers and black-jacks," I replied.

"Yeah, they have. So watch it."

"Say, whatever happened to Raffaella?"

"Still in the can," Gal answered, a look of smugness flitted over her face.

"And I bet you're happy about that, huh?"

Gal erased her expression. "I'd worry about yourself, if I were you."

Before I could respond, Gino arrived, and I was nudged into the back seat.

—

I spent the afternoon locked in my new room. I took a nap, studied the *Rigoletto* score, and worried. Around five, Gal rapped on the door.

She handed me a newspaper. "Check it out," she said and left.

I sat down and opened the paper. Toward the bottom of page eleven was a small article about Ronald Fahey, whose gunshot-riddled body had been found in a deserted warehouse in Brooklyn. The building had been torched at 8:00 p.m. on Monday, a few hours after the coffee/drinks get-together with Joanne in which I'd reported the chauffeur's betrayal. Since Howard was busy with the police then, it would have been fast work to kill Ronald but certainly possible. It was also possible that La Donna had murdered him, using the same arson specialist employed to burn Howard Lowenbaum's theater. Perhaps Ronald's usefulness didn't outweigh the risk of his link to her, a vulnerability that might have been exposed at some future time in the war between La Donna and the Lowenbaums. The article mentioned that Howard was Ronald's employer and also speculated that Ronald had been killed by a professional— no suspects were listed. Would Detective Morris connect the hit to La Donna? I hadn't told him about Ronald's disloyalty to Howard because I'd been under lock and key at La Donna's, but Morris might reasonably assume that she was the cause of anything bad that happened to the Lowenbaums, considering their longstanding animosity.

Either way, regardless of who was responsible, the chauffeur was dead. Just like I would be if I continued to play hopscotch in the middle of Mobster Boulevard. The best I could hope was that Joanne had called Detective Morris, who might decide he had grounds for a search warrant of La Donna's residence and would pay a surprise visit, thus rescuing me, hopefully without a fight. Failing that, I needed to make a plan—some way to thwart La Donna's intentions, which might involve more than my public shaming and the closing of a show.

At dinner, I was let out and seated at the dining room table at La Donna's right. On her left, Gal Friday took a chair. Gal's familiarity with La Donna renewed my curiosity about their relationship, but I kept quiet.

"So, how did the rehearsal go today?" La Donna asked, helping herself to some veal piccatta.

"Fine."

"Was Howard Lowenbaum there?"

"No. Nor was Doris."

"Did you learn anything from Joanne? I know you spoke with her."

I glanced at Gal, who was squeezing a slice of lemon over the meat. "Not really."

La Donna cleared her throat and stared at me. "What exactly did you tell Joanne?"

"That Derek ran away from the car and was safe. That he was house-sitting, and his cell phone was broken."

"Very good, Gil. That was smart of you." La Donna swallowed some white wine. "Anything else?"

"No." Since I had asked for water, I drank that. "After all this is over . . . is it, well, over? I mean, between you and the Lowenbaums?"

La Donna focused on her food and ignored me.

I presumed this meant she was not finished and would never be finished with Howard and Doris until they were six feet under. I also presumed Howard felt the same way toward her, now that he knew she was behind all the recent disasters. I could only hope he was busy with the police and opening night and would delay retaliation. Sadly, my second-act sabotage would align me with La Donna forever, regardless of the explanations I offered to Joanne or Howard. For the rest of my life or theirs, whichever came first, I would be the Lowenbaums' enemy.

"Interesting article in the newspaper," I began, catching a caper with my fork, "about Ronald Fahey."

La Donna squinched up her eyebrows. "Who?"

"Howard Lowenbaum's driver," I replied.

"What about him?" she asked.

"He was shot on Monday night."

"Really? That's too bad." She concentrated on a pile of fluffy white rice, her disinterest unfeigned but not necessarily an indication of innocence.

I had nothing more to add so I, too, ate my rice.

"Gil looked great today," Gal said. "He's got really nice costumes."

La Donna looked up. "Costumes? I don't care what he wore! How did he sound?"

Gal flinched with this sudden rebuke. "Beats me. You know I have a tin ear."

La Donna gave her a disdainful glance. "You do. And you're disgracefully uncultured."

Gal stared at her plate, and her cheeks flushed. I was surprised by La Donna's belittlement of my friend and knew Gal was embarrassed or worse—angry. I decided to patch over the unpleasantness. "So, do you like Mozart?" I asked my kidnapper.

After directing another dart of annoyance at Gal, she replied, "Not especially. His plots are juvenile and convoluted. He needed someone to restrain his exuberance." La Donna cut a piece of veal. "But the music is beautiful."

"Mmm. I know what you mean. I feel like I'm in an *opera seria* of his at the moment."

La Donna startled me by laughing. "You'll be all set to perform *La Clemenza di Tito*."

From across the table, Gal's jaw was still clenched even though some food was perched on her fork. Clearly, she wasn't happy. "I've always liked that opera," I said mildly.

Once on La Donna's pet subject, she ignored Gal and began regaling me with tales of performances and opinions about singers, ranging over four decades of opera-going. Despite my anxiety and Gal's discomfort, I listened attentively and asked questions, figuring it wouldn't hurt to bond with La Donna even though proximity to danger had never held any attraction.

Dinner was concluded with cannoli and coffee, both of which Gal refused. Then, I was escorted to my chambers, and the door was locked.

—

The next day's activities were a repeat of yesterday's, except that I went as Christopher Rose-Wren to Malcolm Earl's theater. I marked my singing again, fearing I would be depleted for *Così*'s opening. That evening, over lamb chops, La Donna interrogated me about the *Rigoletto* rehearsal. Gal looked on in stoic dismay, drinking more wine than the night before. Where the two of them went *après dèjeuner*, I had no idea since I was confined to quarters after performing three Handel arias for La Donna, nor did I know if the two had reconciled.

In my room, I mused on the potential effects of my outrageous behavior as Fiordiligi. With my luck, instead of being lauded for my clever gender-bender, I would be castigated and ridiculed by the music critics, none of whom would bother to review my voice, only my impersonation. Any articles might be illustrated with rehearsal photos, though hopefully I wouldn't be clearly visible, and hopefully they wouldn't appear in the morning print editions where Malcolm Earl might see them and connect the dots. If he did, would he replace me with my cover and ruin my chance to sing a leading tenor role?

I thought of the tickets I had given to Hank and my mother for both operas and to Luis for *Così* and Loretta for *Rigoletto*. My face flushed anticipating the disgrace after the first and the potential humiliating cancellation of my Duke of Mantua. Yet, these were insignificant worries when I considered that people dearest to me might be in the audience with La Donna and her goons. Would she be content with merely closing the Lowenbaum production and destroying his reputation? I'd been thinking small-time revenge, a tit-for-tat squaring of their relationship. That wasn't her style. La Donna thought big.

I tucked myself under the covers, my mind caroming from one possible disaster to another, and raged that I had no phone to warn anyone.

CHAPTER TWENTY-SIX

Overheard and Underheard

I did not sleep a wink. Come to think of it, what is a wink? One blink of an eye? If so, maybe I had two or three of those. At 6:30 a.m. I surrendered to my anxieties and opening-night jitters and climbed out of bed, took a long shower, dressed, and waited impatiently for my breakfast.

A half hour later, I banged on the door to be let out. Finally, Gino came and led me into the dining room, where the cook served eggs, bacon, smoked salmon, and English muffins plus a nice assortment of liquid refreshments. I demolished everything in sight. Fear sometimes has that effect. So, too, does opera singing. You know, it's that oral thing.

Since no one was awake except the cook staff and Gino, I meandered into the sunroom and did what one does in such a place—stare at the sun. It was shining through ominous gray clouds that were piled to high tops. Though I am no weatherman, these appeared to be thunderheads. How appropriate to start the day with a bang, I thought, since the night would probably end with one.

By and by, Gal Friday strolled in but not from the direction of the elevator. She was dressed in yesterday's clothes, which led me to believe she was sleeping on the premises. The question was which area of the premises and in whose bed.

"Good morning," I said. "Just up?"

Gal rubbed her left eye with a fist. "Yeah."

"And from where doth you hail, O Lady in Black?"

Gal made a face, exasperation being the primary emotion expressed. "What's it to you?"

"Though I may seem to be at the total mercy, beck, and call of your employer, my curiosity is my own."

"Well, your curiosity isn't going to be satisfied by me."

"Shucks."

Gal sat down in the chair across from me, rubbed the other eye, and yawned. "So, this is your big night."

"Mmm. The alpha and the omega."

"Huh?"

"The beginning and the end. Greek alphabet."

Gal waved a hand at me. "Can it, Gil. It's too early in the morning."

"You should get up sooner, my dear, so that by this time it would seem late."

"What?" She shook her head and rolled red eyes heavenward. "I give up."

"That's more like it. Now, what's going to happen tonight?"

"You're going to sing. Then, you're going to make an ass out of yourself. Once everyone sees you as you truly are and Howard Lowenbaum has a heart attack and the show closes, we come back here and you sing Handel."

"That's it?"

"Mmm."

"Charming." I rested my legs on the ottoman and sat quietly for a moment, imagining how it would all go down. "So what's your part in tonight's play? Do you get to plug me full of holes after I ruin the performance? Or will you shoot Howard and Doris first?"

"Your job is to sing and screw up, Gil. My job is to make sure you do what you're supposed to do."

"No plans for additional physical retributions?"

"Knock off the questions."

I was unable to persist because La Donna entered the room. She was wearing a silk, floor-length kimono, a beautiful confection of silver and pink butterflies and chrysanthemums. We greeted each other with some formality, although I noticed that Gal and La Donna seemed pre-greeted. I could be in error, but I doubted it.

"Breakfast," La Donna told Gal and returned to the dining room.

After tossing me an inscrutable glance, one that didn't radiate happiness, Gal followed, closing the door behind her.

—

A short while later, I rose from the chair and crept to the door. From the other side, I heard heavy footsteps come near—heavier than

196

Gal's engineer boots. Instinctively, I retreated, but then whoever it was grunted and moved away.

I took up my post once again, and after a few minutes of silence, La Donna said, "Gal, tell the cook I want fruit salad and broiled flounder for dinner. No butter, cheese, or cream. We have to keep Gil's throat clear."

Gal agreed and left.

La Donna lowered her voice and said something, then a man—probably Gino—asked what the plans for the evening were. She replied, but I couldn't hear her answer. The guy spoke more loudly.

"The electrician will take care of it."

Electrician? I was lost in the dark. Hmm. Was that the plot for tonight? If the lights went out in the theater, there would be panic on top of the pandemonium I would create.

A chair's legs scraped the floor, and when La Donna spoke, she was closer to the sunroom door. "Larry will . . . and . . . deal with Gil."

What? I placed my hand on the door knob, about to rush into the dining room to confront La Donna, but stopped. If she realized I knew even a fragment of her scheme, she might terminate me before I'd digested breakfast.

I tried to imagine how to use the sparse information I possessed to foil their plot. With the limits inherent in my incarceration, there was probably nothing I could do before the performance and, I suspected, very little before and during the opera. As I pondered one possible idea, a huge thunderclap made me jump a foot.

—

I was shaking in my high heels when I stepped out of the black 1960 Lincoln Continental, La Donna's replacement for the pink Cadillac. Gal took my elbow and steered me toward the stage door while Gino returned downtown for his employer, who wasn't due to arrive until a few minutes before the eight o'clock curtain.

I considered making a fast break, but Gal, who was dressed as Sol Bleuchek, in a black suit, eased back her jacket to reveal a gun tucked in an under-arm holster.

"Let's keep things quiet," she warned.

We entered my dressing room, and Gal locked the door and leaned against it.

"Gal, please. Don't make me do this."

"You know the deal. Hurry up and get dressed."

I did my vocal warm-ups first, causing Gal's eyes to widen with alarm because of the volume. I thought about screaming for help, but the rooms were sound-proofed so the singers wouldn't disturb each other, and parsing words from the weird noises we all were making as part of our preparation would be difficult. And, most significantly, Gal had a weapon and looked ready to use it. When I began applying makeup, my hand was shaking so badly that I botched the eyeliner. Stage fright on top of fright for life was an unnerving combination.

After correcting the wavery black mess, I added shadow, false eyelashes, powder, and blush and slipped into my pantyhose, starchy undergarments, and blouse. Finally, I fitted the pump shoes on my feet and, with Gal's help, donned the long blue gown. After lacing the front of the bodice together, I lifted the heavy wig onto my head.

When I was suited up, Gal returned to her position by the door. "You aren't planning on doing anything stupid, are you, Gil?"

I turned to observe her. "What counts as stupid? I think the whole thing is stupid and mean. I don't know how you can love that evil woman."

Gal looked at me with surprise. "I don't love her."

"You're sleeping with La Donna. No need to deny that."

"Okay, I won't." She rubbed the back of her neck. "Jesus, Gil, it's too complicated to explain."

I faced the mirror again and applied red lipstick to my mouth. "All I can say is that I'm really disappointed in you." I said this quietly, but my anger was conveyed.

As Gal was about to answer, there was a knock at the door.

"Five minutes," the stage manager called.

"Listen, Gil. La Donna will be in the audience, and she won't be alone."

"Where are you going to be?"

"Backstage, in the rear wings. In front of the fire door."

"So, if I make a run for it, you can stop me?"

Gal nodded.

Or shoot me. On stage or off, Gal would be positioned about thirty feet from the fly curtains, in the main passageway the performers used. At this juncture, the hallway split: one corridor angled

198

around the rear of the stage so singers could enter or exit from the opposite side, and a second led to the fire door and continued past the six primary singers' rooms; the general dressing area, divided into male and female units for chorus, and supers; an administrative suite; Howard's office; and finally ended at the exterior stage door. This hall also served as the emergency exit for backstage and one side of the theater. As long as Gal sat in that exact location, I had no avenue of escape except from the stage itself, though Little Larry and his merry men were probably stationed on aisle seats and outside the building. I wondered how Gal had wangled a chair in that busy spot. A gift of Cuban cigars to Howard? Or had she told him I suffered from stage fright and needed a steadying influence during the performance?

With a tissue, I blotted my lipstick and glanced at Gal. "Wish me *in bocca al lupo.*"

"Huh? Cut the shit, Gil, and let's go."

She escorted me down the hall and through the fire door. Gareth and Ivan were already on stage with Nate Lowenstein, the Don Alfonso, who baits the two boys, Guglielmo and Ferrando, into a wager that their lovers, Dorabella and myself, wouldn't be faithful to them if we were left on our own. The lads agree to the bet, after insisting on our constancy. The plan is for them to leave, don disguises, switch partners, and attempt to woo us from our original lovers.

Joanne came up beside me and gave Gal the "who-are-you" once over.

"Hi, I'm Guilia's agent," Gal explained in a gruff voice.

Joanne looked uncertain but then drew me away from Gal, closer to the stage entrance, where Gal couldn't overhear our conversation. "Are you nervous, Guilia?"

"Yeah. And you?"

"Terrified." Indeed, her eyes were large and unblinking.

Ivan, Nate, and Gareth rushed past us, dripping sweat. The crew hurried onstage to change the set and add props for our scene. This would take about three minutes, but we would need to position ourselves before the curtain rose.

"Did you call Detective Morris?" I whispered.

"Yeah. He wants to talk with you and Derek tomorrow morning. I explained we were opening tonight and that I had no way to reach Derek by phone."

I cursed in silence. No cavalry coming. "What did you tell him?"

"That La Donna tried to kidnap Derek and me . . . that we got away."

"And the theater fire—did you tell the police that La Donna was responsible?"

"Yes. So, did my father. Not to Detective Morris. To the cops who brought him to the station for questioning."

"I see." And I did. Detective Morris would think I was somewhere safe, hiding from La Donna. I had no idea what he could do about arresting her based on the evidence he had, especially if I was prevented from being a witness and Raffaella and Tino didn't talk. And if Morris didn't hear about Howard and Joanne's report made to another precinct, he wouldn't comprehend the larger picture, the one in which I was a central, endangered character, as were untold others currently in the theater.

"Joanne, it's urgent that you tell Howard that—"

She grabbed my hand. "Never mind! We're on!"

Joanne hauled me onto the stage. The set had been transformed into a seaside garden, with painted flats, furniture, and two easels, behind which we took our places. As the prop girl handed us paintbrushes and palettes, my throat closed with anxiety. My first staged opera! In all the confusion created by La Donna and her goons, I'd almost forgotten that I had one act to sing before disaster. One act that should be done with lightness, a comic touch, and ravishing beauty.

As the curtain was slowly raised, I studied the portrait of my lover, Guglielmo, which I was painting. The violins wove a melody through the orchestral music, and I began "Ah, guarda sorella." Although the stage lights were bright, I saw Hank Braylock in the first row. I was so pleased that I almost forgot my next line. Instead, I imbued it with intense feeling and gave Hank a small, private smile, which he returned with a wink. I then checked the fourth row center seat, the one reserved for my mother. It was empty. For once, I was glad she hadn't come.

When Joanne began to sing her part, I experienced a split second of happiness for her and about Hank before I remembered that I might soon be dead, and they might be killed in the crossfire. I did my best to disguise this stab of fear and sang the duet with melting tenderness. Joanne was outstanding, her eyes sparkling with delight.

At the end, the audience roared its appreciation, especially Hank, who was yelling *brava* to me and clapping loudly. My heart swelled at the reception and the special approval of one special man. As I turned to greet Don Alfonso, I wiped a tear from my eye.

Don Alfonso told us that Guglielmo and Ferrando had been called to military duty and would sail within the hour. The two boys entered, and the four of us sang poignant goodbyes. Ivan, my Guglielmo, was eager for his main romantic squeeze and wrapped his large, hairy paws around my shoulders and pulled me tight to his massive chest. In addition to the stench of manly roast beef, his enormous basso sound nearly knocked me off my feet at such close quarters. I set my elbows against him to pry my body away, but the big fellow was so overcome with our operatic parting that my attempts gained me only a few inches.

When everyone was finished wishing everyone else farewell, I was extremely relieved that the "boat" was about to depart, even if it wasn't much of a boat: one large limp sail stuck into a four-wheeled cart hidden behind a scalloped wooden flat painted with waves. As two crouching stagehands began pulling the little ship, Ivan stood on board, next to the mast, which was shorter than he was, with Gareth beside him. The audience was already giggling when the cart lurched toward the wings and unbalanced Gareth, who grabbed Ivan's arm like a baby monkey grasping a thick branch. The crowd erupted in loud hee-haws. Joanne glanced at me, her hand over her mouth, as she tried to stifle laughter.

Shortly afterward, Joanne and I were in a kitchen, joined by Despina, our saucy maid, played by Fiona O'Sullivan. We were sitting on chairs and drinking hot chocolate. From my position on stage, I could see Hank very well, with his short blond hair that glowed in the dark crowd. He was as handsome as I remembered, perhaps more so. Inspired, I hammed up my handling of the cup by flouncing my little finger in the air. He smiled that wonderful smile that was slow and sexy. Would he look at me this way if he had a boyfriend? Maybe I had a chance. If we lived through the night.

CHAPTER TWENTY-SEVEN

Disaster in the Second Act

At the intermission bows, after blowing a two-handed kiss to Hank, I scanned the audience for Little Larry, La Donna, and her thugs, as well as Howard's Russians, but I couldn't see well enough in the dim light nor did I have much time before my exit. My hope was that Howard would praise the cast, giving me the opportunity to warn him about what was about to transpire, if I could ditch Gal, which was unlikely.

Joanne and I left the stage arm in arm. In the wings, I stopped Joanne.

"Quick! Help me find Howard!"

"What's the matter?"

"Everything."

Just as I was about to ask her to call Detective Morris and stop the performance, Gal Friday appeared. I disengaged from Joanne, and Gal threw a heavy arm over my shoulder.

"Hey, great job, Guilia!" she enthused.

Before I knew what was happening, Gal guided me through the fire door and into my dressing room. She turned the lock.

"Gal, please, we can't continue! I don't know what's planned, but Hank is in the front row center. He might be hurt! Others, too. This is no place for a gang war. There're too many people."

"Yeah, but what La Donna wants is what La Donna wants. For it all to go down in the theater, just like it did so many years ago." Gal's voice betrayed a hint of resignation.

Suddenly, I wondered if Gal had been fully informed about all of La Donna's plans, other than about my disruption of the opera. Knowing of my friendship with Gal, did La Donna trust her, and, if not, what would La Donna do about it? And did Gal trust La Donna? After the scene at dinner in which La Donna had humiliated Gal, had there been additional arguments?

"When I ruin the show, will that finish things?" This was the second time I'd asked her this question, but I hoped she would answer me.

"Shut up and strip, Gil."

I gave her a sour look, removed my dress, and toweled off the sweat. Stage lights and costumes are hot, but I was perspiring for additional reasons. Not only did I fear La Donna's reprisal after my second act debauchery, I was afraid Gal might be in jeopardy. I needed to warn Howard and call the police.

"Gal, could you hand me those petticoats?"

As she turned to reach them, I threw the heavy dress on her and fell diagonally on top. Gal whipped to the side, freed one arm, and clamped a firm hand on my mouth. I grabbed the other hand that was struggling to reach the gun.

"Shit!" she grunted through clenched teeth.

I pressed her right arm against the floor and tried to elbow her hand from my mouth. Gal was stronger than I suspected and bucked upward, toppling me to her left. Giving me a wicked shove, she sprang to her knees and reached for the revolver. Next thing I knew, I was facing the business end of a Smith & Wesson.

Gal came to her feet and motioned for me to do the same. She tossed the petticoats at my face and ordered me to get dressed.

—

I had already informed La Donna and Gal when I was going to commit the defilement of *Così fan tutte*. In addition to the human disaster that might befall us and the audience, it was the grossest sacrilege to desecrate this two-hundred-year-old opera, one I greatly revered. But my options to avoid such a travesty were zilch.

After donning Albanian disguises at the end of the first act, Ferrando flirted with me and Guglielmo flirted with Dorabella, my sister, in order to tempt us into betraying our fiancés. Now, in the second act, I dithered and remained true to Guglielmo while my sister caved big time. However, when Ferrando, in his Albanian outfit, threatened death because he's so in love with me, I fall for him. And Ferrando, played to a fairy fare-thee-well by Gareth, would be drooling with excitement to get his hands on yours truly.

We sang the serenades and asides and wistful arias, everyone doing a great job, even though I was having some trouble maintaining my usual long vocal line because my lungs were warring with my brain, which was telling my body to hyperventilate. The only thing that saved my performance was that the music was so firmly lodged in my being. Part of me just kept on, as if this were another rehearsal.

Before the scene with Gareth, I was alone on stage and grabbed Ferrando's military coat and his sword, determined to go to my fiancé and be true. It was my last chance to sing to Hank, and I gave it my all. From his tender expression, I knew I'd communicated more than Fiordiligi's words.

After this, Ferrando arrived, declaring that I must become his or I should run him through with the sword or he would do it himself. Gareth swooned on the sofa, and I, realizing I love him, ran to his side, tossing the coat and sword on the couch.

Gareth was waiting like a crocodile half-submerged in swamp water, his eyes closed to tiny slits. I leaned over and kissed him full on the lips, with shocking force. His eyes popped open, and, as I pulled back, he grabbed me and hauled me in for a repeat. Despite the fact that he was supposed to be contemplating death, Gareth was mad with glee. Forced into his arms, I lay there for a split second before pushing away, standing to full height, and, with great dignity, began unlacing the golden cord that held the gown together. Gareth bolted upright on the sofa and ogled me. We kept singing, though he was stupefied.

As I continued my striptease, dropping the gown and stepping out of it, then unbuttoning the blouse and tossing it aside with a flourish, the audience grew very still. I risked a quick glance to my left and saw that Nate Lowenstein and Ivan, who were supposedly hidden from us in a side room but visible to the audience, were watching in mounting horror, and Fiona, who was standing off-stage by the fly curtains, had covered her mouth with her hands. Joanne stood behind her, eyes wide with shock.

I removed the layers of starched petticoats and bloomers, kicking each in the air, actions that were accompanied by intakes of breath by the crowd. After loosening the bodice, I reached for my falsies and flipped them at Gareth, along with my huge wig. When the bodice fell to the floor, at first the crowd tittered, then laughed, and finally gasped as I turned to exhibit my flat chest and male silhouette, which was clearly revealed in the clingy pantyhose. I further emphasized my masculinity by aggressively thrusting my hips.

Gareth went silent. The orchestra kept playing, although Maestro Cavendish MacDougal's arms had dropped, and he was staring me with astonishment. The violinists were the first musicians to realize something was amiss, and several craned their necks upward to check the stage. Then, zap! The lights went out. A few seconds later, someone shot out the battery-powered emergency "exit" signs.

I had never seen such utter blackness. The theater became the corridor to an unlit hell. Fiona and Joanne screamed, and I hit the deck, expecting more gunfire. Although I couldn't see anyone, I heard the audience's cries of panic and their frantic scuffling. All of sudden a body came tumbling down on top of me. I rolled over and threw a fist.

"Thit!"

I didn't mind that I'd hit Gareth. He had it coming. I shoved him out of my way, crawled to the sofa, groped for the military coat, which I put on to cover my near-nakedness, and then grabbed the sword, the only weapon I'd known would be at hand, useless as it was against guns. The noise had risen to a multi-pitched howl as the theater-goers tried to escape. A minute later, on my left, in the outside aisle, flashlights sliced the dark theater. Gunshots rang out and a loud whoosh of "Ohh!" swept through the air as people squeezed into the spaces in front of their seats. I laid my hand on the sofa and hurried around it, as more shots were exchanged. In the background, Ivan and Nate, both basses, were bellowing like pricked bears, and Gareth, who had apparently crawled toward the orchestra pit, fell over the lip of the stage and crashed into several musicians, who were hollering at each other and at him.

I was about to leave the safety of the sofa, to flee to the opposite exit, when a flashlight beam appeared from the area where Gal had posted herself, which was the side where Howard, Doris, and the cast were stationed—and presumably some of Howard's men—although by now La Donna's henchmen could have also infiltrated backstage. I peered through the open space below the sofa's arm and watched the light move quickly closer. Was it Gal or someone else? Was I about to be shot? I swallowed hard, half hoping it was Gal, who might show mercy, but would she cross La Donna if the woman had ordered her to kill me? Did I, Gal's old pal, rate higher than her fearsome boss, who might also be her lover? In the peripheral glow from the flashlight, it seemed that he or she was holding a gun, though as I noticed this, the person's arm lowered. Should I sneak up from behind and jump whoever it was?

Just as I was considering this, a volley of shots zipped back and forth near the outside aisle, with people crying that they were hit. I ducked, but as I did, I spied a second light approaching. I waited for a pause in the gunfire before risking another peek. The new beam of light shown on the first person, revealing Gal's square physique. Gal spun around, her flashlight's beam striking the person behind her. La Donna. La Donna holding a gun aimed at Gal. The mobster's eyes were fixed on my friend with ferocious, laser-like intensity. I crouched down and clutched the sword in my sweaty hand.

"Where is he?" La Donna shouted, sweeping her flashlight over the set.

Gal didn't answer. I knew the *he* La Donna wanted was me, though she had been training the gun on Gal. The tiny woman suddenly veered and started walking in my direction, the flashlight shining a path in front of her. Although it was difficult to hear over the screaming in the theater, it sounded like Gal said, "Gil ran out over there." Presumably she was pointing at the side exit on my right.

La Donna swiveled her light toward the wings, darkening the area where I was hiding, but then swung the light back on Gal. Instantly, I knew what she intended to do. I gritted my teeth and sprang to my feet. Arcing the sword in a big uppercut, I whacked La Donna's arm. The gun flew out of her hand and skittered across the stage, the flashlight dropped from her other hand, and she staggered to her knees. As the woman groped along the floor for her weapon, I ran forward and stomped on her fingers. La Donna screeched, her face contorted in pain.

"Bastard!" She cradled her mashed fingers and rocked back and forth, her breathing coming in fast bursts.

Gal holstered her Smith & Wesson, snatched La Donna's gun, and ran toward her employer. "You deserve this! For everything you've done!" And, using the gun's butt, she slammed the woman on the head. La Donna pitched over, and Gal hit her again with more force. La Donna's body twitched once and didn't move.

A grim smile spread across Gal's face. She stuffed the gun in the waistband of her pants and turned to me. "Come on!"

I dropped the sword and froze, shocked by Gal's violence, but she gave me a push, which jolted me out of my daze. I stared into the semi-dark theater and suddenly remembered Hank. Oh, my god! Where was he?

"Hank!" My operatic voice knifed through the din.

From somewhere in front came the reply. "Gil! Here!"

"Go to your left!" I thrust my arm to indicate the direction and began running after Gal, who was using her flashlight to shine the way. We hurried to the far side of the stage, where the carved proscenium rose to arch above us. I eased myself over the edge and landed on the floor, wobbling for a moment in my heels. Gal followed, immediately aiming her flashlight ahead of us. Crowded in a writhing, sprawling mass, hundreds of patrons were collapsed in the aisle or were trying to step on or over each other. As Gal's light swept the area, I saw Hank's blond head. He saw me, shouted my name, and struggled to reach my side. When he did, he threw his arms around my shoulders.

"Oh, Hank!" I cried.

"Gil!" He kissed me, long and hard.

"Would you two cut it out!" Gal complained, tugging at us. "Get down!"

We needed no encouragement when more gunshots rang out. The three of us huddled on the floor for what seemed like an hour. Then, suddenly, the rear of the theater was lit with huge spotlights. The police had arrived.

"Drop your weapons!" One of the boys in blue had a bullhorn.

The mobsters ignored that order and decided to shoot at the police rather than at each other. This elicited returned fire from the cops, who were entering the theater, some wearing tactical gear and carrying shields. Reacting to the battle that was forming in the far left aisle, as one massive wave, the audience bolted in our direction, clogging the aisles and trampling one another. Although the uproar was deafening, I heard Joanne and Fiona, who were wailing notes I didn't think they could hit.

The three of us clung together. Gal held onto me, and I held onto Hank for dear life, a phrase I never understood before. The barrage of bullets continued, punctuated with screams when someone was hit, but finally the shooting stopped. Cautiously, we raised our heads to see who had won.

"Do you think it's over?" Hank asked.

"Maybe," Gal said.

A few minutes later, the house lights came on, and the guns remained quiet. It seemed that the police had shot or disarmed the
antagonists. I sat up and turned toward the stage. To my great relief, all the singers appeared unhurt. Nate and Ivan had risen from
behind chairs, and Joanne and Fiona were emerging from the side
of a painted flat. Gareth was still in the orchestra pit, hiding behind
a double bass. La Donna was sprawled where she had fallen. Puddles of red blood surrounded her head and arm.

"I hope Howard and Doris are okay. Did you see them anywhere
backstage?" I asked Gal.

"No. It was pretty hard to tell what was going on. Everyone running around and bullets flying." She paused, then added, "but I did
warn Howard that he and his wife were in danger."

"Huh?" I was stunned. "You did?"

"Well, sort of. As soon as I heard La Donna would be at opening night, I told Ronald Fahey. I didn't know what she had up her
sleeve, but when Ronald was killed—"

"By whom?"

"Little Larry. Anyhow, once Ronald was dead, I decided to stay
on the QT. I didn't want La Donna to know that Ronald and I were
pals. She was seriously paranoid and was watching everyone.
Later, I suspected she had a plant in the backstage crew—I didn't
know who it was—so I had to make things look realistic. You know,
about guarding you."

"But you pulled a gun on me in my dressing room!" I protested.
"Were you really going to shoot?"

"No way, Gil. I just wanted you to go onstage. Figured you'd be
safer there if La Donna and her boys charged down the aisle and
through the emergency entrance, though I was only guessing what
she intended to do—she never told me. Anyway, that's why I sat
where I did. To keep you from getting your damned bloomers shot
off. "

"Why did you come onto the set, then?"

"It was too hot for comfort where I was, what with Howard's
Russians and La Donna's gang sniping at each other. And I knew
La Donna would be after you, once she took out Howard."

"So you were protecting me? Is that why you turned on her or
was it because of that night at dinner?"

"Huh? Oh, yeah. She pulled that kind of crap a lot, constantly
criticizing everything I did. Bossing me around. That stuff was

really bad, but what flipped me was watching how obsessed she became about killing Howard. La Donna had always been careful. Stayed home. Let her guys do the work. But this time it was too personal. This time she crossed the line into full-out, bat-shit crazy. No one was safe, me included. And neither were you."

"I'm lost. What's going on?" Hank asked. "Who started all this?"

"La Donna—my employer—wanted Howard Lowenbaum and his crew dead because of an old grudge," Gal answered. "And they were after Gil because he pissed her off."

—

Although the police were ordering everyone to stay seated so that the perpetrators couldn't escape in the crowd, the audience, once they realized the gunfire had ended, was in no mood to remain in the theater a second longer and began frantically rushing toward the front entrance.

Gal rose to her feet. Over the increasing noise, she shouted, "The EMTs are coming."

Hank and I stood. Although we couldn't see well, it appeared that Little Larry was being strapped onto a gurney and Howard was on another one, his jacket off and blood oozing through his white shirt. A medic was tending to him, as was Doris, who seemed to be okay. Several people were slumped over seats, and from the number of gurneys rushing down the aisle, I guessed dozens of people had been wounded or killed.

"I knew this would be a disaster." Gal surveyed the audience and then focused on the bloody body of her lover. "La Donna's always been smart. This time she said was different." She wagged her head sadly. "Well, yeah, it was."

I commiserated with Gal and gave her arm a comforting squeeze. Then, I turned to Hank, my wonderful Hank, and hugged him, notching my head over his shoulder. "I didn't think I'd ever see you again."

"I'm sorry for not calling."

I held him tighter. "I was so upset after I saw you with that guy—"

"What guy?"

I told him about what I'd witnessed from the bus. Hank was quiet, and then he kissed me. "Oh, Gil! That was my brother, Kenny."

I felt like a fool and said so.

Gal edged closer. Using me as a shield, she removed La Donna's gun from her waistband and pulled a handkerchief from her pocket, using it to wipe the weapon clean. Once she was finished, she slipped the gun under a nearby seat and did the same with her revolver.

"Just in case," she said. "Now, come on, lovebirds. We got to get out of here."

Hank and I followed her, keeping tight to the swarm of people. Through the bullhorn, the police were commanding everyone to take seats, but as one, they surged forward through the police line, and with them, we did, too. Hank held my hand tightly in his.

In the lobby, we bolted, shoving open the big glass doors. The sirens of police vans and ambulances were shrill in the night; blue and red lights crisscrossed the street, which was mobbed with on-lookers as well as escapees.

Once outside, Gal put her hand on my shoulder. "Gil, sorry, but I got to split. Don't forget, you owe me." She gave me a crooked smile and touched two fingers to her forehead. "See you soon." She started to leave, then rounded on her heel. "Hell, maybe I got that wrong. Maybe I owe you."

I nodded.

It was tempting to follow her since I had dozens of questions, but I knew I would run into Gal Friday some day when I needed a marguerita and a friend.

I turned to Hank. "Your place or mine?"

"How about my place," came a voice to my left. Before I knew what was happening, I felt a powerful grip on my arm. Detective Morris stood beside me. He didn't look pleased. "I was wondering where you've been," he said. "You have a lot of explaining to do."

"Please, can't we do it tomorrow?" I looked at Hank hopefully, but the policeman was not in the mood for delays.

"Come on, Gilbert, it's time to fess up to everything." Morris stared at my military coat and the semi-nakedness underneath and laughed. "Nice outfit. I'm sure you'll tell me all about it."

Despite my protests, the detective pulled me to his unmarked police car. Hank trailed along, unsure what to do.

"What precinct are you taking him to?" Hank asked.

Detective Morris told him and then stuffed me in the back seat.

CHAPTER TWENTY-EIGHT

The Fabulous Finale

I received a gray blanket at the police station that did nothing to re-lieve my embarrassment. It's one thing to dress in women's clothes at the Purple Plum, quite another to be in theatrical makeup, almost naked except for a weird coat, and sitting across from a detective with a tape recorder.

"So, I'm listening," Detective Morris said, tapping a pen on his clipboard.

I had no idea where to start. Finally, I decided to tell the truth. I told Morris every detail I knew about La Donna's organization, about the "accidents" during *Jungle Fever*, how Howard had ruined her career, and how both warring parties were retaliating against each other, including who had killed Ronald. I also related that La Donna—contrary to her usual avoidance of public appear-ances—had become unhinged by the chance to take revenge on the Lowenbaums, that she had joined her men and even run on stage to shoot me and Gal, even if everyone in the theater could witness her murdering us. I then reported my kidnapping by Eddie and Gino, but when I reached the part about the light bulb store, Detective Morris' eyebrows nearly flew off his head.

"So you know something about Little Larry?"

I said I did.

The policeman's face creased into a huge grin. "I bet I can get a warrant to search the store since the business is owned by Larry and maybe La Donna, plus you were abducted from there. Your description of the activities in their shipping department also sounds like stolen goods were passing through the place. After all, it's pretty suspicious that a light bulb emporium is unloading TV sets." He chuckled. "What will they think up next . . . light bulbs for chrissakes." Morris wiped his forehead with a large hand. "So, will you be willing to ID the guys you saw there?"

I wasn't sure about this if it meant testifying against them. Everyone knows that witnesses to mob business were soon dead or missing. I'd already come close to annihilation in the scenic wastelands of New Jersey. "Do I have to? I mean, I'll look at a line-up or through photos, but I don't want to get into more trouble."

Morris leaned back in his cracked leather chair. "Well, maybe you could testify dressed as a woman?" He laughed. "Okay, let me see what I can do. It may not be necessary to involve you. We have enough evidence on La Donna and Little Larry from the theater. Murder and attempted murder for starters. Lowenbaum is already charged with selling stolen merchandise and now with shooting several people, even if his lawyer is swearing Howard was acting in self-defense. My guess is that most of these characters will be in the slammer for a long time."

I nodded and then explained that Gal Friday was innocent of everything.

"Really? Are you sure?"

"Yes," I nodded again. "Have you heard how Howard and La Donna are?"

"They're in the hospital, with quite a few others. No preliminary reports are in yet."

After my statements were typed and signed, I thanked Detective Morris and was offered a ride home. Before I accepted, I checked to see if Hank was waiting for me. He wasn't. Since he had been told the precinct address, I was upset by his absence. I tried calling him from the police desk, but he didn't answer. Feeling exhausted, I returned to my apartment, driven there by an officer who picked the upstairs locks after we had been let in downstairs by one of my neighbors.

—

About ten o'clock the next morning, I woke from a violent nightmare in which I was being chased by guys in black, and the faster I sprinted, the faster they ran. Sound familiar? Anyway, the dream made me realize that my life had to change. All of the disguises and false identities had to stop. Even singing soprano, which I thought would be a lark, was all wrong. What was right was a relationship with Hank and being a real tenor.

I swung my legs over the side of the bed and switched on the computer to check my e-mails. No word from Hank. What was going on? Was he pulling another disappearing act?

After breakfast and a shower, I logged in to *The New York Times*, figuring the digital edition would contain the news from late last night. On the front page was a report about the opening night mêlée, which was accompanied by a photograph of the people fleeing the theater. The article said that five people were dead, including a policeman; nine members of the Gabrielli and Lowenbaum gangs were in serious or critical condition and others were wounded; and Howard had suffered a gunshot to the shoulder. The cause of the battle appeared to be mob-related. A number of people had been arrested. More information to come.

I was horrified by the carnage. All wrought due to spite and jealousy simmering from a decades-old feud, a feud that had escalated into the brutal shooting of innocent people. And, even if I hadn't caused the catastrophe, I felt guilty that I hadn't disrupted La Donna's plans. Had I been too eager for my big chance to sing? Or too chicken? My heart burned with remorse.

I re-read the short article, feeling sicker. Then, with increasing anxiety, I linked to the music review. The headline: "A *Così fan tutte* with a Twist." The critic deplored the appalling violence, regurgitating some of the front page account, then wrote: "The Fiordiligi of the evening, Guilia Hancock, a newcomer to the New York opera scene, sang with conviction and poise. Her voice is securely supported and unique, almost unearthly, of a type that resembles a countertenor, only finely wrought and decisively female, despite the gender-bending interpretation that occurs in the middle of Act II." He described my striptease as ingenious and provocative, saying that it stunned the audience just before the lights went out. He followed this with glowing praise for Joanne. Gareth received a commendation for the clarity of his voice but not for his performance, which the critic deemed insufficiently commanding. Ivan was described as well cast, with a serviceable bass instrument, and Nate and Fiona were lauded for their roles.

Joanne and I had walked away with the kudos, and, perhaps due to the abrupt ending, my vulgar behavior had been completely misunderstood. The live-dress publicity photo, which accompanied the article, featured Joanne—no doubt chosen by her father—with Gareth and Ivan behind her. I was to the side, my back partly turned to the photographer. This was a godsend because no one would recognize me from the Purple Plum or connect me to the *Rigoletto* cast.

I checked two other New York newspapers. In one, the music reviewer wrote a brief paragraph about the performance itself. She, too, had been fooled about my gender, loved my singing, though she criticized the production as an ill-advised and overly sensational interpretation.

I had escaped censure and public embarrassment. I fell against the bed in shock, but shortly thereafter, returned to eviscerating myself for what happened at the theater.

—

Finally, exhausted, I ran through *Rigoletto* to refresh my memory and mentally rehearse some stage moves. When I finished, the day was almost gone, and I still hadn't heard from Hank. I borrowed a neighbor's phone and called him, leaving a message about tonight's performance and inviting him to a private cast party—his and mine. I tried to sound cheerful, but I was worried and upset. Next, I checked in with Detective Morris. He was tired yet excited by the progress being made against La Donna's operation after years of frustrating pursuit. He said that Little Larry's light bulb store had been successfully raided, many of Larry's remaining affiliates rounded up, and sufficient evidence amassed that I would only need to testify against Raffaella and Tino. Since the State Police troopers at the scene were corroborating witnesses against them, killing me—if there was anyone in La Donna's gang left to do it— was a waste of time. Morris promised to return my clothes from La Donna's penthouse after all the evidence had been gathered.

—

Opening night was a dressy affair at Malcolm Earl's theater. The crowd was very Upper East Side, decked out in tuxedoes and gowns, and apparently enthralled with having a little opera company on their doorstep. In my dressing room were flowers from Luis, Loretta, and, yes, Hank. His note said, "Bravo to the Duke! I'll see you after." Even Gal had sent a bouquet of white lilies—a wry reference to my missed funeral? And despite Joanne's family tragedy, she, too, had sent red and white carnations. Propped against my mirror was a card from my mother: "Congratulations on Your Graduation." The type and tassel were rendered in silver glitter, the mortarboard in gold. I supposed it was the best she could do.

As I warmed up for Act I, my distress slowly lifted. The moment I set my toe on the stage, I knew success would be mine. I swaggered, I seduced, I sang. I was so in the zone that I hardly remembered anything, although I know the applause was loud, long, and enthusiastic, especially for me at the bows.

Afterward, my dressing room was mobbed with well-wishers, all helping themselves to the French Champagne supplied by Malcolm Earl. Joanne came by, her eyes red from crying on and off for the last twenty-four hours. She explained that her father would be okay, though his discharge wasn't expected for a few days, at which time he would be taken into police custody. Then, Joanne threw her arms around my neck and thanked me for saving his life.

"How did I do that?"

"By having your friend warn him." Joanne smiled and kissed me.

I started to say that I hadn't, but she continued. "And Derek Guilia Christopher Hancock-Rose-Wren . . . I forgive you for all your disguises and pretenses, although I must say I nearly died of shock when you stripped off your clothes."

"Add in Gilbert. My real name." I took her hand. "I'm so sorry. And sorry for pretending to be straight."

"That's okay. I knew something wasn't right. I guess I wanted to believe in Derek."

I gave her a big hug. "I didn't mean to lead you on. Things got crazy. I hope we'll be friends . . . maybe even sing together again?"

Joanne's eyes filled with tears. "I'll be your leading lady anytime."

—

After everyone left, Hank arrived. He gave me a huge smile and said, "You were the best Duke of Mantua I've ever seen. The reviews will surpass those from last night."

"Do you think so?"

He nodded. "And I apologize for not coming to the station. I was called because Kenny was caught dealing cocaine again. He'll be in prison for several years, if he survives AIDS."

"Oh, Hank. That's really sad."

"It is," he agreed, pulling me into his arms, "but there's nothing I can do to help my brother." He stared at me with such affection that I almost fainted. "Tonight, no interruptions."

—

Although I am tempted to give each and every delightful detail of our lovemaking, I simply must respect the sanctity of the bedroom. Trust me, however, when I say that bells and whistles and fireworks resounded throughout the night, and that Hank, my dear Hank, was totally, totally fabulous!

In the morning, while he slept, I examined his face, observing the lines around his eyes, mouth, and forehead. These might have made Hank look old, but they didn't. I read them as signs of empathy and experience and character.

His bedroom had character, too. It had a high ceiling with bleached oak beams, tall windows, and a collection of original paintings arranged on the white stucco walls. In a full-length glass cabinet were museum replicas of Greek sculptures. I recognized Apollo, Poseidon, and Zeus, but these gods didn't compare with the one lying next to me.

As the sun peeked through the windows and fell upon his face, he woke.

"Good morning," I said.

"Good morning." He kissed my lips gently.

I gazed into his green eyes, observing how they absorbed the golden light. Would this be the first of thousands of mornings? Joy spread its warm wings in my chest.

"What are you thinking?" he asked.

"About serious things," I began, watching as a look of concern furrowed his brow. "Oh, don't worry. Good things."

His frown relaxed into a smile. "I'm glad. Will you tell me?"

I leaned over and whispered in his ear, "I'm remembering what Madame Clara said."

"What?" He rose to one elbow. "Who's Madame Clara?"

217

"Madame Clara is my very own, personal, wonderful psychic medium."

"Really?" he chuckled and shook his head. "And what did your own, personal, wonderful psychic medium say?"

"That it was just a matter of time," I proudly announced.

Hank stared at me for a second, waiting for the rest of the explanation, his face struggling to maintain its composure. "Is that it, Gil?"

"Yes."

He gasped, fell back against the pillows, and burst into helpless laughter. "That it was just a matter of time? That makes no sense at all! That could mean anything!"

I smiled wisely, a smile I'd practiced many times in front of the mirror. "Oh, no. I know exactly what she meant. Now more than ever." I gave him a long kiss. "And, Hank, she was absolutely right."

ABOUT THE AUTHOR

[photo credit: Vicki DeVico]

Laury A. Egan is the author of *The Outcast Oracle*; a collection, *Fog and Other Stories*; and a psychological suspense novel, *Jenny Kidd*. Her stories have appeared in numerous literary journals and anthologies. Four poetry volumes, *Snow, Shadows, a Stranger*; *Beneath the Lion's Paw*; *The Sea & Beyond*; and *Presence & Absence* were published in limited editions. She lives on the northern coast of New Jersey. Her website: www.lauryaegan.com

ABOUT THE PUBLISHER

Tiny Fox Press LLC
5020 Kingsley Road
North Port, FL 34287

www.tinyfoxpress.com

CPSIA information can be obtained
at www.ICGtesting.com
Printed in the USA
BVHW08s1526031018
529171BV00002B/186/P